LUCKY
FISH

Reviva
Schermbrucker

First published in 2003 by Jacana

5 St Peter Rd
Bellevue
2198
South Africa

2003 © Reviva Schermbrucker

ISBN 1-919931-73-2

Cover design by Disturbance
disturb@mweb.co.za

Printed by Formeset Printers

See a complete list of Jacana titles at www.jacana.co.za

CONTENTS

My thanks to Peter,
Lesley, Jill, and in
fond memory
of Ivan.

Acknowledgements

The early chapters of this book were written with the help of a grant from the Council of Arts and Culture.

The family and most of the events portrayed in this book are based on fact. However, the main character originally asked that I keep his identity confidential and I have used fictional names for him and the other characters. This also gave me the freedom to shape the story my own way including making up people, events and a chronology that suited my intent.

THE YEARS OF THIS STORY

1964

BY 1964 THE SOUTH African Government had won its fight against the movements that wanted to overthrow it.

AT THE END of *The Rivonia Trial*, which lasted seven months, eight men were given life sentences including Nelson Mandela and Walter Sisulu. Suliman Saloojee fell seven floors from the window of the South African Security Headquarters in Johannesburg during interrogation. He died from multiple injuries. The magistrate found "no irregularities" at the inquest.

THE BOXER, CASSIUS CLAY (later to change his name to Muhammad Ali) knocked out world heavyweight champion, Sonny Liston, in Miami, Florida.

A LAW WAS passed that forbade African women living in rural areas from coming to join their husbands working in the cities.

FROM 1963 TO 1990, there were more than 80 deaths of people who were being detained by South African police.

AMERICAN MILITARY INVOLVEMENT in Vietnam escalated.

BRAM FISCHER, a leading figure of the South African Communist Party, went into hiding.

SOUTH AFRICA WAS not allowed to take part in the Tokyo Olympics because of its policies of racial segregation.

MARTIN LUTHER KING won the Nobel Prize for Peace.

THE UNITED NATIONS recommended that complete economic sanctions against South Africa was the only feasible way to end apartheid.

JOHANNESBURG HAD ITS first recorded snowfall.

THE SAFARI SUIT caught on as both business and leisure wear in South Africa.

THE CATHOLIC CHURCH agreed to exonerate Jews for their guilt in the crucifixion of Jesus.

A RIP-ROARING AFRICAN adventure yarn, *When the Lion Roars*, by the local author, Wilbur Smith, was banned by the South African censors.

THE BEATLES' FIRST film, *A Hard Day's Night*, premiered in London.

1965

THE SINGER, DUSTY SPRINGFIELD, was deported from South Africa because she sang before a racially mixed audience.

SOUTH AFRICAN POLICE were allowed to detain people for 180 days without charging them and taking them to court. The previous maximum period for detainment had been 90 days.

A NEW LAW, *The Bantu Laws Amendment Act*, stripped seven million black people of their rights in South Africa. They were made into "temporary dwellers" without any rights. Black workers were allowed to live only in certain limited areas.

THE MINI-SKIRT appeared in London. Designed by Mary Quant, it ended 15 centimetres above the knee.

BRAM FISCHER WAS captured by police.

AS A PROTEST against apartheid, the schoolteacher, John Harris, hid a time bomb at Johannesburg Station. It detonated, killing one person and injuring another 23. John Harris was arrested and executed.

THE SPACE RACE between America and the USSR "hotted" up. Both Americans and Russians were able to execute their first space walk (separately).

SOUTH AFRICA ENTERED the nuclear era with the opening of the first nuclear power reactor outside Pretoria.

MODS AND ROCKERS, gangs of warring rebellious youth, descended on the English seaside town of Brighton, forcing pedestrians off the street.

WHITE RHODESIA BROKE with Britain. The Prime Minister, Ian Smith, declared UDI (Unilateral Declaration of Independence).

SOUTH AFRICAN SWIMMER, Karen Muir, just 12 years old, broke the world 110-yard backstroke record.

THE YEAR'S BIGGEST box-office success was the syrupy *The Sound of Music*.

THE WORDS "PSYCHEDELIC" and "flower power" became common usage.

1966

THE SOUTH AFRICAN Prime Minister, Dr Verwoerd, was stabbed to death in Parliament by Dimitrio Tsafendas.

IN THE TWELVE months ending 30 June, 479 114 Africans were prosecuted for offences against the pass laws.

BRAM FISCHER WAS sentenced to life imprisonment. He developed cancer in prison and was released only a few months before his death in 1975.

JIMI HENDRIX BURST upon the international music scene and The Beatles' movie *Help!* was released.

THE GROUP AREAS ACT led to the forced removal of many communities. District Six, the suburb close to central Cape Town, home to about 60 000 mainly coloured people, was proclaimed a "white" area.

SANDRA LAING, AN 11-year-old girl whose parents were classified white, was reclassified coloured and forced to leave the boarding school she was attending which was for "whites only".

THE HIT SINGLES of the year included "Yellow Submarine" and "Eleanor Rigby" by the Beatles, "The Green, Green Grass of Home" by Tom Jones and "California Dreaming" by The Mamas and the Papas.

THE LAW WAS changed so that political prisoners could now be kept in detention for an indefinite period without recourse to the courts.

THE GENERAL ELECTIONS showed increasing support for the Nationalist Government from the all-white electorate.

YVONNE CHAKA-CHAKA was born.

RACE RIOTS FLARED up in the US cities of Chicago, New York and Cleveland.

A LAW WAS passed in South Africa that abolished all interracial political parties.

THE FILM *DR ZHIVAGO* starring Julie Christie and Omar Sharif was released.

1967

DR CHRIS BARNARD performed the first heart transplant at Groote Schuur Hospital, Cape Town. The operation was a success but Louis Washkansky, the recipient of the new heart, died 18 days later.

THE PRIME MINISTER, Mr Vorster, tightened up the press laws so that the South African press's freedom to publish articles critical of the government's policy was severely limited.

THE DEFENCE AMENDMENT ACT made military service compulsory for white males.

OLIVER TAMBO, LIVING in exile, became ANC president.

CHE GUEVARA, THE revolutionary hero of the counter culture, was shot dead in the Bolivian jungle.

RENE MAGRITTE, THE Surrealist painter, died. One of his most famous paintings is of a solid-looking pipe with the words, "This is not a pipe", written below in French.

THE BEATLES' MANAGER, Brian Epstein, committed suicide by taking an overdose of sleeping pills.

MUHAMMAD ALI WAS stripped of his world title by the American Boxing Association for refusing to fight in Vietnam. "No Viet Cong ever called me nigger," he said.

THE SIX-DAY WAR between Israel and her Arab neighbours had South Africans glued to their radios.

RAYMOND ACKERMAN BOUGHT four small Cape Town stores – the first in what is to become the giant "Pick 'n Pay" chain.

CHIEF ALBERT LUTHULI, the Nobel Peace Prize winner, died.

IN SOUTH AFRICA, campaigners against the mini-skirt were vocal in the press. "Until the shameful parts of women are covered, I am convinced God will not fill the Vaal Dam." (Gert Yssel)

NEW GROUPS TO break into the top of the pop charts were – The Doors, The Seekers, The Monkees, The Who and Procul Harum.

THE BIGGEST EVER demonstration against the war in Vietnam took place in Washington DC. A dozen protestors were injured and hundreds arrested.

ONE

I knew he was taken when it was Rose who fetched me from school that Thursday. From where I stood leaning against the tennis-court fence, I could see Rose's red Mini turn jerkily in through the main entrance gate and bumble up the drive, making for the front. Her head was swivelling about, looking for me amongst the knots of boys kicking loose stones on the tarmac, amongst the groups lounging on the stairs. I started at a half-run on a diagonal path across the lawn to try to intercept her, the heavy kit bag banging my knees with each stride. I wanted to wave and shout, to flag her down, to race to her. I wanted to get it over with, her telling me what I knew she had to tell. But I didn't. I couldn't risk it. It was too theatrical, especially in front of the very public space at the main door.

Nothing was overlooked by the boys hanging about on the stairs, boys whose blank stares hid a sarcastic and nasty streak. To show enthusiasm for anything in their company, to be caught acting in any way but with studied cool or outright violence, was to expose a weakness you could never live down. Tomorrow – I could see it clearly in my mind's eye – Cedric van Zyl and his sidekick, Baby, would catch up with me outside the tuck shop at break and make loud comments about running after women in *fast* cars. Guffaws and sniggers would burst out from the rest of the boys crowding round the counter, cowered into joining in even when you sensed they were uncomfortable with it. Who knew for sure which one of us would be next? I had learnt that it was best to laugh with my tormentors, trying to deflect their attention, and hoping like all hell that some other silly thing, a vest sticking out of a school shirt or a beggar wobbling past on the road outside the school, would soon catch their attention.

Rose wasn't to know the spot on a side street near the tennis courts where Dad picked me up after hockey practice every Thursday. Although I had never told him of the bullies who held court on the steps after school well into the late afternoon (did their parents not care where they were, I wondered, mildly envious) he seemed to know that the best way to be fetched from school when you are thirteen, was as inconspicuously as possible.

I slowed down to a casual saunter as I reached the edge of the parking lot. I could feel the eyes of Cedric, Baby and Co. boring into my body. It was almost a challenge to feel as I did, to feel as if the world had stopped and yet to walk normally, super-cool, gliding as if in slow motion. I dared not look up. There was a sort of slow song going in my head: I hope Rose stays in the car, I hope she's seen me and isn't tempted to ask for me, I hope it isn't true.

In another part of my head there was a different kind of conversation, a fast flashing type of thinking. Maybe Dad couldn't make it because something came up at work. Maybe his car had given up the ghost. Yes that's it – the gearbox had been making a ghastly grating noise for ages now. Wasn't that fixed last week, though? Maybe ... maybe what? I couldn't think of any other feasible excuses so in those few moments it took to cross the car park a whole lot of ridiculous ones came in a flood. He's gone off with another woman, he's left the country, he's gone fishing!

But of course, deep down, I knew. It wasn't as if it was unexpected. We had lived with the possibility for over a year. Dad had discussed it with my sister, Jane, and me, not often, for that would have been morbid for someone of his basically cheerful nature, but often enough for me to know that it was not one of the dramatic flights of fancy that he sometimes had. When, every single morning, a man goes to work with a little suitcase packed with a change of clothing, a toothbrush and a razor, and kisses his wife passionately before he leaves; when his friends suddenly flee the country or disappear; when he sits his children and wife down and begins with "If I'm no longer here..." it's obvious that something is going to happen, isn't it?

And yet, until I saw Rose's Mini that Thursday, it hadn't been obvious to me. I had heard Dad speak of the missing friends, the Rooses, the Flints, the Fleichers. I had seen the embarrassing kisses in the morning and cringed. I had listened to the "little talks". But at the same time, I hadn't. I nodded when, after explaining the implications of their political work, my parents had asked, "Steven, do you understand what we mean?" Of course I had, what did they take me for? And yet, I hadn't really seen, hadn't heard, hadn't wanted to see or hear. That afternoon, walking over to the car, it felt as if I had been shaken from a waking sleep. My skin prickled, the edges of my ears burned, my bones grew taut in my body.

It is a contradiction but at the very same moment I recognised how, without knowing it, I had rehearsed this moment many times before. When Dad drove off in his station-wagon every working day, when the police raided our house in the middle of the night, or the worst vision of all, a snippet of a daydream, one that only now I remembered having at all: Reggie Nutfield coming bounding down the Yeoville street we live in just as I return from the corner cafe with a haul of toffees in my pocket. Have you heard? They came and got your father. He's been fighting for the kaffirs, hasn't he?

They'd got him. He'd been arrested.

Then all of a sudden I was in the car and Rose's face was close, inches from mine, and I could see that she had been crying.

"When did they come to get him?" I asked.

"In the morning, at the newspaper offices."

"Does Lucy know?" I've always called my mother by her first name when talking about her to other people.

"Of course. She had an exercise class she couldn't cancel, otherwise she would have come herself to fetch you."

"Jane?"

"Lucy phoned the school."

A hoot from behind and Rose started up the car. She was quiet for a long time, all the while it took to reverse, turn around and head out into the main road to join the lines of cars edging out of the city to the suburbs. Rose was concentrating fiercely on the road, too fiercely. I knew that she was holding back a flood of words; I could feel the pressure build. It was a family joke. Rose talked and talked: Rose said so herself.

At the intersection to Rockey Street she burst out.

"I can't believe it. Steven, oh Steven!"

It was a weird sing-song cry and the tears were rolling down her puffy face. I sank deeper into my seat, cringing, hoping the passengers riding high in the cars beside us wouldn't notice. Rose was a friend of my parents, someone who worked with Dad on the newspaper, someone who was in the movement, as they called it. She was especially close to my mother. They liked to go shopping for materials and furnishing together. Once or twice when I woke up in the morning she'd be asleep on the sofa in our lounge, having stayed too late to make it home the night before.

The tears stopped and the words tumbled out.

"He spent most of the morning writing away at his desk, clearing away papers, doing the accounts like he always does. Everybody was about as usual, no panic, no frantic discussions. I stepped over that little suitcase on the floor by his desk, oh, about six times, and still no-one said a thing about his going. Then, just when we all thought maybe not today, Katachi came rushing in. 'They're outside, the police are outside,' he was yelling and he was rattling the chains on the door trying to lock it. Your father got up and walked over and said 'Don't be a damned fool, Katachi, what the hell do you think you're doing, are you demented?' Then he opened the door and they came in, about five of them. Your father took charge, he asked, 'Yes, officer, what can we do for you?' He was so calm, Steven. He was fantastic, absolutely fantastic."

Tears were rolling down her face again.

"What's he got? Ninety days?" I asked.

"Probably. No-one's sure yet."

I was thinking, the words going in my head: here are the cars, the same cars as every Thursday. Here are all the people walking on the pavements. See the chap with the jaunty red suit, a zoot suit. Here is the newspaper boy dancing between the lanes of traffic at the robot. So this is what it's like. It's just the same. Now that the dreaded thing had happened, it was a kind of relief. We could begin a life without him. It was awful but it had a shape.

Ma was at the house after all. Her blue Beetle was in the driveway. Rose parked under the cascade of twigs which was the mulberry tree at that time of the year. I opened the passenger door, climbed out and then burrowed halfway back in to free my satchel and kit bag and hockey stick, which were jammed into the tiny space for your legs. When I emerged, Ma was standing near the car. Under her skirt and jersey she had on the leggings and leotard that she wore when she ran her exercise classes. She looked fine.

"Lucy."

"Rose."

They hugged each other. Ma tried to put her arms around me and I slipped out of them. She took my satchel from me and started talking in a light voice. "I can't tell you much. Abie's doing all he can to get permission for me to see him, he's got the lawyers working on it. It's unlikely that they'll allow it, though."

We walked into the house, Ma first, then me and then Rose following in the wake of the kit bag I was dragging. Jane came out of the bathroom and went over to the dining-room table where her homework was spread out. She grunted a greeting in my direction. I could tell she had been doing battle with a pimple on her chin.

Then she saw Rose.

"Were you there when he was taken, Rose? Did Dad give you any instructions? Anybody to contact?" She continued in that vein, reeling off the names of friends, lawyers and others from the movement. "Has Steven's teacher been told? What about the headmaster? We don't want him going into one of his dog-yapping phases again, you know, the stress getting to him and his marks dropping. Auntie Grace?"

I glared at my sister. She was only two-and-a-half years older than me and bossy from the day she was born.

"Tell your own bloody teachers," I snapped.

Ma turned to her. "Jane, Daddy and I decided beforehand who should be told. Here, Steven, take your satchel to your room." She looked at the heap I'd dumped at the base of the table legs. "All your stuff," she added mildly. She turned to Rose. "Thanks for getting Steven for me. Will you stay for tea?"

Rose and Ma went off to the kitchen conspiratorially. I could hear Rose sobbing again and laughing too, "I should be comforting you, Lucy." Jane was back in the bathroom, banging the door behind her.

I kicked my stuff into a corner of my bedroom, pulled off my hockey boots and socks and flopped on to the bed on my back. So ... now what? The ceiling with its familiar struts and patches of rust glared back at me. My room was once an enclosed porch. It still had frosted double-glass doors and red *stoep* cement under the carpet. It wasn't the shape of a bedroom either, more an entrance hall, small and narrow. From my bed, it felt as if it was a cabin. A wave of rough green foliage had climbed up from the back garden and threatened to spill in through the only window. A row of wooden cupboards, a foot taller than I, lined one side. On top lay my guitar.

Okay, so it's happened, I said out loud. I screwed up my face and held my balled fists in front of my eyes. I tried one or two punches at the pillow. No-one else was about so I could test the situation without an audience. It was no easier to know how to set my face in front of my mother, Jane or Rose, than it had been with Cedric, Baby and Co. In fact, it was worse. They seemed to be searching for something in me, demanding something of me I could not give – a show of emotion that I was unwilling to manufacture. In truth, I had no idea how I felt.

I needed to test myself, to see if I had any reactions I didn't know I had. Thirteen-year-old boy, father gone to jail, *unjustly* sent to jail. I said these words very slowly, purposefully to myself. I thought of throwing myself on the bed with grief but I was already on it. I experimented with a cry, "ahe ahe", not too loud, of course. I touched my eyes to see if they held tears. The skin-tingling, the tight bones, the adrenalin rush I had felt at the sight of Rose's Mini at the school were gone. Maybe they had come as a result of the pressure of hiding the tiniest shred of the news from Cedric and Co. There was an element of thrill and danger in keeping the shield up between home and school when they were about to collide. They were two very different worlds, which were to be kept separate at all costs.

But what I now felt was neither rage nor grief, only the usual feeling of tiredness and boredom and waiting. I toyed with the idea of bringing down my guitar to practise the new chords Peter had shown me, but it was too much effort to get up and reach it on top of the cupboard. I felt pinned to the bed by a mood of nothingness. The fact that Dad was in jail was outside the feeling, outside me. It was on the ceiling in the rust spot shaped like a crocodile, on the dust on the window-sill on which I scribbled rude words. It was perched on the bookshelf in a shoebox where I had stashed an illicit collection of Tubby comics. Me? I was safe. I pulled a blanket over myself and pretend-snoozed: having a zizz, my family called it. My body fitted into the hollows of the mattress and a stray sunbeam warmed my shoulders. Although the window was shut hard against the straggly winter growth, I thought I could hear the pool filter suck and water plop against the cement sides. Pigeons whirred and cooed. The air in the room went in and out with my breath. The afternoon light seeped away.

TWO

"Steven? Aren't you hungry?"

Ma stood at the doorway. Had I slept? It didn't seem as if I had but the suddenness of her appearance told me I had. She came in, sat down on the bed and passed me a plate of food. I half sat up and leaned my head against the headboard. This was not a special treat; I often had a small meal before supper in my bedroom or anywhere else for that matter.

"Where's Rose?"

"Left."

I heaped some orange-brown mince on the slice of whole-wheat bread and pushed one end into my mouth. Gravy dripped on to the plate.

Ma looked at me while I chewed.

"Would you like me to inform the school? With exams next week, it's going to be difficult."

I shook my head.

"They will have to know at some stage. You tell me when."

"Wherf ey gotim?"

"What's that?" Ma's face crinkled and for the first time I could see the strain behind the cool skin. A delicate blue vein on her temple fluttered.

I swallowed. The mince and bread slid down my throat in a warm gush. "Do you know where they've got him?"

"The police station in Fordsburg. That's where most of them land up at first. Abie's checking for us. I expect he'll phone any time now."

"Not the Fort?"

"No."

I had imagined Dad in the Fort in Hillbrow with an intuitive certainty that was difficult to set right, even when Ma told me otherwise. I had a clear picture of the Fort's surreal presence in my mind: a small regular hill on a rise, something like a miniature mine-dump with aloes and succulents planted on it, right in the middle of the shops and flats and high-rise buildings in Hillbrow. The only way you could tell it was a building was by the huge doorway in its middle. Then you could see it was a jail because it was blocked off by a large sheet of studded metal that had been painted grey. In the lower left corner was a man-sized door. When I was small Dad liked to tease me and say that it was for the dwarfs who mined gold in the hills.

"Where in Fordsburg?"

"I'll show you. You can come with me when I drop off some clothes if you want."

"Has he got 90 days?"

"90 days," she said, looking away.

"How do you know? Rose wasn't sure."

"Abie's pretty certain. They can renew it after the 90 days are up and give him another 90. They could release him but it's more likely they will lay charges and there will be a trial. Let's take it a day at a time, Steven. Don't you think it would be better if I contacted the school? Next week's exams, isn't it?"

It wasn't like Ma to repeat things like this, to ask when she already knew.

The phone rang.

"Ma! It's Mary," Jane shouted across the house.

"I'm not going to nag you. Change out of your hockey kit. It's making the bed muddy."

Ma left. Abie, Mary, Rose, Rita, Solly, Alfie, all of those who weren't in jail or had not left the country, not yet anyway, they'd be phoning to ask after the baby or to loan a lawn mower. Those were the codes that were used to pass on messages on tapped lines. They were like bees whose hive had been upturned, buzzing, talking, circling about helplessly. I smiled at the picture that I was forming of Abie driving to Rita's house who'd be on the phone to Lilian who would be visiting Alfie who would be in earnest discussion with Mary, etc., etc.

When I got up for supper proper, the sun was gone and an icy Transvaal night was closing in. Jane had propped up a biology book against the tomato-sauce bottle on the kitchen table. Under the table, a three-bar heater glowed near her sock-covered feet. Ma was eating a heap of green stuff.

"What's that?" I asked.

"Seaweed," she answered a bit sheepishly.

"Vile," said Jane, not looking up from her book.

"Yugh," I said, helping myself to mince and chips from the stove, William's stock supper. William had worked for us for over five years.

"Did someone explain to William?" I asked.

"Yes," answered Ma, "he just shook his head and kept saying *aikona*, over and over." She lifted up the edge of the tablecloth and looked under the table. "For God's sake, Jane, you'll get chill blains if you put your feet so close to the heater!"

There was a loud knock at the front door. Jane jumped up.

"Sounds too polite for the police," she said, darting out.

"Too early," Ma added. She too got up and walked out of the kitchen, a distracted look on her face. I listened out for the front door opening and the familiar rhythm of Abie's voice came to me, the unhurried careful tones of a born lawyer. "Tried the door a few times ... where are you chaps sitting?" I thought I heard him say.

I helped myself to the uneaten chips on Jane's plate and chewed thoughtfully, letting the fatty softness under the crisp skin of each one dissolve in my mouth. When we were small, there was a time when I couldn't walk down the passage without Jane jumping out at me from behind the lounge door where she had been lying in ambush. I would walk down the passage, well aware that she was there, knowing it because the game had been on for hours, and yet, when she did, I'd still get a fright. BOO! It would drive me crazy that I'd fall for it again and again.

Police raids had a similar effect. It made no difference that we knew that they could happen at any time: they always caught us unawares. During normal waking hours they were a hassle but when the security police banged on the door in the dark hours of early morning... BOO! And I'd jerk awake, heart bumping in my chest, eyes flying open into a rigid stare in the dark.

It would take a couple of seconds to place myself in my own bed in the familiar short-hand pattern that was my room at night: a craggy hill (a heap of clothes over the chair); a straight edge (the cupboard); the slick crescent in the centre of a dark plane (its handle). Only then would the pounding and rapping and tramping become recognisable. It's them again, a little voice would say, and I would sink back into my pillows getting ready to get up yet again but at my own pace.

Once I knew that it was only another raid, the menace was gone. I'd join my sleep-rumpled family as they shuffled to the front or back door, wherever it was that the assault seemed stronger, or congregated at the bathroom door using the opportunity to take a pee. The lights had been snapped on and walls and furnishings were stained a night-time yellow, dull and stale. Dad, having hastily bit into the teeth he had fished out from the glass by his bedside, would be dressed in a pair of crumpled, mismatching pyjamas. "The only thing the bloody SAP have ever forced me to do is wear pyjamas," he liked to say. (And now, Dad, in jail?)

With an air of resignation he'd open the door and let them in, a bunch of fully dressed strangers, men in cheap, ultra-conservative suits and loud ties and rough voices. We'd watch them as they swept the same books off the shelves, tipped out the same drawers, emptied the same cupboards. For the hour or two they stayed, Jane and I were under orders to choose a policeman and stick with him as he went through the house, making sure that banned books or incriminating documents were not planted amongst our possessions.

"But you went through that already, last week Tuesday," Ma would protest.

The young sergeant grinned. "No madam, that wasn't me. You must have been dreaming." And it was true; we had been, until they'd arrived. The young policemen who came barging into our house once a month, lately more often, all young, ruddy and moustached, were interchangeable. They lacked an individual identity but they weren't particularly malicious, either. In fact, they reminded me of some of the matric boys at school, more foolish than bad.

"Hiya, Steven."

It took a while for me to register that it was Abie's face as it peeped round the doorway. When I did, I had to swallow a laugh. His head was swathed in a grey scarf knotted under the chin like the babushka of a Russian peasant woman. His eyes searched the room before making contact. He was trying to find the "right" words. "Ivor's strong, you know that. He was prepared. He'll be all right." A hint of cold-air smoke came from his mouth.

"Sure. What's with the *doek?*"

"Toothache." He stepped into the kitchen. "I should have the lot of them out and be done with it but that's neither here nor there. Your father..." He paused and his eyes went on the roam again. "He's known that it was bound to happen. It was a choice he made, to stay and face the music. He refused to leave the country, but you know that, Steven, don't you?"

I nodded and watched the colours of Abie's knuckles as his hands gripped and let go the top of the chair, greeny-white under the liver-spotted skin. He must be at least ten or fifteen years older than my father, I decided.

"It's not a choice most of the blacks have and so it's not a choice your father would make. He's a brave man, an honourable man." Was it the pain in his teeth causing the nasal twang to his voice?

"Is there any chance anyone can see him?" I asked.

"No, but they've given permission for a food parcel and clothing while he's in detention. That's the only good thing about being in the hands of the security police rather than the prison authorities. You can drop off fresh laundry and pick up his dirty clothes every day."

Abie was backing out of the kitchen as he spoke. He left me with a vague wave of the hand and I lifted the plate to my face to lick up the last bits of gravy.

"Oh, by the way," his comical face was once again at the door, "don't you think it's a good idea to let your school know? I know your father is concerned about your schooling."

I groaned. "Steven's schooling" – I heard the words too often. Okay, so I wasn't the all-time academic success. So I wasn't quite up to my sister's standard.

I didn't answer and Abie left the room again. I could hear him talking softly with my mother in the passage and then using the phone.

William came into the kitchen from outside to do the supper dishes. "Is Jane finished and Madam?" He motioned to the table.

"Umm, I suppose so. Yes," I answered. Mine was the only empty plate. I passed the dishes to William at the sink.

"*Hau*, Steven," he said, scraping the seaweed directly into the bin, "your father – she did not steal, she did not stab people with a knife. Those police, they're wrong to take your father." Like so many blacks for whom English was a second or third language, William often muddled he and she. It was as much a feature of African English as confusion over "is" and "are" in the English used by Afrikaans-speakers. I looked into William's face hovering quietly above the busy hands, searching for the source of the calm and wisdom that always seemed to radiate from him.

23

"It would be better to look for *tsotsis* for them to catch in the street. There are too many in the street, stealing, fighting." William steered the conversation along well-trodden, comfortable paths which made it easy to be with him in the kitchen. Suds drifted up his dark arms as he stirred the dishes about. The subject of *tsotsis* led him to his son, George, who was back in Johannesburg without a pass. He had just been released after a two-year sentence for petty theft. Worries over George were a favourite topic of conversation between William and me. "No good, that boy. Bad friends," he would often say to me.

Suddenly, it was night. Reflections of the bare electric light bulb which Dad had promised he'd cover with a shade, shone out from the black squares which were the kitchen windows. There were no curtains except for a little frill which covered the bottom quarter. In the panes above, a couple of stars glittered sharply above a wave of dark trees. William opened the back door and left it open as he carried out the rubbish. I shivered as a blast of chilly air pushed its way into the kitchen. I had read that it was dark and cold in deepest space, darker and colder than can be imagined. With no cloud cover, the dry night air on the Highveld seemed to suck the warmth out of every living thing.

"Goodnight, Steven."

William had returned, washed his hands and untied the womanly apron he had chosen over the more conventional options my mother offered him, hanging it up on a hook near the sink. It was a sign that he intended to go to his outside room off the courtyard.

"Goodnight."

Not long after I too left the kitchen. I unplugged the heater, switched off the lights and turned down the passage to my room. I could hear water gushing into the bath. I stopped at the open door of the lounge. Ma was sitting alone in an armchair bathed in a pool of light thrown by a standing lamp.

"Ahh." A small noise escaped her lips as she looked up at me in the doorway from the heaps of papers and accounts lying in a semi-circle at her feet. There was no-one else with her. Abie seemed to have left; Jane was in the bath.

I fell into the closest armchair and Ma went back to her silent shuffling and sorting. I closed my eyes but then suddenly I had a question. "Ma, did Dad say I should do anything, something particular for him?"

Ma thought a moment.

"You could help with the pool. Dad did show you how to do that, didn't he? You could scoop out the leaves and muck and put in chemicals so that we'll be able to swim in summer without problems. You could make a start after the exams, during the holidays."

"Did Dad tell you I should do that?"

"No, not directly, but it would be helpful if you did."

"Will Dad be back in the summer?" I asked.

"I don't know, Steven. Maybe."

"Okay." I got up, ferreted out Dad's cat, Puss, from the couch where she had burrowed under the cushions and went off to bed.

THREE

So many visitors were at our house that weekend that Ma had to go out twice to get milk, bread and biscuits at the corner cafe. Jane and I were supposed to be studying for exams so she kept apologising and sending people off as they arrived. Yet more and more came and eventually the house was full and we were sent to our rooms with strict instructions to get on with it. I left the little hugging flocks commiserating with my mother and lay on my bed, strumming my guitar, practising. I'd got the chords for "Where have all the flowers gone?" from a book of folk songs Dad had bought me. One change was a little tricky and I got stuck time after time at the same part.

"For God's sake, Steven, give it a break," Jane yelled from her room. I got up and slammed the door shut.

Ma put her face in through the door. "Steven, we replaced that glass last year. If you think… Coming!" A guest came drifting down the passageway. "Lucy, Lucy, where can I find some more saucers?"

Ma lowered her voice. "I'm not having you and Jane screaming across the house. Why haven't you got your books out?"

"What did I say? I didn't say anything." I strummed away furiously.

She closed the door again. I heard one lot of people (the Shapiros?) taking their leave.

"Come and say goodbye, Steven. Jonathan is leaving." This time it was Jane who came swinging in through the door, her bent arms jammed above the doorknobs on each side as if she was on parallel bars. I ignored her.

"Where have all the flowers gone, long time passing, long time ago… Gone to young girls every one," (the difficult transition here) "when will they ever learn, when will they ever learn…"

"Learn another song," she spat out before crashing out of the room.

Next to pop in was Rose. "Mind if I come and listen?" she asked and leaned against the cupboard. I was pleased. I'd never really played for anyone else before except my family and I tried hard to do it well.

Rose hummed along with me for a while, and then sang softly, all through the verses – the young girls, the young men, the war and the graves.

Then, very loud, from the lounge, came the voice of Joan Baez singing "John Reilly". It was Jane, spiteful as ever. I gave up and Rose and I left my room. There was still quite a crowd in the lounge. Jane was at the record player looking guilty. Ma was on the couch flanked by Abie and Hilda. She was crying and laughing a bit in between. "I know it's stupid, I know, but it's Ivor's favourite record. No, don't take it off Jane, leave it. I like it, I really do, it's just that … oh, here I go again. I miss him already and he's only been gone three days… Sorry, it's so silly of me."

"Not at all, not at all. It's good to cry." Abie patted her hand. Hilda stroked her hair and gave Rose a look above my mother's head. "Get a glass of water," she mouthed.

Jane had turned down the volume and was looking undecided about what to do next.

I left for the kitchen with Rose, who filled a glass under the running tap and hurried back. I didn't want to return.

Around the table, on which several ashtrays overflowed, a huddle of men and a single woman, Rita, my father's colleague, were talking politics. Ropes of cigarette smoke curled and rose to the ceiling, like a djinn from a bottle. Peasants, capitalism, the market place, class warfare, the terms tripped off their tongues in the earnest, argumentative way I'd been hearing ever since I could remember.

Bennie made space for me on the wooden bench along one wall of the kitchen. "Join us, Steven," he said. I knew that if it weren't for Dad being in jail, he'd have ignored me, allowing me the freedom of listening in – or leaving – as I liked, which was the way it always was. It made me feel uncomfortable to be singled out.

"Gotta study," I mumbled and headed back into my room.

I kept up with "Where have they gone?" until everybody had left.

"Whew!" Ma slumped into the chair near my bed. "The good wishes are well meant, but all these visitors are exhausting, aren't they, Steven?"

I grunted.

"And distracting. I feel I should have chased them away sooner. What are you writing tomorrow? English comprehension and composition. No swotting needed for those. Poor Jane's got her first maths paper."

"Are you going to the Film Society? What are they showing tonight?" Sunday nights were Film Society meetings.

"It's about Chinese peasants again. I forget the title – 'Blossoms on a Bough', 'The Breaking Bough' – something like that. You're not thinking about going, are you? I really don't…"

"No, Ma, I'll study history for Tuesday's exam, if that's what you're asking. You go, though. Phone Dulcie and she'll fetch you."

"I'll leave you the number, in case there's another police…"

"We'll be fine, Ma."

"I'll check if William is in his room. Maybe he's back early…"

"Ma!"

"Yes?"

"Go!"

And she did. Before she left she went to the neighbours and asked them to listen out. She left a list of phone numbers sticky-taped to the wall near the phone. She made us put on all the lights, lock the doors and windows and check them over and over. And she left a huge cheese omelette in the oven (it was William's night off) which Jane and I ate straight off the serving dish, both spooning from opposite ends at the same time.

After supper, Jane went to her room to study and I was left to my own devices. For a little while I paged through Paul Kruger's problems with the *Uitlanders* leading to the Jameson Raid (pages 78 to 83, Van Jaarsveld) before the urge to escape won over conscientiousness, and I headed back to the kitchen, perhaps for some more food, I'm not sure. I didn't have anything in mind. Nevertheless, in that way that often occurs over exam periods, I found myself only a minute or two later engrossed in something as unrelated to studying as could be found. A box of green jelly, Royal Jelly, greengage flavour, winked at me from behind the tins and packets on the pantry shelves. I hadn't made jelly for years (we hardly ever had it for dessert) and suddenly it seemed the most desirable thing imaginable.

I remembered that I'd seen a fancy copper-coloured mould somewhere in the kitchen cupboards and rummaged about amongst the baking sheets and cooking pots till I found it. Jane shouted out from her room but I ignored her. Then it was done. The jelly in the fridge was waiting to stiffen. It had only taken a few minutes after all and I knew very well what I should be doing next. I poured out a saucer of milk for Puss who'd been brushing up against my feet and yowling, and left the kitchen. Oh, well, nothing for it. Back to Van Jaarsveld.

I ignored the open mouth of my guitar on the floor saying O, sat at my table and flipped through the dreaded textbook looking for a place to start that was neither too boring nor too long and complicated. Finally, I settled on the 1820 Settlers for I thought it would be easy to summarise. Point One: the 1820 Settlers were... Eventually, one-and-a-half foolscap pages of writing lay before me, a bit untidy (blame being left-handed) but done.

I heard Jane padding about in the lounge and rushed off to talk to her. She was cutting her toenails. "Bugger this bloody maths," she said to me. "It's *che sera, sera* at this stage. I've either got it or I don't."

I flopped down on the sofa next to her.

"Me too," I said.

"Steven!" She dropped the scissors and grabbed my ear.

"Ow! What?"

"You've got a whole lot of blackheads in there."

"No! Where?" I pulled away but she held on.

"Here, there. I don't know. You should wash more, you know. With soap. They're ugly, really ugly."

"Rubbish." Still, I didn't break away completely. I knew a boy in my class whose ears had a crop that both disgusted and attracted me. The urge to look at them, if not to say something, was overwhelming in his company.

Jane tugged at my lobe, pulling the body attached to it closer to her prying gaze.

"If it's sore, I'll stop, I promise. You just have to say stop."

"How much will you pay?" I asked.

"Tomorrow's tuck money."

"All of it?"

"Half." With the negotiations over, she finally let go. She got out a matchbox from a drawer, removed two matches and pushed me down onto the sofa, my head pressed hard against the armrest. After adjusting the angle of my ear to catch the light from the standing lamp, the surgery began.

"Little black piggies needing just the slightest prod to burst out of their pens," Jane said in a reciting way.

"Sis, Jane!" I said, snorting with laughter.

"Hold still, you," she said. "They're massive. Here I'll show you." She brought down one of the matches to my eye level.

"It's tiny, man."

"No, they're not. If only you could see the inside of your ear. They always look small when they're out. I just got another one."

"Ouch! You're hurting!"

Eventually, I rolled off the sofa. "I can't anymore. You're a bloody butcher."

"Bedtime, then." Jane stretched out like a cat. "I'll do the rest tomorrow."

"Not on your nelly. And don't forget I'm taking your tuck money."

"Half."

I heard Lucy come in soon after I went to bed. Closing car doors and engines idling outside, the latch on the door, then her voice. "Bye, Dulcie. Yoo-hoo, everything's fine. Jane's still up." Another car door slamming shut and the engine making off down the street, and then I fell asleep. I must have because the next bit I remember *I* was driving a car and the roads were getting narrower and narrower until I was driving through rooms in someone's house. I passed what looked like a nursery with a crib-like thing in the middle and even drove up some stairs, the car wheels adapting to the vertical and horizontal of each rise in a most ingenious way.

FOUR

When I got back home from school in the afternoon I was chuffed with myself. Not only had I cleverly managed to adapt one of the choices of essay titles in the exam to my favourite genre, horror, but I also thought I'd done a pretty good job of it. All the way home in the car (my mother fetched me) I went through the plot in my mind, enjoying the bits I thought I'd written particularly well.

There was the majestic beginning with a single man on foot in the middle of a desert, which I had described in my favourite cowboy-book language: "Like an ant in an empty oil drum, he found himself in a vast dusty plain, the towering mesas and buttes, the merciless sun," etc., etc. I had the man parched, half-starved and already partially hallucinating, stagger into a ghost town and, failing to find a single drop of water or food, collapse at an abandoned railway siding on the edge of the town. He willingly invited Death to take him but Death declined because (I thought this bit was close to brilliant) "Death had eaten his fill that day and like a bored baby who was tired of swallowing spoonfuls of mashed carrots, he was ready to play with his food, to roll it around on his feeding tray, to smear it into the cracks, to make it fly into the air for a laugh."

"Seems like it went all right today," my mother said. "What are you writing tomorrow? It's history, isn't it?" She was in a breezy mood, her chirpiness expressed in the perky movements of the Beetle.

"History *and* maths."

She put on a sympathetic face.

"When's your lesson with Dave this afternoon?"

"At four thirty."

I went back to the buttes and mesas of the south-west, where the sun was setting in a spectacular fashion, splashing the rocks and soil and the empty clapboard houses in an array of stunning colours. My man, lying in the sand, eyes wide-open, taking his fill of this glorious sight for what he knew to be the last time, waited for the end.

"You've done all the preparation one can expect," Ma was saying.

The train had almost pulled into the station before he realised that the rhythmic pounding he had been hearing for some while was outside him. The metal tracks had been singing, the ground reverberating. The train had stopped just in time.

"What was that? Did you say something?" Ma hummed to herself, the warm wind from the open passenger window blowing her hair, parting the mass of blonde curls to form a whirling crater. Reluctantly, I broke away from the West and studied her for a second. She had taken the decision to put a brave face on things, I decided.

"Uh-uh."

The Beetle scooted along through the streets of Yeoville. The strings of houses painted in pastels, the grilles and crazy-paving slasto stoeps, the Beware of the Dog signs lopsidedly wired to front gates, all swam past in the same order that they did every day, as meaningless and catchy as the melody of a pop song. My mind wandered back to my essay.

Absolutely the best part, I was thinking, was the phrase, "sensing the imprint of past lives burnt into the icy metal skin". I repeated it over and over, enjoying the deliciousness of the words. That was how I had described the feel of the inside of the car into which the train driver and the conductor had put the man, once they had revived him with a drink of water and the train had set off once again. Lurching around in a completely dark, sealed metal box, the man had come to his senses, only to realise that he was imprisoned in a refrigeration unit hurtling through the night to an unknown destination. My last sentence put the train back into the landscape at daybreak, a scorching heat beginning to build up over the immense desert through which the train crawled like a tiny black caterpillar. I had kept the ending open-ended. Whether the man was dead or alive and whether his journey was the delusion of a dying man or not, were for the reader to decide. I, sure as hell, didn't know.

"So what was your essay topic?" Ma asked, steering the car into the driveway and gliding to a stop under the mulberry tree.

"A Train Journey."

"Not terribly original, is it? But easy enough," she mused.

"Ja, I just hope Sir hasn't read too many Louis L'Amours. I have a feeling I got the idea from a book or comic I read, but I can't remember."

"Comes from wasting your time on such rubbish," Ma said, her tone cheerful. She slipped the key into the front-door lock and let me in. "Yoo-hoo, we're home, Jane," her call bounced through the interior of the house and resonated off the walls.

"She must be in the garden, "Ma muttered and went off to her room.

Once I'd dumped my satchel in my bedroom, I made my way to the kitchen and opened the fridge door, a habit on returning from school as automatic as pulling off scabs from my knees in bed at night. Immediately, I remembered the green jelly. It had been whole when I had last looked before setting off for school; I had put the mould in hot water to loosen the jelly from the sides and tipped it over onto a plate. Now there was only a sunken heap. Someone had helped themselves, torn into it, gorged on it. I stared at the battered remains. The beautiful fairy-castle shape, the colour of extra-terrestrials and boiled sweets, was gone. I imagined the sound and feel of the first spoon carving a smooth scoop into its fluted roundness, the combination of sweet and tart flavours as I sucked it off the spoon, the wobbly, shimmery feel of it.

Jane. It had to be her. She had come out earlier than I because of the exams and she had helped herself without waiting to ask me. It was a childish reaction, I know, but I was furious. Mad as anything. My cheerfulness evaporated in a single moment. I stood in front of the open door letting the fridge hum and clammy cold escape into the kitchen. I could have murdered my sister there and then. I stood very still. I was scared that my anger would blow me apart. And then I snapped.

It started with a vicious kick to Jane's shin when I eventually found her in the garden sunning herself on a blanket with her books. The proof was sitting on the ground beside her feet, an empty white bowl tinged with green, the spoon lying in it as innocently as a cent in a child's palm. She jumped up in shock and anger.

"Ow! What d'you do that for? Ma! Steven kicked me. Ma!" She chased me round the garden and when she couldn't catch me she threw anything she could lay her hands on, books, stones, half-bricks, a small garden pot. I ducked and weaved, avoiding getting trapped in the dead end created by the garage and the house wall by crashing through the hibiscus, an escape route that we had discovered on the many wild chases we'd had in the past. I bashed through the thick, woody branches,

33

uncaring of the scratches and spikes. She was waiting for me at the other end and flew at me biting, scratching and kicking.

"You ate the whole thing, you guts. I made it and you didn't ask," I screamed at her, pulling away and trying to break the grip of her hands from around my leg and neck. I broke free and faced her a safe distance away. Tears were streaming down my face.

"Cry-baby, cry-baby!" she sneered, kicking a small branch in my direction.

Ma came out of the house.

"What's going on here?"

"He came and kicked me for no reason. Look! I'm going to have a terrible bruise here." She clutched at her leg.

"You ate my jelly, you fat cow!" I yelled back, diving behind a tree trunk as a stone came hurtling my way.

"Stop this, you two. Stop now!" Ma raised her voice. "Come into the house this instant!"

"I didn't know it wasn't for everybody. It was in the fridge," Jane whinged. "How was I to know? Can you believe it, thirteen and crying over spilt jelly."

I ran at her, fists flailing. Ma stepped in between us and made an attempt to catch me in her arms.

"This is it," she said. "I've now had enough. Each of you go to your room this second. I'm taking you to a maths lesson in half an hour, Steven, so go and get ready. You, young missy, you're in standard nine, not that one would believe it from your behaviour!"

She held tightly on to my shirt, which she had bunched into a handle between my shoulder blades and frogmarched me in through the front door. Jane followed, swearing and complaining, issuing little kicks at me which weren't meant to connect and didn't.

FIVE

Before we left for my maths lesson, I washed my face in the bathroom and Ma put some Mercurochrome on a scratch I had on my forearm. We climbed into the car in a sullen silence. The cough of the starter and the responding series of tones sung by the engine filled in for conversation: a fart-like burst in first to near the corner, a shift as we swung left into Innes, a hiccough on the bend and then the building up to the usual Beetle doofa-doofa as we sped downhill. Only a block away from the corner, however, Ma turned into the parking lot at the sports club near the golf course.

"Hey, what're you doing?"

"We're in plenty of time for Dave. I want to talk to you, Steven."

She pulled up in a bay, switched the ignition off and turned to me in the passenger seat.

"Don't, Ma," I began, knowing what was in store.

"I'm not going to lecture you," she answered gently. "I want to ask you if you're struggling with things, with the uncertainty, Dad being in jail, primarily."

"Ma, Jane and I fight, we always have and we always will. That's the way things are. Don't make a thing about it."

"Are you worried about the maths exams? It's not unheard of to ask for leniency for special circumstances. I can phone the school so they can take it into account when they mark."

"Don't! Please let's go. Dave was going to show me how to do these equations that we're getting in the paper for sure."

"We'll go now, I promise." Yet, we didn't. She swivelled around in her seat and her eyes sought mine and locked in.

I turned aside. "Jane deserves everything she gets," I began. "She's such a bossy know-it-all, and she gets into my stuff all the time. She couldn't be bothered to find out if it was *my* jelly." The crisscross pattern of the tennis-court fencing I was facing acted as a sieve to my words, straining out everything but the anger, which ran through it in buckets.

"Wait!"

Ma had raised her hands and was motioning with her taut palms as if she were holding back a shuddering attack in the air. She took a deep breath, modulated her voice purposefully and willed me to listen.

"Let's not get into that again. I know this will sound like a lecture, but it would help if you think about what I'm going to say. I understand that things are difficult for you. It's been a stressful time for all of us. Not knowing when Ivor's coming back, what is happening to him, things going through your mind at night – it feels like the family's falling apart but it's not, you know. I know it sounds like a cliché, but we have each other and we have to try be kind to each other. It would be better, healthier, if you came out and expressed some of what you feel, instead of bursting out with ugly scenes. No, listen, Steven. Please try and talk instead of acting out your frustration. Try and find suitable words instead of punching and kicking and making noises like rundy-bundy and speaking like Mickey Mouse. And this childish fighting with Jane … I know it's asking…"

"I don't have any words!" I shouted. "I don't know what you want from me, but I don't and that's that! Now, start the car."

Ma looked at me for a second or two, as if she were thinking over whether it was worth continuing or trying a new tack, then faced the front again and turned the ignition key. As we reversed out of the parking lot and made our way through the streets to Dave's house in Cyrildene, I glared out of the side window. The strain on Ma's face hung before my eyes and already I felt guilty. This was not the way to act when you were the "only man left in the house", a phrase I'd heard quite a bit lately.

I didn't know what it was that had made me so difficult. I find myself difficult, I decided. As for the angry attack on Jane, the jelly seemed such a puny reason to have shouted and fought and cried, especially to have cried. I felt ashamed. How could it have been the jelly itself, a silly mound of green gelatine sitting in the fridge? A pudding, for goodness sake. A rhyme from babyhood came singing back to me: "Jelly on the plate, jelly on the plate, wibble-wobble, jelly on a plate." An irritating, teasing falsetto.

I stole a glance at my mother from behind the maths book I was pretending to read. She seemed a great distance away at the wheel. I was making a big thing of looking for the chapter on equations, reciting the snippet of maths pummelled into me: "Order of operations: BODMAS, brackets of division, multiplication, addition, subtraction." One of the small, ineffectual life belts thrown to those who drift in maths confusion year after year, this was a hopeless distraction from the forgiveness I both yearned and could not ask for.

I shot another look towards the driver's seat and my mother's profile was marble.

Snapping the book closed with my knees, I tipped my head back and rested it against the vibrating window. Light swam over the rosy skin of my closed eyes in bars of green and speckles that bloomed a crazy purple. I watched each effect intently, as if I were following a film on a screen, except that I was in control to some extent. Squint and the lines turned into zigzags, relax the muscles around the eyes and they expanded into fiery sea-anemones spitting white-hot sparks.

This was an old trick of mine, a private display that I had often turned to as a child in boring situations where escape was not possible, at political meetings, in class, on long trips. Today, though, the fireworks were more than mere entertainment. They seemed to echo a rage that I recognised was running deep within. A blazing fire burned out of control, threatening to break through to the surface at any time, surprising me with its fierceness. While the lights went on and off in pretty patterns in my head, down below all was molten and hot and confused.

I opened my eyes.

"Ma," I began, "I think ... umm, I think I'm going to..." I searched for anything to say, for some words to fall out of the sky and give me a direction, a shape. I felt the powerless feeling I had had as a young child when I was at last given the chance to break into the conversation at dinner parties, only to find that I could not remember what it was that I'd so urgently wanted to say. I'd cover up by talking absolute rubbish, quickly filling the hushed hole in the talk before it closed up again, locking me out.

"To do what, Steven?"

"I think..." I continued helplessly, "that maybe, if I get into the B team this term, well, you know, then maybe..." At the edges of my awareness, almost out of view, something insisted, something small and weak, making its way to the front of my mind, tip-toeing gingerly forward.

Ma sat as still as anyone can when they are driving a car, waiting for me to come out with it. But it was no good. Just like all the other times, the minute it got close and I was on the point of identifying it, it was gone. Something in me made a loud noise, screamed, punched, hit out, scaring it off again. Like a timid little animal, it darted away; like a field mouse twitching in the grass and scampering behind a rock at the slightest movement.

"Ag, nothing," I said.

What was it? I was too angry to care. The fire crackled.

SIX

In the last week of school after the exams were over and the long mid-year holidays lay ahead, everyone, boys and teachers alike, was present in the classroom in body only. The geography teacher set up the 16 mm film projector at the back of the class, chose a dusty reel from the top of the cupboard at random, got it threaded and going and left for the staff room ostensibly to finish our reports. Left to its own devices, the class exploded, drowning out the tinkling music and loud commentary on the paper industry in Canada and mocking the endless shots of fir trees being felled and log-jammed rivers.

Peter Schiff stood up in his seat, hands by his side, taut and unbending as a board. Silhouetted against the projector's light, he dropped forward on the floor in the aisle between two rows of desks, boom, just like that, saving himself from surely breaking his nose only at the last second with a deft spring of the hands.

"Timber!" we yelled, falling over each other, stiff like trees.

Mike Lecanides ran up in front of the screen and staged his death from a hail of bullets, his form a moving black shadow against a backdrop of a chipping machine in a sawmill. Everybody followed, jostling and pushing to get their chance of a minute or two of fame on the screen.

Reggie Nutfield took out a half-finished cattie from his suitcase and mimed what was supposed to be the stalking of prey on a hunt.

"That's no cattie, it's your two-pronged peepee," someone called out from the back.

"Pass it to me," I shouted to him when he returned to his seat. I had noticed the wood shavings and sawdust building up on the floor under his desk earlier in the day.

"No, why should I?" he shouted back, but he threw it over anyway. I caught it over Mike's head. It was a beauty, thick and strong, just waiting for a bit of pink inner tube.

The bell rang well before it should have, leaving the great rollers shooting out miles of paper on screen and the music, now a mechanical, jazzy sound, to play to an empty classroom. Obviously someone had persuaded the secretaries or headmaster that restraining three hundred boys under these conditions was pointless.

The business of the extra-long break was rumour-mongering. Christopher Plumstead wasn't coming back next term; boarding school in Potchefstroom was a distinct possibility. Someone passed on the tidbit that one of the boys from form five was planning to drive his mother's car to Durban and Baby and Cedric van Zyl were hitchhiking a week later to join him. Barney Sundelowitz said he was going to use his *barmitzvah* money to buy the number 10 Meccano set, which he'd seen at the toy section at Stuttafords in town. Oh really, we put in, adding a dash of theatrics to the sarcasm to emphasise our lack of interest in such mundane and childish matters. Reggie Nutfield was planning a visit to his uncle's farm in the Free State.

"I'm gonna finish it with *lekker dik* rubber," he was telling us near the toilets where I reluctantly handed the cattie back to him. Eric, Reggie and I were at the back behind the urinals, a favourite spot of ours in winter where a nice sunny heat built up from a bank of high windows.

"There's all sorts of animals to hunt there. There are snakes and birds, even springbok. When the bush is low, you can see them easily. Best time for hunting, this time of the year – No Place to Hide," he boomed, invoking the title of our favourite serial that played at quarter-past-seven each week-night on Springbok Radio.

I snorted. "Don't forget to bring me a piece of biltong."

"No, man, Wheels," Reggie said. "I didn't say I was going to get a springbok with a cattie. My uncle's got guns, plenty. You should see my cousins, man. They can shoot like bloody – I don't know – like soldiers or something."

A troop of boys came into the toilet, unzipping their pants, talking loudly, gesturing. We walked out, down a short flight of steps and out of the building. There was a chill to the air that was surprising, considering the cheerful sunshine pouring over the school and its grounds. Crossing over from the tuck shop to the tennis courts, we took a short cut through the rugby field. The grass was a torn, scuffed yellow, shrivelled dry by frosty nights and sunny days. Flakes of it always stuck to our jerseys and pants when we sat down and were kicked up on to our grey socks when we walked.

"So what are you going to shoot with your cattie then?" Eric asked Reggie.

"I don't know, just aim at meerkats and stuff."

"Are you gonna get a chance with the guns?"

"Ja, of course. My uncle takes us out in the veld with air guns and he says, be my guest. If it moves, shoot it."

"Gee."

"Shoo!" We were all suitably impressed. My granny, who had lived on a sugar-cane farm, wouldn't have let us do anything as exciting as this. And my parents disapproved of what my mother termed "blood sports".

"Have you ever, well, shot anything? Before, when you've been there before?"

"An owl."

"Owl? Are you mad in your head?" Eric was besotted with certain animals.

"Why not? Why not an owl?" I confronted Eric.

"They're birds, remember," he said. He was thinking about the pigeons he and I had kept in a coop in the back of our house for over a year. It was his unhappy lot in life to live in a block of flats where the caretaker refused her tenants the privilege of pets, even a budgie. Eric had loved those birds. He had once punched me in the stomach when I had forgotten to feed them. Since then he had come by our house every weekend, even when we were out, to check on them. A week after my father went to jail my mother finally put her foot down and ordered us to get rid of them. Rats were being attracted by the sacks of feed, and the smell was wafting into the house from the *hokkies*. Eric was still sore about having to sell them.

"This is different," I said, not knowing in the least why it was different. Eric was pulling at a scab on his arm, remembering anew the hurt of losing the birds.

"Your dad wouldn't have minded about those birds. Your mother waited until he was out of the house and the second he was gone, she got rid of them." The bitterness in his voice made me want to defend my mother, but why? He was right.

"Where's your dad gone? Run off with another woman?" Reggie Nutfield was not as close a friend as Eric. He hadn't heard.

I laughed and changed the subject. "What kind of owl was it? One with a face like a heart? Hooooot! Hooooot!"

"But where's your father gone, Steven?"

"Tu whit, tu whoooo. Tu whit, tu whooooo."

"Has your dad left the old woman? You can tell. We don't even know where mine is."

"His father's in jail. For politics," Eric said.

It was Reggie Nutfield's chance to be impressed.

"Wow! What'd he do?"

I shrugged. I wasn't actually too sure what my father had done to get arrested. I knew my parents were involved in fighting apartheid. I knew they organised protest marches and speeches and boycotts, spent Saturdays collecting signatures for petitions. They wrote endless letters to the press and posted illegal banners in public places. I knew my father ran a newspaper that kept changing its name. Every time it got banned he brought out another edition with a new name: *The Guardian, New Age, New Vision, The Progressive View.* What was memorable about this work for me were the stories Dad told us of the trips all over the country to collect money for the paper; the characters he met; the strange places, getting lost and found; the high adventure of it, not the politics.

Dad also had another business, which raised funds for the movement (Ma was now running it between exercise classes). Uncle Willie's Christmas Hampers worked like this: agents went around the township and got people to sign up for the scheme. They paid a small fee each month which ensured them a big hamper of food, sweets and crockery at the end of the year. It did a roaring trade.

"He must have done something," Reggie continued. "They don't lock people up 'cause they don't like the look of them."

I looked away. What on earth could I say?

"Ag, I don't know – something about fraud. Stealing money from the newspaper," I lied.

Eric gave me a sharp look.

"Ja, his dad stole all this money from the bank by diddling the books and they caught him red-handed."

"I thought you said it was politics," Reggie said.

"It is, you fool," Eric continued, "the newspaper he works for secretly supports the, umm," and here Eric's voice broke into a hoarse whisper, "the Nazis."

"What?"

"The Nazis. I said the Nazis. They're here again in South Africa planning a big showdown, stockpiling arms and stuff. You know the Drill Hall in town, the one across from Joubert Park? Well, underneath it are these miles and miles of tunnels and that's where they're hiding it all." I avoided looking at Eric as he spun this marvellous tale that grew more elaborate with each sentence.

"They've got tanks they managed to ship here after the war, you see, and they drove them through the veld from Walvis Bay, *at night*, and…"

Reggie gave Eric a small punch on the forearm.

"You're talking *kak!*" he said.

Eric shrugged. "We're not chaffing, promise. Okay, don't believe it."

We walked on in silence. We could sense Reggie chewing over things at our side. Eventually he broke out.

"That was in the Second World War. The Nazis are over and done with, man. They were beaten by the British and Americans at the end of the war. Anyway, what's that got to do with Steven's dad?"

"Well, where's he then? Have you see him fetch Steven lately?"

Reggie caught my sleeve and pulled me round to face him.

"What d'you say, Wheels?" he demanded.

I clicked my heels and shot up a stiffened arm into the air.

"Jawohl, mein Führer!"

Reggie's face broke into a broad grin. We spent a couple of minutes giving each other the Nazi salute and laughing. A tiny whirlwind blew up, an icy wind chasing chip packets and papers across the field in a dizzy dance.

"Check that!" I said, pointing. I did a little spin, hugging my blazer tight around me as the wind lifted the debris and flung it against a bush.

"How long has he been in chookie?" Reggie persisted.

We reached the farthest point of the school grounds and turned round to make our way back. This break was unbelievably long, I thought to myself. Had they given up on maintaining even a semblance of school time?

Eric was shameless. "About two weeks. They've tortured him with water torture and electrical probes and pulled out some of his teeth to tell them where the guns are stashed but he didn't tell them a thing."

"Ja. I believe you."

A little later, I caught Eric's eye as he bent over to pick up a bare jacaranda branch lying on the grass. As our eyes met, it was difficult not to snigger. Reggie saw it, though.

"You're laughing, I can see."

"No, I'm not, it was just a cough. See," and I coughed two or three times in a row.

We were walking on the path between the tennis courts and the prefabs where kindergarten children were hanging on to the fence, shaking back and forth in the wind and calling to us.

"Go have your biscuits and hot milk," Reggie barked at them. They ran away with whoops and shrieks, only to rush back again and begin the game afresh. We walked in silence until the bell rang.

"Don't tell anyone about Steven's father. It's top secret. And bring us springbok horns for a trophy, hey?" Eric half broke the stick he'd been beating through the air and held it to his head to approximate horns.

"I dunno," Reggie was saying, "it didn't feel so good when that owl dropped out of the tree. I felt pretty bad afterwards, I can tell you."

Eric's desk was near to mine in the classroom. I wanted to thank him but I didn't know how, so instead I made a face behind Reggie's back and we both laughed.

SEVEN

On the second last day of school, I was called out of class to the headmaster's office. I went through a quick mental checklist of all the offences I might have committed over the last weeks and drew a blank on any that might have been seen. I came to the conclusion that Ma's threats (they always felt threatening to me, even when voiced with concern) to phone the school had finally materialised. For the second time in my short high school career, I found myself waiting in dread outside that panelled door with the brass nameplate.

I forced up the knot of my tie and combed my hair with my fingers, tucking the straggly growth at the nape of my neck into my collar where I hoped it would not show. The first time I'd been to the Boss (this was what Mr Muirson was called behind his back by staff and boys alike) was at the beginning of the year when I had fought with Jason Freed at the bus shelter outside the school and his mother had phoned to complain that her son needed two stitches above the eye.

"Come in."

The response to my timid tap came immediately. I took a deep breath to steady the nerves, twisted the handle, pushed on it and almost fell into the office. The door looked heavy but it gave hardly any resistance. As I regained my balance, trying to disguise my lurch into a perfectly natural movement, I saw that the Boss was busy on the phone and had kindly averted his gaze from my unspectacular entrance. I needn't have worried about the hair and scuffed shoes either. When he put down the phone and swivelled in his chair to face me, I could see he had on his concerned expression: soulful, heavy eyes set in a long, brown face framed by a lot of wiry, black hairs which sprouted in equal quantities from his ears, cheeks, nostrils and temples. He stretched his thin lips into a half-smile.

"Well, Carter," he began, "do come in. Close the door, my boy." I did as I was told and walked across the carpet to his desk, sensing the wrinkles in it with my shoes.

"Sit down."

On my side of his desk was a chair set at a slight angle to appear welcoming. I arranged myself gingerly on it and fixed my gaze on the floral curtains behind the Boss's head. They were a swirl of cream, russet and olive-green, a rendering of autumn leaves.

"Carter," he said.

I focused in the direction of his chest, noticing that his face was reflected in reverse on the polished surface of the desk that yawned between us. He sighed, and began the spiel I was expecting.

"Your mother phoned me yesterday about the spot of bother your family is in at present. She asked me not to make a big fuss about this. She was uncertain whether you would find it easier if we just ignored the whole matter but I'm a great believer in talking, my lad. Talking and talking, getting it off your chest, speaking your mind."

Usually his voice reminded me of a strangled turkey, a strident, gobbling sound that tried, but failed, to carry authority. Now it had mellowed to a lower, more sympathetic register.

"So that's what I thought we could do, boy. Have a little chat."

I glanced up but immediately fixed my eyes on the curtain once more. How many coppery leaves on each repeated sprig running diagonally down the folds, how many streaked with orange? The dance of the patterns took my full attention.

"Have you anything to say, Carter? View me merely as a concerned adult, someone who wants to help you if he can."

Yet another person was imploring me to talk. What could they possibly want me to say?

Eventually, to cover the silence that was threatening to swallow us both, he continued in a firmer, starchier voice.

"I want you to know that if there is anything we can do, you should not hesitate to approach me or any other member of staff in the remaining days of this term and next term."

There was a pause like a channel of water sinking into the sand before he re-navigated his course and set up in more familiar territory.

"I have had a brief look at your exam results, which are barely average, although I don't have the full set as yet."

He shuffled some papers on the edge of the desk. Now that he was sounding more like the headmaster I knew, I was encouraged to try to make the contact I was being asked, almost begged, to make. I nodded and mumbled a few words.

"Yes, sir. Will try." Something like that.

Heartened by this shred of interaction, Mr Muirson softened his position.

"Don't get me wrong. I don't view this set of marks as the final word. By no means. I'm sure it will be way up there in no time at all. Your teachers inform me that they think you're no monkey. Quite clever, in fact. Creative, imaginative. But, it's not the right time to worry unduly about schoolwork. You have three weeks of holiday ahead and I want you to have a good time."

Following this came a comment that seemed in direct contradiction: "A father in jail is not an easy situation for an adolescent boy who needs a father's love and firm direction at this stage of his life…"

Was this an allusion to the Jason Freed incident? It had been strong words and four cuts with the cane on that occasion. Plus a letter to be taken home and signed by my parents in which they were informed of the incident and the school's disapproval. "An unfortunate beginning to Steven's high school career," was the way it was expressed.

What neither Mr Muirson nor my parents knew was that I had beaten Jason up because he had called one of the school gardeners a fucking kaffir to his face. I, like my father, had been fighting for the rights of the oppressed.

"One doesn't need to support or even understand your father's political involvement to feel sympathy for you and your family. My door is open at all times."

I was awash with embarrassment.

"Pop in any time you want a chat. There's nothing better than getting things off your chest," he repeated.

I shuffled in my chair.

"Or Father Williams. Many boys find that he has a sympathetic ear and provides good guidance. It's not only spiritual matters that he deals with. A practical man, understands boys. Do you attend church?"

I shook my head.

"Does your family, er, ever, attend?"

I shook my head once more, and squirmed.

"Well, don't let that inhibit you in any way. There is always a first time, yes? Father Williams is…"

A word bubbled from my lips.

"What's that, Carter? "he asked.

"May I go, Sir?" I managed to mumble. Ending this torture was all I could think of. I could not endure another second of it.

"Of course, son. Of course."

I hoofed it out of his office.

On the last day of school, there was a single period with the class teacher, a break and then the final assembly of the term. Mr Muirson addressed us from the podium on the stage, accusing us of all sorts of plots for the coming holidays before we'd even begun to hatch them. No straining for the psychological this time, no glimmer of sympathy. It was reassuring to hear him addressing us in his normal school manner, the usual public rant.

"Don't let me hear of a single incident in which a boy from Rand High has let the side down, where his behaviour has been anything less than impeccable. Remember this: whether you are wearing a school uniform or not, you are ambassadors for this school AT ALL TIMES."

But the reddening face, the heavy pauses, the strain for effect, all the dramatics he threw at us, were wasted; for everybody knew that during the holidays he was fundamentally powerless. Then we sang the school song, a silly tune that led breaking voices into croaking, hoarse highs, ending with the Latin *semper sersum, in iternum*, we shall serve forever.

Filing out of the hall, shushed without much conviction by prefects and teachers alike, we burst out of the school into freedom and the heady feeling of discipline fallen apart. It had been shown up as a sham. We had left it behind in the form of a helpless little man with a turkey's voice gesticulating on the stage.

My mother fetched me at the tennis courts. She was in a hurry, between two exercise classes. As she raced me back home, plunging the car round turns with gusto, I began to lay my own plans for the holiday.

"Can I take guitar lessons?"

"Yes, of course, Steven, if you want."

"Is Jane home already?"

"No, she's getting a lift with Marie's mother. Have you got your report?"

"No, they're posting them."

What I would have done to have had a peek at the papers lying on the Boss's desk, to know just how average "average" was. This anxiety was the only bit school owned of my life for the next three weeks. Before me lay the prospect of checking the post box daily for that distinctive brown envelope. Maths was a particular worry. Please God, Lucy doesn't get it into her head to send me to maths lessons right through the holidays, like last year. Please God, let me have passed.

EIGHT

Every morning after her first exercise class, Ma drove into town to deliver food and pick up washing at the police station in Fordsburg. During the school holidays, Jane and I joined her more often than not. The cells in Fordsburg where Dad was kept were in a single-storey brick building on a corner of a built-up city block. The guarded entrance was on one street but the cells faced the other. A band of small, barred windows ran along its length at the height of one-and-a-half men. I don't know how Ma organised it when she went in to drop the food and washing but when she'd come back out again, she'd make us wait outside a stationery shop opposite the cell windows. Eventually we'd spy a hand, just a hand, waving furiously behind one of the panes.

"Wave back," she'd say, "it's Dad."

And all three of us would wave for as long as the hand was visible, even though it was obvious Dad couldn't see us. After we did this a couple of times the lady who worked at the stationery shop could no longer contain her curiosity. She brought out a cloth and edged forward, dusting racks on her side of the glass front. It was obviously killing her to know whom this little blonde group was waving to. A murderer? A felon? I suppose that working across the road from a jail hardly ever provided the entertainment and excitement she expected.

Later in the evenings, at home after her exercise classes and long stints at Uncle Willie's Christmas Hampers, Ma went through Dad's washing very carefully. She'd get out her sewing tin and patiently unpick the seams of his shirts and pants with small scissors. Then she'd sew them. It took her nearly an hour each time.

A week and a half into the holidays, and on the very day my report arrived (I passed all my subjects, including, by a mere one per cent, maths), Ma was picking through the clothes she'd collected in the morning, Jane was reading and I was learning the chords of "Little Boxes", when I heard a small shout from my parents' bedroom. It wasn't a shout exactly, more an exclamation broken off quickly. I heard it above

50

my guitar and above my tuneless singing. Our household was like that at this time. Minor changes in routine, sudden periods of quiet or unusual rhythms in conversations held even on the opposite side of the house, registered immediately.

I ducked out of my room into the passage. Ma was already on the phone in the hallway, the receiver clamped between her ear and shoulder. She was holding a tiny strip of paper up to the light.

"Could you, Abie? I'd really appreciate it. I can't get the damn thing started and I've got work tomorrow. Yes, tonight. Thanks."

She put the receiver down, turned round and saw me.

"What's wrong, Ma?" I asked.

"I've got a message from Dad," she answered gravely. "It's not good. He's being tortured."

I gulped. This was unreal. Torture!

"What kind of torture?" I asked.

"They're making him stand on a brick night and day. They're questioning him constantly and not allowing him to sleep."

My first reaction was relief, maybe even a touch of disappointment.

"Why on a brick? A single brick?" I asked.

To me, torture was water drips on your forehead that eventually drove you mad. It was bamboo shoots growing through the soles of your feet or under your fingernails. It was being hung up on meat hooks in dungeons. If your father was a hero as mine was, should not his tribulations and trials be on a heroic scale too?

She nodded.

"That doesn't sound so bad."

"It's meant to wear him down, to crack him, Steven. It's very serious. Abie is on the way. Maybe we can bring an interdict against the police."

"Can you do that?"

"I don't know," she answered, "but we must do something. We can't just let it go."

Despite the measured tones, the control in her voice, I saw her shudder involuntarily, as if an ice cube had been dropped down her blouse.

"The bloody bastards, who the fuck do they think they are!" Jane said after joining us a few seconds later. Together with Ma, she pored over the tiny scrap of paper that had been unpicked from under the waistband of

Dad's flannel trousers. They read the message over and over. "It says, help! Then, torture, no sleep, standing on brick night and day, contact IT. Capital I, capital T. Finally, do something!"

"What's IT? An organisation? International what?" Jane asked.

"Maybe it's a matter of who's IT?" I countered.

"I can't think," my mother agonised.

"Maybe someone with the initials IT?"

"Iris Trent!" My mother and sister exclaimed in unison.

Iris Trent was a well-known politician, the only member of the legal opposition party in Parliament. "A lone voice in the wilderness", was the way she was described by the liberal press.

"But what the hell can she do?" Jane asked.

"Bring it up in Parliament?" I suggested.

The triumph at successfully deciphering the message was momentary. Ma was already distracted. She had the look of a *dassie* caught in the headlights of a car on a country road at night.

"What good will that do?" Jane said. "They're just a bunch of liars. They'll deny it."

"Ma," I began, with no idea where I was going. Yet I carried on, trying to reach my mother with anything, absolutely anything. "Maybe, Dad's being, you know, a bit dramatic."

This is not what I intended to say at all and I regretted it the second I heard my words out loud.

"Ah." A little sighing noise from Ma, nothing else.

We had not moved from the dimly lit passage. All three of us stood in it, around the telephone table, like actors who had been given poor instructions by the director.

Jane pointedly ignored my comment.

"They can't bloody well treat people like that," she was saying. "It's not as if he's a common criminal. And yet they can."

Her voice wavered, then burst out with renewed anger.

"That's the problem, isn't it? They can do anything they want and there is nothing we can do about it. They've seen to that by passing laws that give them the protection to do anything they bloody please. Maim, kill, dispose of people at will, like those they throw out of windows, or those they shoot and pretend were escaping, or those where they don't even bother to hide their handiwork ... electrical shocks or beaten up so badly..."

I watched Ma's face crumple and Jane come to her senses all in one instant.

"But of course, that's not what's happening to Dad. They aren't exactly *physically*, I mean, they're not *assaulting* him, or anything. He's strong, you know. He won't let them get to him, I'm sure."

Her ranting thankfully petered out and a look of shame flooded her face. It struck me that neither Jane nor I was very good at these situations: an ostrich with his head in the sand and a hysteric, neither very helpful.

The noise of a car pulling up outside released Ma from the passage. She rushed to the front door.

"There's Abie at last. We'll discuss our options with him."

I don't know what Abie recommended but I do know that the discussions went on till late that night, well after I went to bed.

In the morning, Ma cancelled her exercise classes and got ready to set out for the prison a little later than usual. She wanted Jane and me to go with her but I refused.

"I can't understand you, Steven. You act as if you don't seem to care, when I know just how much you do. Surely, you want to, now more than ever."

I shook my head. "Eric's coming over. We made plans ages ago."

"Sorry, but you can't. I need you and Jane to come with me to Iris Trent. She's seeing us at ten this morning at her house after I've dropped off the food and washing."

"But Eric's got all the rope and stuff, Ma. We're going to build a raft at the golf course, on the dam."

"A raft?"

"Yes."

Ma looked at me, or more accurately through me, and kept quiet.

There were tiny lines around her eyes. Clearly she hadn't slept much.

Then she said in a small, firm voice, "It's your decision, Steven. Will you come?"

I shook my head. The guilt of failing her was heavy but the will to escape was stronger.

"Okay," she flashed, "Jane will."

She turned aside and left the kitchen.

I followed her down the passage to my parents' room, wanting to smooth things over. She was sitting on the edge of the bed pulling a brush through her hair.

"Ma," I began, but she was talking out loud to herself.

"I hope all this food is getting to him. If they're doing ... *that* to him, then one wonders whether they're passing on all that splendid food I've been buying and cooking. Frankly, it's absurd." She dropped the hand with the brush on to her lap.

"Ma," I repeated, knowing that she was waiting for an explanation from me. With my parents one always had to give a reason for one's decisions. It wasn't important if the reason was feeble, unlikely or even obviously false, it was accepted without further discussion if you made the least effort to dredge up an excuse.

"I'd rather not go. I wouldn't be any good with Iris Trent – you know that. I can't talk to strangers at the best of times. Jane does it well enough for both of us."

Ma had tipped out her handbag on a towel she had spread on the bedcover. She repacked each little intimate thing of hers into it with single-minded intent: a couple of lipsticks and a comb, a red leather purse with the clasp that clicked, a little zippered bag where she stored the tissues you needed in a hurry in public, a letter folded in an opened envelope (I recognised Dad's handwriting) and other odds and ends. I'd noticed this habit of hers before: while life seemed to be falling apart around her, there she would be counting the pennies in her purse or carefully folding her tissues into thirds.

When she had checked it all to her satisfaction, she looked up at me. From the way she spoke I could tell that she was digging deep for her response.

"Don't be paralysed by your embarrassment, Steven, for it cuts you off from people, from asking and getting what you need. Now, look what you've done. You've got me starting up on your problems when I have a million other things on my mind."

She gathered up her things and slipped on a pair of shoes that she hooked out from under the bed with a stockinged foot.

Jane came bounding in.

"Are you two done?" she enquired and then to me, "God, haven't you changed yet?"

"Steven's staying," Ma said matter-of-factly and they left.

It was true that I was easily embarrassed. I refused to return sour milk Ma had bought from the cafe and wished that she would pour it down the drain so that I did not have to witness her tackling the café owner over a replacement pint. I died a million deaths when Ma wore a revealing dress the day Dad and she came to the school sports day, but who wouldn't with all the boys in the school pretending not to look but looking all the same? The simple act of phoning a stranger in response to an advertisement in the newspaper caused me pangs of discomfort. And sure, the prospect of being a member of a family party throwing themselves on the mercy of Iris Trent caused some trepidation. But I hadn't told Ma the whole truth. How could I? What words could I have used?

It was the little scene outside the stationery shop which had caused me to balk at going. I had woken up that morning with the fearful notion that it wasn't Dad's hand waving to us as we stood outside but an imposter, a policeman or warder, one of *them*, who had cottoned on to the little subterfuge and was having us on. I could imagine the torturer in Dad's cell, a smile on his lips, as he motioned to Dad to keep standing on his brick, while he himself climbed on the shelf, or table or bed or whatever it was that enabled him to wave at window height. Once the idea popped into my mind out of nowhere, I couldn't shake it off. It had a grotesque attraction.

How would we know the difference? No clue, not even a cuff was visible from the pavement. One should know a thing like that, how one's father waved, whether his fingers were parted or together, whether he only bent his fingers as some people do or whether he held up his hand, open-palmed, and moved it from side to side, flexing at the wrist, as I'd seen the queen do on *Pathe News*.

The problem was that in the few weeks my father had been gone, he had kind of disappeared from my mind. I could see his situation but not him. Most nights when I lay in bed before sleep I found myself recreating the walls of the jail outside his cell, brick by brick, row by row until I got to that high long window, barred as if with a metal muzzle. I put myself below on the pavement, alone, at night, hiding in the shadows from the guards, darting a look at the get-away car parked a little way down the road. I saw myself taping gunpowder to the wall, or tossing it in through the window, or putting it in a dustbin at the base. Almost too easy, eezy-peezy-puddy-sticks. Once the thing had been done, though, once the explosion had burst the wall and the dust had settled in the gaping hole I had blasted through and I waited for him to emerge, then … nothing. My mind just point-blank refused to put a face or a body to the man I called Dad. Even in the image of the charade played in the prison cell, the man standing on the brick was hazy, like an underdeveloped blob in a photograph.

A week or so before they went to Iris Trent, my sister and mother brought down the photo albums from the top of the bookshelf in the lounge and spent hours poring over them. I busied myself with a geography project in my room.

"Remember when I did you up in beads and shoe polish and you won the fancy dress at the hotel as a Zulu boy? And Jane went as Mrs So and So. What a sight. I thought I'd lost the photographs for good, but they were slipped into the cover of our wedding album."

Ma was wiping her nose absent-mindedly with her sleeve as she stood at the frosted glass doors of my bedroom, waving the loose photographs at me. Behind her, I heard explosions coming from the lounge where Jane was convulsed with laughter and screaming, "God, how could you have worn a hat like that! Dad must have been tempted to run off with someone else!"

I looked through the small pile Ma placed on my desk, quickly turning over the photographs where Dad was in the picture. You see, it wasn't only that my mind could hardly picture him but also that my eyes refused to linger on him. I went back to my textbook. On the margins of the page on which typhoons were explained, the previous owner had scribbled tapering swirls in ink. They inspired me to fill the surrounds with my own brand, sucking me into a pleasantly repetitive and comforting activity that blocked out the noises from the lounge.

Some confrontations were unavoidable, though. Once by mistake I caught sight of Dad in the framed photograph hanging where the passage did a 90-degree turn at the bathroom door. His face, lit up by the bragging joy of landing the whopping great mussel-cracker he is hoisting in the air, looked straight at me from behind the glass. It was like a punch in the stomach. From then on I made a point of walking by fast or looking at my feet when I turned that corner.

Ma and Jane came back from their appointment in a sombre but calm mood. "Mrs Trent promises she'll do whatever she can. She says there is a possibility that they'll stop torturing him if she poses a question in Parliament," Ma informed me.

I don't know whether Mrs Trent's question did the trick and stopped the torture but a week later Dad smuggled out another message in his collar and it was about something completely different. Thus the torture scare faded and other matters surfaced, such as getting Uncle Willie's Christmas Hampers functioning smoothly again. Ma roped us in to address envelopes and lick stamps in a mail order frenzy to recruit more agents to sell the hampers.

The method they had used to torture Dad continued to intrigue me. One morning I fetched the stopwatch from the drawer on Dad's side of the bed that he had used for timing my sister and me doing lengths in the pool, and a single brick from the garden. I retreated into my bedroom, closing the door firmly behind me. I placed the brick in the middle of the carpet and timed myself standing on it. Three minutes … three and a half minutes … five minutes. I tried balancing one foot on top of the other, I tried fitting both feet side by side, and I lifted one foot off the brick altogether. Eight … nine … ten minutes, ten minutes and thirty seconds, ten minutes and fifty five seconds… I stepped off the brick, eased it quietly under the bed, and went off to find something else to do. While I undid ganglions of tight knots from a hank of rope Eric had brought, I thought it over. It had been boring standing there, not even uncomfortable. Could you torture people by boring them to death?

NINE

The raft was a way to keep Eric from mourning over the birds that Ma had forced us to sell and give away. But it wasn't the crowning achievement of the holiday. All we had to show for it was a leaking barrel and a pile of scrap which we ditched on the edges of the shallow, muddy dam, thankful that it was hidden from view in the woody, wildest regions of the golf course. Quickly putting this failure behind us, we turned our attention elsewhere.

Making gunpowder was a kind of fever that overtook us periodically over the years, ever since Eric found the recipe in one of the pile of second-hand technical magazines he had stashed in his bedroom. Our first attempt failed when we couldn't think of a way of getting hold of the ingredients. We couldn't ask just anybody where to get saltpetre. It would be a dead give-away and we stewed over this for a good while. But while dipping into the magazines again, we found a clue. Under the heading "Veldcraft for Youngsters", Eric found a method for drying leftover venison. Saltpetre was one of the ingredients.

Jane, still a partner in our schemes back then, asked at the Yeoville Butchery but the butcher laughed and told her that butchers hadn't stocked saltpetre since the Middle Ages. He threatened to tell our mother if we were playing around with gunpowder. The idea faded and we spent most of the holidays camping at the bottom of the garden.

This time round, we were older, smarter and more confident. Eric and I caught the No. 20 bus to Hillbrow and, in a carefully planned exercise, split forces once we got there. While Eric walked nonchalantly into the first chemist he came across and asked for saltpetre, I went on ahead to the next pharmacy to get sulphur. The small packets were handed over to us without a murmur. Signalling our success to each other with nods and winks, we met up at the bus stop, and were back home within half an hour.

Behind a screen of Zululand shrubs that Ma had planted to remind her of her childhood on a sugar plantation near Eshowe, Eric and I started the process by grinding charred wood into what we hoped was the powdered or granulated charcoal required by the recipe. It was a clear, cold morning. William was painting the courtyard, Jane and Marie were inside swotting for their matric prelim exams and Ma was at Dad's office. We dug bits of burnt wood out of the ashes of the braai, laid them on a cement paving stone and crushed them into a sooty dust with a stone. We swept it up into a heap with our hands and over it showered the remaining ingredients we had bought.

The colourless saltpetre had a bitter, salty taste when I put my tongue to it and the pale yellow sulphur had an unmistakable, eggy, stink-bomb smell that did not encourage tasting. In a few finger-swirls, this unpromising-looking combination was mixed. A small cooldrink bottle was the receptacle for our home-made bomb. Only a fuse of some kind was needed and this we pulled out of a cracker that had survived since the last Guy Fawkes.

Then it was time. A stretch of yellow veld belonging to the Scout Hall adjoining our garden was the perfect site for our experiment, and we chose an open area in its centre where rubble and frost had prevented any grass from growing. It was safer, Eric insisted, in case of sparks. We wedged the bottle upright between two small lumps of concrete which would contain the explosion to some extent. With much fiddling over the matches, Eric eventually lit the end of the six-inch fuse, turned and ran like hell, yelling, "It's alight!" He dived in through the thick umbrella of leaves clothing the giant loquat tree on the border of our own garden, from where I was watching.

We waited and waited, peeping out from behind the leathery, felted leaves to see whether the fuse had gone out or simply taking its merry time. Eventually, impatience drove me out to the periphery of the clearing. Sure enough, the fuse had gone out and it would do so at least three times more. It was now I who re-lit it, again and again, running for cover each time. Finally, the fuse stuck out only half an inch from the bottleneck and after I lit it, I hardly bothered to run.

The explosion took me by surprise even though we'd been aiming for it. For the first fraction of a second, I didn't know who or where or what I was. A large noise and energy had taken possession of me and the sky was black inside my head. It was a delicious sensation, like fainting. The next feeling I had was a kind of coming round, place and light and identity returning but in a bit of a muddle, as if someone had stirred up the world with a spoon. I saw Eric's face close to mine. The light was a spiky frame around him and something hard was digging into my back. I realised that I was lying on the ground.

"Are you alright? Steven, are you alright?"

I grinned from my glorious position, a baby's eye-view of the world with life wheeling around and above me in great shimmering sweeps. It felt great.

Marie materialised out of nowhere and helped me into a sitting position. She lifted me up by my arm, while my sister hovered nearby. William was there too. I could tell from a range of deep clicks and sympathetic sounds and the powerful smell of whitewash in the air.

"Ow! What's that?" I asked.

We all looked at my bare arm. A big piece of jagged glass stuck out from the skin, just above the elbow.

"God!" I said, frightened.

Marie, whose father was a doctor, did a very brave thing. With a grim look on her face (it was her expression I fixed upon), she pushed my arm straight, wedged it hard against her body with one hand and with the other grasped the piece of glass. She pulled it out with a short, sharp yank that had me shouting with pain. At the same moment I saw the glass shard she had extricated, at least half an inch longer than when it was in my arm.

A new problem emerged. Blood was pouring down my arm, over my hand and into my lap. Jane recovered from shock and grabbed my arm, pulling it up into the air. "Hold it up," she ordered. William and Eric were dispatched to the house to fetch bandages, as I was helped to the tap. I staggered along on rubbery legs.

"Don't tell Ma," I was blubbering, "she'll kill me. Promise, Jane."

"I promise," Jane said. "Was that gunpowder you guys blew up?"

I nodded.

"At first I thought it was an earth tremor from a collapsed mine shaft or something, but then I heard Eric shout." Jane led me to the side of the house. I refused to walk over anything except the lawn in case Ma might see the evidence.

"Keep it up," she warned me, as my arm dropped. "I hope the Branch isn't outside. They'll think it's revolutionary forces at work." Security policemen often sat in parked cars on the street outside our house, watching our visitors arrive or following our cars when we left. Our parents had given us strict instructions to behave as if they weren't there. Eric and I hadn't given them the slightest thought when planning our experiment.

Marie thought the cut was deep enough to need stitches but that was out of the question. After dabbing it with a stinging dose of mercurochrome and then Dettol (William's contribution), Jane and Marie bandaged up my arm as best they could. Immediately, the bandage went a bright red colour.

"Honestly, Steven, you should get to the doctor. It most probably needs five or more stitches," Marie repeated.

I disagreed vehemently. "It will stop bleeding in a while, I'm sure,"

William was still standing around, shaking his head, saying, "Shame," over and over. His overall was speckled with white paint, and his hands covered with drying flakes which he was shedding on the ground with all the wringing he was doing. Obviously, the only adult around, he felt responsible. I could see his mind ticking over.

"Don't phone Lucy, William. It's nothing. Look, I can move my arm perfectly."

I wiggled it about. How could I buy his silence?

Before Ma was due home, I sought him out in his room where he was taking his post-lunch rest. He was sitting on a chair rolling a cigarette. A spoon and the empty enamel plate from which he had eaten his meat and *pap* was placed neatly on a doily on an upturned box at his side.

"Is the blood still running?" he asked me.

I undid the cuff and rolled up my sleeve to show him the bandage, which was mostly brown. "William," I began.

"Has Eric gone home?"

I nodded. Eric had left after picking up all the glass scattered by the explosion and hanging around long enough to ensure that I did not bleed to death. He also helped wash the blood out of my shirt and shorts.

"William, that time when George came here after the fight with the *tsotsis* and you asked me not to tell Dad, remember?"

I felt terrible doing this, it was a despicable thing, blackmail. To hide my shame, I made a thing of looking around William's room: at the cupboard which mirrored the dark little room in its central panel; at the

61

shelf above the dresser which was lined with newspaper cut into patterns; at the photographs on the wall; and at the most wondrous item of all, the large bed with its snow-white cover embroidered by his wife, Martha. It stood halfway up to the ceiling since it was raised up on paint tins (to thwart the *tokolosh*, William said) and it had the presence of a religious shrine.

I explained how badly I didn't want Ma to know.

"She said that we weren't allowed to do it. She made me promise I wouldn't, after that time Eric and I started that fire and nearly burnt down the Scout Hall. Please, William."

William laughed. "You're naughty, you and Eric. You do a lot of nonsense together. Alright, Steven, but if she sees your arm, you must say, I didn't see. I wasn't here."

I was embarrassed. It had been unnecessary to threaten to tell his secret. We sat around in his room chatting about this and that until he got up to start his kitchen duties. I took a last breath of that pungent odour I so loved, a mixture of cigarette smoke, Lifebuoy soap and whitewash, and went inside the house myself.

Both Jane and William kept their promise and didn't let on. For the two weeks I wore the bandage, I was careful not to be seen without a long-sleeved shirt and a jersey that covered the bump the bandage made when I bent my arm. Ma was a bit puzzled when I didn't take off my jersey, even in the car when the midday sun beat through the windscreen, but it was a minor thing. By the time she took me off to the shops for a new set of school clothes the day before term began (I looked like a war orphan with sleeves riding up my forearms and shorts bursting on the bum, she said), I could pass off the scar as a scratch I got while climbing a tree. In the dark, stuffy cubicles at Emdin's where I reluctantly tried on three sizes of every item, it was difficult for her to tell and she was mainly concentrating on surviving the ordeal of taking me shopping, anyway.

TEN

When I got back to school after the holidays, it was obvious that nearly everybody knew about my father and the torture, too. A newspaper article had appeared on the second page of *The Star* on 26 July. The headline said: "DETAINEE ALLEGEDLY TORTURED". The story that followed (Ma cut it out) went like this: "In a snap debate in Parliament today, Iris Trent, sole member of the Progressive Party in Parliament, once again questioned the Minister of Security on the matter of the torture of prisoners detained under 90 Days. It had come to her attention that Ivor Carter, business manager of the newspaper *New Age* and a prominent political figure among left-wing circles in Johannesburg who has been detained since early June, is being maltreated. According to his wife, Lucy, her husband is being denied sleep and forced to balance on a brick for unreasonable periods of time, causing him to become increasingly confused and distressed. It is not known if Mr Carter will be brought to trial or released after serving 90 days, but she remains optimistic that he will be released."

As I approached a group of friends, I'd notice a break in conversation and, when I joined them, someone would start up on some new, jolly subject, casual-like. Then there were sideways glances from behind desks, or from across a field, when boys' eyes would catch mine and instantly pull away. I recognised this look (not looking, really) from when Mark Dubb's older sister was killed in a hit-and-run accident. When he got back after missing two days of school, we buzzed around him in the same ignoring way. Having a father in jail standing on a brick wasn't anything like a family member dying, but it was the kind of thing most boys couldn't come straight out and ask about. They waited for you to bring it up.

Reggie Nutfield gave me a big grin and a Nazi salute when I greeted him on the first day, which was his way of saying something, I suppose. His holiday with his cousins on the farm in the Free State had not been a success. "I got flu, man," he told us. "I've never been sicker in my life. I thought I was going to bladdy die."

Cedric van Zyl was the exception. When I came across him unexpectedly in the third week of the term, it was too good an opportunity for him to miss.

"Heard about your old man. Pity he didn't do something deserving to get into chookie, something like MURDER."

He swerved ahead of me and backed me up against a wall. I threw a desperate look right and left but there was no help in sight. Empty corridors on either side ran off in heightened perspective like aeroplane wings lifting off from the ground.

Cedric rammed his head inches from my face. He had a real sense of the melodramatic; he was acting the way they do in the flicks. I'm sure the pity for him was that there wasn't an audience to witness his performance.

"But then he's not a BIG, BAD fighter like his son, is he? The father of the form one champion boxer, the guy who'll *moera* the bravest in his class? Wheels the Great? No, he's a man with his head in books, RED books, hey? COMMIE books. Can't take it when they make him stand on an itty-bitty brick."

His face was so close to mine the cheddar cheese and gherkins from his lunchtime sandwiches hit me in great, smelly blasts. No part of his body was actually touching mine and, theoretically, I could have got away fairly easily. But the force of his aggression was immense. I was mesmerised by the microscopic texture of the skin on his cheek which filled my sight nearly from horizon to horizon. His eyes swam in a fog above but a row of three ripe pimples at the junction of nose and cheek were distinct and unavoidable, like mini-volcanoes on a Martian landscape. His spit was shooting in flying drops onto my face.

I could feel my heart thumping in my chest. My legs felt a bit wobbly but, at the same time as being very frightened (and who wasn't terrified of the biggest bully of form four?), I could see Cedric's point completely. It was clear and direct. He was the only person who hadn't beat about the bush, who'd actually said the words.

This was preferable by far to the looks, to Mr Muirson and his lecture, to the sympathetic little noises from my parent's friends. An urge to laugh gripped me. Maybe it was part of the fear, maybe something else.

"Ja, I agree. Totally. You're right," I stammered.

Words of betrayal? Punching Jason Freed was one thing, Cedric van Zyl another.

"You don't mean to say you also think your old man's daft?"

I heard a string of feeble sounds, something like, "uuuh, ummm, blug, mm", come out of my mouth. I think I closed my eyes. When next I was aware, the threat had somehow dissolved. There was an air of contemplation on Cedric's face.

"Wait until Baby hears you disown your old man," Cedric said, and the overwhelming power of his presence ebbed away. I knew it was the time to escape and I ducked quickly under his lifted arm which been pinning me, psychologically if not physically, to the wall.

Cedric's voice followed me down the corridor.

"Enjoy visiting your Daddy in chookie. You can dance and sing together on the bricks. One-a-clock, two-a-clock, three-a-clock, rock, we gonna rock around the clock tonight."

I was round the corner and up the stairs and in my classroom before the thought struck me that someone should set him right. Under 90 days no visits are allowed at all. Only food parcels and washing to be picked up and dropped. It seemed important to me that Cedric should be told this, I don't know why. Secretly, I asked my father for his forgiveness for being such a coward.

ELEVEN

I finally managed to get down to the bottom of the garden to clean the swimming pool that weekend. I had noticed a few times over the holidays that it was in a bad way but had successfully ignored it. Ma hadn't said a word either. I can't believe she had been too busy to notice. Most probably she had instructed William to leave the pool and was waiting for me to make a move.

The pool was in an even sorrier state than I had thought it would be. I could see that the minute I rounded the "Zulu hedge", as we called it, and walked around the slasto surrounds. The cold nights had ensured that it was not full of algae, but the water was filthy from weeks of neglect. There were leaves floating on the surface and some suspended halfway down, hanging motionless in the water. Others, torn and rotten, had dropped right to the bottom, drowned. A pattern of settled dust and earth decorated the floor of the pool. The water itself had an oddly oily sheen.

I stirred up the pool with a long-handled leaf scoop which I fetched from the shed, following up the leaves that escaped from each scoop with another and yet another scoop. I banged the head of the scoop on to the slasto to empty each load and dipped again and again. It was a kind of cat and mouse game, with the smallest particles somersaulting away from the front of the scoop.

Next came the chemicals, the pool *muti*, we called it. I was relieved that the water wasn't really murky or green. But I also knew that without doctoring it soon would be. September the first is the day the public baths open in Johannesburg, the official start of the swimming season. It was only two weeks away. I hauled out the chemicals Dad had stashed in the shed and lined them up. There was a small plastic bag with some white powder in it that said "hydrochloric acid", a sack of chlorine, a couple of bottles labelled pool toner and a variety of rusty measuring cups. There was also a pool testing kit in a box with many of the parts missing (one could tell by the empty spaces in the contoured packing).

I really had no idea how to begin. I had watched Dad doctor the pool quite often but I had never participated or paid attention to what he was doing.

Just then I heard Ma coming out through the kitchen door.

"Ma! Lucy!" I shouted a few times. "Do you know which chemicals do what?"

Eventually she came through the Zulu hedge and made her way to me.

"I wish you wouldn't shout, Steven. Come and find me if you need something."

She looked at the chemicals and the pool and said something I couldn't quite hear and then walked off distractedly. "Ask William," I thought I heard her say.

I went inside to look for William. Jane was home. She was practising reciting a poem in front of the hall mirror.

"I am the Smoke king, I am black. I am swinging in the sky, I am ringing world on high: I am the thought of the throbbing mills, I am the soil tole kills, I mean soul toil kills, what do you *want*, Steven?

"D'you know where William is?"

"No."

I made my way back to the pool via William's empty room. I looked through the pile of chemicals once again and began haphazardly sprinkling and pouring them into the little drain attached to the filter. I was sure it didn't matter one way or another, as long as I put something in. I replaced the cover to the drain, checked that the filter was on and then carried the lot back into the shed.

Jane came through the shrubbery, biting into an apple.

"I think Lucy wants to tell you something. Go."

"I just saw Ma. She didn't say anything."

"It's about Dad. There's going to be a trial in November. He's been charged."

I went to find Ma.

"Jane says that they're taking Dad to court for a trial," I said as I pushed open the kitchen door and made a beeline for the large salad on the table set for dinner. I lifted a piece of tomato out of it and dropped it into my mouth from above. Ma was peeling the onions submerged in a bowl of water.

"Yes, Abie told me just a while ago. They've laid charges – belonging to an unlawful organisation, dissemination of banned materials, the usual."

She transferred the onions to a chopping board and started cutting them, all the while leaning away and back to avoid getting the onion vapour in her eyes.

"As from November, he'll be classified an awaiting-trial prisoner."

She stopped to wipe her face with her apron. Her eyes were red despite her efforts.

"It means we can write to him, Steven, and see him on visits. From the first of November. Isn't that fantastic?"

"How long will the trial last?"

"No-one can tell."

The onions made a great sizzle as they were dropped into the frying pan.

"Will the public be allowed – I mean, will you go to it?"

"Yes. Jane and I will go whenever we have the chance. They won't let you go though. The rule is you have to be over sixteen. I could try to get you permission."

"Don't. I don't want to go."

"We'll see. It's still a while. Maybe you'll change your mind. You'll have school, mind you." Ma washed her hands at the sink.

"When can I write the first time?"

"You could write now if you want but he'll only receive it on the first of November because that's the date his status changes, from detainee-under-90 days to prisoner-awaiting-trial. Why don't you? He'd love having a pile of letters waiting for him. But nothing about politics or jail or anything like that. The letters will be read by a censor before he gets them and his letters to us as well."

William came in with a basket of groceries. He was agitated.

"Hau! The police are at the shops. Pass raid. Where's your pass? Is your pass in order?

Many are in the vans. You! You!" He put out the loaf of bread and carrots on the kitchen counter as if marshalling rows of pass offenders. Ma looked up at him with concern.

"No, Mam, I'm all right." He chuckled. "I keep my pass here, always."

He patted his chest, then to emphasise his point he retrieved the small green book from the inside pocket of his jacket and opened it on the last page. "All up to date, all signed up. The others, Mr Petrie's boy, they took him away in the van. That one, she shouldn't come here to Johannesburg. She should be living with his mother in Hammanskraal."

"But there's no work in Hammanskraal, William. He'd starve," I said.

We had been trying to raise William's political awareness ever since he'd been with us, but it was useless. He was a stickler for the rules. Whether they were just or not was of no interest to him.

"No, Steven, no, his mother will feed him at home."

He took off his smart jacket, slipped the top of an overall over his shirt, tied an apron round his waist and took over the cooking from Ma, who had rushed off to answer the phone.

Over supper, Ma told us that she was sure that I'd get a special visit with Dad because of being too young for court. Abie was sure he could swing it.

Jane snorted. She was filled with a sense of her superiority in being allowed and even wanting to go to court. With her matric exam only a few weeks away, she had her eyes set on university, on the adult world. I didn't rise to the bait. I took a huge helping of salad on my plate and scooped up the fried tomato and onion sauce on a hunk of white bread, which I folded over and pushed into my mouth.

TWELVE

3/10/64

Dear Dad,

How are you? Did you know that Eric Sundelowitz and I had to sell the birds and break the partnership? Ma complained that the smell from the *hokkies* got into your bedroom even in winter and I couldn't write to you then about how unfair it was. William and I made a big bonfire of the *hokkies*. They were filled with vermin.

A man from the bird association came in his van to buy the rollers. We gave the others away to a boy who keeps birds down the road. Eric has been visiting him a lot lately, maybe he wants to go in with him. I was sad to see the birds go, specially the white rollers. Eric got R10 from the sale and I got R7,50, because I owed Eric for the feed which he bought the last two times.

I immediately went out and bought the latest Beatles record *Beatles for Sale*. It's terrific. Also a Rolling Stones album. I don't think you'd like that as much. Mom doesn't.

The filter of the pool got stuck but William and I have sorted it out. We added acid and chlorine for a few days and I spent Sunday morning brushing the sides where the green stuff was growing so that the filter would get at it and that seemed to help. But I'm still the only one who swims because it is still cold. Also, I think Jane thinks I've poisoned the water.

Oh, by the way, you (and Ma) bought me a new guitar for my birthday. Thanks! I went to guitar lessons all through the last holidays and have improved considerably.

Lots of love,
Steven

8/10/64
Dear Dad,

It was nice that you wrote to us. Could you write a letter to me alone? Jane grabbed your letter and read it out as if everything you wrote was for her and she insists on keeping it in her desk. Did I tell you that I got into the first tennis team in my last letter? Well, the season is nearly over, but I did. Next year I'm going to try for the cricket team, even if I only get into Social Cricket. There are some damn good batsmen in our school, quite a few are in provincial sides. Exams are coming up and the extra maths lessons are helping. We went to see a Peter Sellers movie. It was all right, actually a bit disappointing after *The Party* which you remember we saw at the beginning of the year and was hilarious, especially the scene where he fishes his shoe out of the moat.

Eric Sundelowitz says we should breed guppies. You can make quite a lot of money selling them back to the pet shop and his cousin has some empty tanks he thinks he could persuade him to part with. Mom says why don't I ask you? We could use the back room, the one near William's room.

I have just been reading a book about lost gold and mislaid fortunes in America. There are some jolly interesting accounts about money that has been mislaid in the most obvious of places but for unknown reasons just cannot be found again.

Lots of love, Me, Steven

28/10/64
Dear Dad,

We have all got into a complete tizz about the hampers. The crockery has still not arrived. Ma put in the order 3 months ago and the suppliers keep saying they'll be getting them next week and next week and next week etc., but still no crockery!

Ma says we we'll have to send the hampers out without any cups, saucers and plates otherwise people won't have them in time for Christmas and just imagine what a stink there will be! Perhaps we will fill them up with extra sweets or tins.

Jane and I have been helping with the paperwork, marking names and addresses. You would be very impressed! Ma seems to be rushing about a lot what with Jane's matric, exercise classes, hampers and court. She's got quite thin! Not Puss, though.

With love... Steven

19/11/64

Dear Dad,

I'm sorry about not being able to read some of my last letter. I'm going to make it easier for you – and the censor!

ISN'T THIS BETTER? THE PLAN ABOUT THE GUPPIES HAS FALLEN THROUGH BECAUSE ERIC'S COUSIN ACTUALLY WANTS THE TANKS TO DO SCIENCE EXPERIMENTS. TOO BAD.

MY EXAMS ARE NEARLY OVER. SO FAR THEY'VE BEEN OK EXCEPT MATHS WHICH WAS A STINKER. EVERYBODY SAID SO. BRIAN MY NEW MATHS TEACHER SAID HE WOULD HAVE STRUGGLED WITH IT WHEN HE WAS IN STD 6 AND HE'S A BOFF.

I'M SORRY I DIDN'T WRITE LAST WEEK, TOO BUSY WITH EXAMS. I AM MAKING PLANS FOR THE HOLIDAYS. IT'S ONLY THREE WEEKS BEFORE WE BREAK UP.

I THINK I'M GOING TO GO TO PLETT WITH DENNIS SHAW. DO YOU REMEMBER HIM? HE'S THE GUY WHO CHAINED HIS BIKE TO OUR DINING-ROOM TABLE BECAUSE TWO OF HIS PREVIOUS BIKES GOT STOLEN. HIS PARENTS SAID IT WAS FINE FOR ME TO STAY WITH THEM AT THEIR HOLIDAY HOUSE. BUT ONLY FOR THE LAST THREE WEEKS OF THE HOLIDAYS. WE AREN'T LEAVING TILL AFTER NEW YEAR.

MA WON'T BE ALONE. JANE HAS NO PLANS TO GO AWAY. SHE IS GOING TO DO A SPEED WRITING AND TYPING COURSE AND WANTS TO READ HER BOOKS FOR NEXT YEAR. ENGLISH 1. WHAT A SWOT!

Lots of love,
Steven

26/11/64
Dear Daddy,

After our special visit, I forgot to tell you that I think you are smashing! Also, my marks last term:

Science	65%
History	80%
Geography	74%
Biology	69%
Latin	62%
Afrikaans	54%
Maths (boo hoo hoo)	43%
English	66%

I'm sure you agree that except for maths they're jolly good.

I have learnt to play some tunes on the mouth organ. On my guitar I'm learning hard chords. How does E flat major sharp nine sound? I am also learning to drive the Volkswagen and already know how to drive it up and down the lawn. I know all the gears too. That's all I have to say. Mostly wanted to get my last lots of marks to you, so that you can lavish me with praise in your next letter!

Your loving son
Steven

1 December 19 hundred and 64
Dear Daddy,

It's been raining so much here everything's been swamped out including the swimming bath. After a big storm water from the street drains started to pour through the front gate, through the garage and into the swimming pool. It made the water so black that it took me all week to clean it, although I did put in a lot of chemicals!

We all went to see a film called *The Victors* which was terrific and on Sunday we saw *Ivan the Terrible* which was great. After the society we went to the Orange Grove Hotel and had a huge feed.

The underwater camera that Eric and I and Guy have been experimenting with is working great and I have already got some good results of Guy gliding through the water despite it not being too clean.

At school I have to decide whether I am going to take French or Geography for next year. Jane says that French is easier but Ma is going to phone the school secretary and see what she can find out. I think maybe it will be Geography because I am quite good at it and it's not new like French.

My tennis racket had to be re-strung because a "slight" dampness loosened the strings and made them weak, but I am sure that when I bought the racket the strings were useless.

Only a few days before the holidays start!

Love

Steven

P.S. I'm sure Ma's told you but at last the crockery has arrived, so big rush to pack it in!

15 December, I think, it's hard to keep up during the holidays

Dear Dad,

Lately everybody has been shopping for Christmas presents and small funny-looking packages. Last week I went all over town with Jane looking for a pair of pants but I couldn't find anything, they all had too many fancy designs on, Carnaby Street style. We are getting a genuine Christmas tree from Norway out of somebody's garden.

We found a book of folk songs in a book shop in President Street. They really are terrific. The swimming pool is fine, hardly any algae left. Izzy says that he can get lots of fruit from somebody he knows – for free, we'll send you some. The film of My Fair Lady is coming to His Majesty's in about 2 weeks time and we are going to see it with Izzy. I suppose you have heard of the Boksburg MURDER. Well they found the head in the ZOO LAKE of all places. Jane is trying to keep to a diet so that she can get thinner but she keeps on nibbling at little bits of food.

Love Steven

Boxing Day

Dear Dad,

Well Christmas has passed and we missed you very much. On Christmas Eve, Jane and I swam at one o'clock. It was quite warm. We got to bed late, then of course got up early and opened our Christmas presents on Ma's bed.

Thanks for the money and Jane is very pleased about the bit of Victorian jewellery you got her. She will wear it to court once the trial starts up again.

On Christmas night, we went to a midnight show with friends. It was good fun called the Black Demon with bodies and money and love. It ended at 2:45. Ma nearly choked when we came out and said, great, there's another on Thursday.

I think Ma was a bit worried specially since William is so very, very HAPPY at this time of the year. His wife Martha paid her annual visit today, decked out in full tribal regalia. I don't know how she can move with all those metal bangles around her ankles and even more around her neck. Yet her shoes are sensible, snow-white tennis tackies!

I leave for the holidays with the James's in a day or two. Ma has given me three stamped and addressed envelopes, two are for her and one letter to you, so I won't forget. We are driving down and sleeping over once on the way.

I'm taking your cane rod, the big one and the Penn reel. I hope you don't mind. I will look after them, I promise, and I'll catch a whopper!!! And yes, of course I will be careful.

Love, be happy
Steven

16 Jan

Dear Daddy,

This letter is all about my holiday, which is nearly over. Back to Joburg tomorrow and school starts on Tuesday. I don't have any excuse about not writing sooner, just a good time.

Plett is the same as when we were last there except for more houses. When will they run out of places to build? Dennis's parents have a *lekker* place there. They are very kind to me. We had a bathroom all for ourselves – can you believe it?

Dennis is very musical and he and I have decided to start a band when we get back to Joburg. He has taught me all sorts of songs and chords and I'm getting a lot better. What do you think of the name "The Driftwood" for the band?

There was still lots of time for fishing and tanning and hanging around the discos at night, looking at the talent. I did catch a *blaashoppie*, a dogfish or two and a few rock cods from the rocks, but not much, because most of the time I was showing Dennis and his mates the ropes. They'd not done too much fishing before. I know, excuses, excuses!

I bumped into Jonah, your favourite gilly. He asked about you, wanted to know when you'd come on a fishing trip again. I said, maybe next year.

Ma and Jane have phoned me twice and they tell me that court just goes on and on but they're not complaining, because they can see you and write to you nearly every day. I have let my hair grow right through the hols and it's gone so blonde in the sun, I think I am going to cry when I have to cut it for school.

Love Steven

8/2/65
Dear Dad,
We've been back at school nearly a week and already being hounded by the teachers about the July exams! I do not take French as one foreign language is enough for me! Instead I take Geography and Biology, both quite interesting. I have bought new records, The Beatles and Rolling Stones. I read in a magazine the other day that each of the Rolling Stones is insured for one million pounds! Hear our sins: with Jane at the wheel and me pushing from behind, she drove into the wall of the house but the only damage is a large chunk of plaster and a slightly dented bumper so neither of us will be having driving lessons for some time, so Ma says. After those brilliant matric results you've got to forgive her.

The white powder you told me to throw away is the only thing that kills the algae in the pool. We put in about 5 cups every three weeks and after two or three hours, all the algae is dead and can be just swept off with no trouble at all.

The band is going well. Dennis (lead) and I (rhythm) have auditioned for a drummer and another member, and a terrific guy called Neville is joining us. He lives in Highlands North and goes to school there but he is very committed.

Did you know that the first people to discover the trampoline were the Red Indians of South America? They placed a piece of springy wood over two supports and began bouncing up and down!

Lots of love
Steven

21/2/65

Dear Dad,

Well Happy Birthday to you. I hope you get lots of books and things. How old are you? Ma is very cagey about telling me as then I can work out her age and that is apparently not needed. I think it's funny that you can't remember which day is your real birthday the 22 or the 23. I can never forget mine 8 SEPTEMBER, in case you forget that one too.

The other day we saw a film called *That Man from Rio* not a cowboy but a French James Bond. The film had everything in it from aerobatics to kidnappings and ancient Incas to skyscrapers.

I am busy reading *The Rise and Fall of the Third Reich*. I've never tackled such a long book before. I have reached the part where Hitler's party has come to power and is already in control of half the country. It is amazing how he wriggles out of all the Allied Conventions. Have a happy birthday with hundreds of huge slabs of chocolate!

Love from Steven

25/3/65

Dear Dad, Sorry for not writing for a while. No excuse. In just four days we break up for Easter.

I am now captain of the junior tennis team and have got into the social cricket team. It's quite a lot of fun even though we don't play against proper teams, only each other. All the fatties and boffs are in the team so there's a lot of joking. No-one takes it a bit seriously. For most of them it's their only sport. The rule is that all boys must do at least one team sport per term.

On Tuesday they launched the first two-man space flight from Cape Kennedy and on Wednesday a lunar probe crash-landed on the moon, sending all these hundreds of photographs back. But last week the unmentionables pulled off the greatest feat of all. They made the first ever space walk. Tethered only by a lifeline the astronaut moved about 16 feet away from his rocket. So you see the race is hotting up. One of these days they're going to get a man to the moon. I wonder if he will find it's made out of green cheese after all.

Jane says that you look at her and Ma all the time through the trial with a grin on your face and that makes it worth it. It's gone on and on, hasn't it?

The science teacher showed us how to blow glass. You just heat the glass till it is soft and then blow until a bubble forms. You can also make a thermometer out of the glass while blowing it when it is full of mercury. Hope the howling cats who've been keeping you awake leave soon and that your cold is better.

Lots of love,
Steven

4/4/65
Dear Dad,
So this is it. Judgement day on Thursday. Perhaps this will be the last letter and you'll come back home! Goody. I don't think I can think of anything more to write to you about.

Today it was autumn or near winter. The grass is browning and the leaves are blowing from the trees and there's that faint smell of charcoal burning.

Jane has been working jolly hard doing one varsity essay after another. She likes African Government and Politics but English isn't well taught. She says it's most disappointing. I don't know why I am telling you this. Her letters to you are mammoth. I see pages and pages. Ma lets us read her letters to you and vice-versa. We think they're awfully slushy and repetitive! Jane won't let me read hers, of course.

The Rand Easter Show opened on the first. I went with Dennis and Neville. It was the same as usual: prize bulls and pigs and merino sheep, pavilion after pavilion filled with stuff to buy and brochures to nick, fun fair, nothing new. Except for one thing: if you could swallow a live white mouse and keep it down for 15 minutes, you could win a car. I never saw anybody do it but I heard one farmer did, vomiting just as he drove away in his new car!

Start wearing your woollies. Holding thumbs.
Lots of love,
Steven

P.S. I forgot to tell you the most important news of all. The Driftwood have their first engagement to play at a *barmitzvah* in Norwood!

THIRTEEN

In all of the six months of the trial, I had been to court only once. This had been as a result of a request for special permission made by my mother and Abie.

The morning started off well as it always does when you miss a day of school, and it's not spoilt by being sick. It felt as if the weekend had come early and best of all, only for me, Jane having been packed off to varsity at the normal time.

I woke up late, put on civvies and ate a leisurely breakfast. "Death Touched my Shoulder", a Springbok radio programme which I rarely caught because of the time, provided light relief as I dipped my toast into the eggs Ma had fried for me. This week it was a story about an Allied pilot and a mysterious "presence" which guided him through the mist over enemy territory when he had lost radio contact with the other members of his squadron.

William came into the kitchen in his overalls and he and I talked a little. Then Ma and I drove off just after nine. The pleasure of zooming about in a car through the streets to town was heightened by knowing that at that very moment everybody else was stuffed up in their classrooms, already into the second period.

Even so we arrived at the Magistrate's Court Building near Diagonal Street a little early. Ma did a bit of shopping at one of the Indian shops (she was looking for some German print for a skirt she planned to sew for Jane) while I moseyed around the streets. I stopped outside an African *muti* shop where I could swear there were desiccated monkey carcasses hanging from hooks on the eaves. A peek inside through curtains of unrecognisable pelts and plants revealed shelves full of bottles of luridly coloured powders and liquids. The smell of the place was not unpleasant, a little like scratching your own unwashed scalp and sniffing under your fingernails. It was all rather exotic and agreeable. It reminded me of Dad's stories of his childhood in a trading store in the Transkei or the collections of traditional African stories my parents bought for us.

I wondered if animal "qualities" were what was really for sale in this shop: the wisdom of a hare, the strength of a lion, the wiliness of a warthog, the courage of a wildebeest. Which would I choose to buy? Patience? Superhuman strength? I couldn't make up my mind. Maybe, I could get an extract of all, an all-animal tincture. I laughed inwardly. Spying Ma coming out of the Indian shop with a parcel in her hand, I made my way over to her.

"You go for natural remedies, would you use any of those?" I pointed across the road.

"No," she said, "but I remember my mother using a poultice of some herbs for snakebite which she got from the headman on the farm."

"What snake?"

"*Boomslang*, I think."

"Jesus, did the man survive?"

"Yes, if I remember correctly. It was a woman, though, a neighbour's wife."

"What luck to make it."

"Yes," Ma said as we crossed the main road and walked up the wide skirt of stairs that lay at the foot of the court building. "We could do with some ourselves," she added quietly.

"You mean Dad?"

She nodded.

Dad's trial was in Court 12 towards the back of the building. To reach it we went down a series of wide passages, turning right and right again, and then finally left. We could have been following the route of a question mark, going around in a semi-circle with a dogleg to end it off.

The floors were of worn linoleum and the walls were painted in two tones, cream above and from the floor to head height, an official brown enamel, scratched, smeared and sticky from all the people dragged unwillingly past them. Signs above the doors warned the public of heavy fines for spitting, swearing or removing government property. "Whites only" signs were stuck up at strategic points. Ashtrays (could they be spittoons?) the size of bedpans balanced on wooden stands that were screwed into the ground. Like giant crabs, they dominated the hallways and overshadowed the handful of people we came across: the cleaners leaning on brooms which had rows of bristles stretching halfway across the corridors, a sorry-looking wedding party and a legal man illegally grinding his cigarette *stompie* into the floor. A pantomime white wig the kind judges wear sat skew on his head.

The public gallery of Courtroom 12 was nearly full when we entered. There was quite a hubbub and milling about. We scanned the crowd and what was surprising for me was that I hardly recognised a soul. I knew that Dad was being tried with a whole lot of other "accuseds", but why did I not know these people whom I presumed to be supporters? We eventually spied Rose who motioned that she had kept two seats for us and Ma and I squeezed past a row of seated people to get to our places.

"Steven," Rose said with a note of surprise. "I thought it was Jane who'd be coming."

"She had an important tut. She'll be here this afternoon," I told Rose.

"Anyway, it's nice to see you. Girls flocking to hear you on your guitar?"

I was saved a reply when the judge entered to a call of "All Rise". A troop of handcuffed prisoners emerged through a sort of trap door in the floor. It was odd to think that prisoners were being kept hidden in the holding cells below our feet. Dad was the third or fourth in line. It was kind of unbearable to look at him, but I had to.

He was scanning the crowd, his eyes searching and finding us almost immediately. He gave me a sheepish, apologetic kind of look as if to say, sorry about the drama, boy, but what can we do? I find the thing almost as embarrassing as you. And then he was led to some seats tucked away on the right of the room where he and the other prisoners sat for the rest of the day.

The proceedings started up in a rather humdrum way and then continued, on and on. A lot of the time I couldn't hear what they were saying. It wasn't a bit like courtroom scenes in books or films. The small bits I could hear didn't seem to have anything to do with anything. The judge looked like he was asleep most of the time.

The most exciting thing that happened the whole morning was when they were questioning a downcast, dark-haired young man whom I'd never seen before. He was a state witness who had agreed to testify against Dad and the others in order to avoid getting charged himself. The prosecutor asked him the most inane questions and I couldn't hear his answers. His voice seemed to get swallowed up in his shirt.

"Do you reside in Morningside? When you left your aunt's house in Page Street, where did you move next? What exactly did you see? Were these cardboard boxes kept in the safe? Where were they kept? Are you sure that these were the same boxes you saw the previous day? Could someone conceivably have swopped the papers in the box?" and so on.

"What are they going on about the boxes for?" I whispered to my mother.

She shrugged.

I wondered to myself if what they were talking about were the boxes filled with papers that Dad had brought home about a month before his arrest. We'd burnt them together at the bottom of the garden in a bonfire. It had made a big impression on me, feeding pages and pages of printed matter into the flames, watching the pages separate, curl, shrink and blacken before being consumed in an orgy of blazing sparks and acrid black smoke. I had sensed that they were somehow dangerous (why would Ivor be destroying them otherwise?) but I wasn't in the least bit curious then about what they were or what they contained.

There had always been an un-discussed rule that for my own safety it was better I didn't know about some things. It wasn't anything as sinister as a code of silence, just an attitude of common sense with which I willingly complied. More often than not I did not want to know.

After that it was more questions which seemed to lead nowhere and mumbling answers and then an adjournment while the lawyers discussed things amongst themselves. Even the odd looks I cast to Dad's corner when I thought he wasn't looking at us revealed nothing. It was all so utterly boring that I was very glad that my age had saved me from having to go more regularly.

The visit with Dad that had been specially arranged for me during the trial was not a success either. Ma fetched me early from school and drove me into town. For some reason we got into a terrible traffic jam and got to the court ten minutes late. This left Dad and me about three minutes together before he was taken away by the guard.

I saw him in a funny room with low wooden benches. He got up when I came in and tried to get his arm around me. He was wearing the smart suit Ma had bought him at the beginning of the trial but it flapped about his arms and legs a bit comically. At the same time as he made a move to reach out for me, the guard barked out, "*Geen kontak!*" and I tripped over the bench and got a sharp smack on my shin. I held on to it while Dad was trying to talk to me. He was saying, "Are you alright? Let me see. Just a bruise," and then my name, "Steven, my boy," over and over. Then he seemed to get hold of himself and asked me a few questions, single words, I think, "School? Ma? Bicycle? Being careful?" which I answered in monosyllables, the pain in my shin helping me to avoid looking him in the eye.

"Sit down, my boy, sit, my boy, "he said but it was already time to leave. The guard got out the handcuffs, snapped them around father's outstretched hands wrists and led him out. Before he disappeared, Dad twisted around in the doorway and gave me a wink. I think it was a signal to say, relax, don't take it too seriously, boy, it's all a bit of an act.

Yet it wasn't. It was horribly serious. In April, the trial came to an end. My father was found guilty of belonging to an illegal organisation and sentenced to five years. He was transferred to Pretoria Central Prison. As a category D prisoner he was limited to one letter (both the letter he would write and the letter he would receive were to be 500 words only) and one visit every six months.

FOURTEEN

It rained and rained that weekend, the start of the Easter holidays. People said it was the last of the summer rains. The newspaper headlines were about carnage on the roads and lost revenue because of poor attendance at the Rand Easter Show. Photographs of horrible smashes showing wrecked cars crumpled into weird shapes decorated the front pages.

In English class at school, we'd learnt about how writers and poets attach human emotions to non-living things and the weather most of all. Our set-work was *Macbeth* and whenever something really bad was brewing in the castle, there would be a massive storm outside. It added to the atmosphere of evil and drama. The teacher gave us a weird term for it, "pathetic fallacy". It sounded more like a useless lie but because of its strange name it stuck in my head.

The rain drumming ceaselessly on our tin roof was a similar thing. When I got up to pee in the bathroom in the middle of the night, I could hear Ma crying under her blankets. Jane was in her room a lot of the time, ostensibly working. I think we were all in shock.

Five years, my God! Five years! As long as high school from beginning to end. As long as it had taken me to get from standard two to now. When I was in standard two, I still half-believed in Father Christmas. In five years, it would be 1970, the start of a new decade, I'd be 19, I'd have been legally driving for a year, I'd be finished school, maybe even started university. I'd most probably be fully grown. In five years I'd be shaving, earning money. I might even have had sex with a girl.

I spent much of the time on my bed, guitar idle on my chest. The noise of water gushing down the gutters and bouncing on the roof was very loud. Still, I could hear the cars as they went past on Innes Road with a whoosh – more like speed boats than cars, especially in the dip which had quickly filled with water. A row of ants was crossing the far wall, like an army on a forced march through the desert. For three days the line had been unbroken, one ant streaming after the other. Could there be so many of them or was I seeing the same ones coming and going? Their nest outside must have been flooded.

I got up and went to forage for some food in the kitchen. On an impulse, I decided to go look at the swimming bath. It was sure to be overflowing, even though William had built a little cement wall up on the slope above it after the last flood. I fetched Dad's rain jacket from the hallway where it was still hanging on a hook and went out the back door, careful of the slippery steps down into the garden.

It was coming down in buckets! It's always such a shock that first wetting. I fought it, trying to avoid the extra dollops of water that splattered from the shrubs on the way to the pool. But one look at my shoes into which muddy puddles were already seeping from below and rain from above and I sat down, plonk, on a bank of sopping wet grass, letting the rain fall on me. It stopped being unpleasant, the balmy water plastering my hair to my head, splashing down my face, running down inside my collar and rising from the seat of my pants which the rain jacket didn't cover. It was a delicious sensation once I gave myself over to it.

I had a clear view of the swimming pool (not counting the stripes of rain racing diagonally through the air and the dance of water as they hit the surface). Eric told me what it was like coming down to land at Jan Smuts airport. He'd gone to Durban after his *barmitzvah* and was returning home on a clear summer's day.

"All you see are these Lego houses and each house has got a little patch of bright blue at the back or front – the pools of all the Joburg whities. Hundreds and hundreds of them, all shapes, kidney-shaped, square, rectangular, on and on, as far as you can see."

I'd never flown myself, but I could easily imagine it.

The swimming pool decided my parents on buying our house. It was where we spent summer weekends, eating lunch, entertaining my parent's many friends and acquaintances and our own friends too, swimming, diving, cavorting. The summer I turned eleven, I got up every morning at dawn to practise doing breaststroke underwater. By the end of the season I could do four and a half lengths without having to come up for a breath.

As I sat there getting wetter and wetter, I remembered the weight of the water I had pushed through and my stinging eyes as I battled on in the lonely blue-green until I could take it no longer and kicked up to the surface. Then there were Jane's or my birthday parties where the invitations said bring a cozzie and a towel. When pin-the-donkey, musical chairs and other games organised by my mother on the tennis court flagged, everybody would land up in the pool, screaming, throwing balls, jumping or playing a version of underwater hockey with more arguments about the rules than there was playing.

I remembered being alone on the water, bobbing about on an inflatable Lilo Dad came home with it one year but it didn't last for more than one summer. I would close my eyes as I lay on my back, catching a tan, being gently wafted from one side of the pool to the other. The sun glare and the lapping of the water put me into a daze. I'd squint up into the sky from time to time, a sky so blue it made me ache. Sometimes there would be great Joburg clouds about and sometimes a delicate silvery trail left by an aeroplane slowly streaking through the sky. I'd find myself thinking, I wonder if they can see me from where they are? And I'd reach through the miles of space and what Eric described would become my own experience, what I had seen for myself. I'd add myself as a single dot in one of those pools, a speck of dust in one of the many blue-irised, whitey eyes.

Still the rain came down. It was incredible. There was a constant stream of water running from the tip of my nose on to my knees, which I had pulled up under my chin. I heard a sharp rap of someone banging on a window, then the scrape of metal against the window frame. My mother's voice came from inside, "Oi! Come inside. Steven! What are you doing?"

She was at the kitchen door when I got back. She made me take off my clothes at the sink by the back door.

"Steven, what the hell were you doing out there? Are you alright?"

"Of course, it was sort of fun, that's all," I answered.

The rain jacket and my shirt were in a sodden heap and I was now sitting down on the linoleum pulling off my squelching, oozing shoes.

"I don't know what to think about you two, honestly! Jane did the same thing when she was your age, sitting in the garden under an umbrella in the pouring rain, except she was reading a blue book she'd got her hands on. *Candy*, I think it was."

Ma laughed. It was a good sound.

"Get into a hot bath," she ordered.

I lay in the bath for a long time, adding more hot water now and then. Water seemed to be the medium of the week. Jane came inside to pee. I looked away. We had only one indoor bathroom with the lav in it, not separate.

Before he was taken to Pretoria, Dad sent a special letter to us which was delivered by his lawyers. Someone had typed Dad's handwritten original. Ma read it out in a strong, clear voice to Jane and me and a small group of my parents' friends who had congregated in our lounge after the sentencing. There was Rose, Izzy, Abie and Dulcie, all looking pale, helpless and wet! Dad's sister, Aunt Grace, was also there.

It was sterling stuff Dad had written: he knew that political change would come to South Africa, it was inevitable, it was only a matter of time. It would be hard but he was determined to survive jail, more than survive, triumph over it. Our cause was just and it was the laws of the land that were wrong. He would be able to endure it because even if we had few opportunities to express it in the hard times ahead, the ties of love between the four of us were a given, they were unquestionable. We were to carry on leading a full life, filled with fun and parties and adventures and holidays and hard work at school and varsity. This last part was underlined. He said we must not become bitter. The time would pass and we would be together again. Of this he was sure, he said, he would land another mussel-cracker off the rocks of Robberg if it was the last thing he did.

Aunt Grace wiped a few tears from her eyes, and everybody said what a good letter it was. They could hear Ivor's voice coming through loud and clear, his modesty, his humour etc. Then it was a round of tea and biscuits and it all became like the usual social occasions, only a little more subdued and polite than normal. No-one knew how to hold on to this particular day with words or actions that would not seem forced or trite. The big words had already been expressed in Dad's letter.

Then Abie said, "What would Ivor say if he were to see us with these long faces? It's not his bloody funeral, for God's sake," and the liquor cabinet was opened, and people stayed until quite late, hugging Ma, talking about this and that.

I went over the words in Dad's letter as I lay soaking in the bath and breathing in the clouds of warm vapour that were building up and condensing against the walls and clammy tiles. Courage. Justice. Triumph. Endurance. They were spectacular words, those of a hero, a freedom fighter, of a political visionary. They were my father's words. He was a great man.

And me? Gripped with self-pity, I looked down at my puny body, so undeveloped for a fourteen-year-old compared with others, I thought, the little willy completely hairless and as innocent as a worm, my chest caved in where others bulged. My fingers and toes were crumpled and white with frog skin from such long exposure to water, and the cuts and scratches on my legs and arms confirmed that I was a mere child. What about me?

FIFTEEN

Winter set in. It was back to long pants and hockey and waking up in the dark. To help with the finances, Ma took in a lodger who moved into the spare room. Perry Scher was a university student studying psychology and doing a thesis on the behaviour of bush babies. He spent much of his time rushing back and forth from our house to the university to check on his "pets", as he called them, which were his sole responsibility.

When he was home, he would sit reading a weighty tome in our lounge, pipe in mouth, well dressed for the part of serious intellectual in a corduroy jacket with leather patches on the elbows. He addressed Jane and me in a thoughtful, measured way, as if each of his words were little polished stones, offerings which we should store up and treasure. Although he was nice enough and well-meaning in the extreme, it made me uncomfortable when he asked if I minded if he sat in the armchair by the fireplace, Ivor's favourite spot. We were not used to being handled so carefully.

Ma had wound up the Christmas hamper business and thrown herself into a hectic schedule of exercise classes which were often held at the house. It was not unusual to come home from school to find the driveway blocked with cars and the floors of the house shuddering to the rhythm of a-one-and-two-and-three as Ma put her "ladies" through their paces. A glimpse through the window as I wheeled my bicycle to the shed revealed my mother and her students doing a yoga stretch which made them look like cormorants hanging out their wings to dry.

I had a vague sense of other things going on as well: phone calls at night, conversations breaking off when I entered a room, my mother inexplicably absent from meals. There were more arrests. The newspaper called it "A major crackdown on the left". The police raids in the middle of the night did not stop. The day after a particularly long and unpleasant raid (one of the policemen sneered at my mother and said he would tell Dad she had a man living with her), a strange thing happened.

I was trying to roast pink marshmallows over the stove in the kitchen, when I heard voices accompanied by an unusual noise coming from the garage, which shared a wall with the kitchen. Then I heard a dragging sound, followed by the characteristic click of the unlocking and opening of the boot of the Peugeot.

"Ma? Is that you?" I called, only mildly concerned. There was no answer so I left the sticky burnt mess that I'd been trying to scrape off the stove and sauntered over to the back door of the garage. It was closed. When I opened it, I was faintly surprised to see Rose and Ma at the back of Dad's dusty station-wagon in the semi-darkness. They were whispering and piling quite a lot of luggage into the boot.

"Oh, hullo, Rose. I didn't see you come. What's up?"

Rose looked at Ma and Ma looked at me.

After a pause, Ma answered softly. "Rose is going to get out of the country. Help us with this case, Steven. What have you put inside, Rose, rocks? Instructions were a light case, for goodness sakes. Get us a blanket from my bed, Steven. I think the large green one will do. Is the Branch parked outside? Did you notice?"

"No," I answered, "but I'll go check."

I fetched the blanket, then made my way back into the house to the front door, picking up a tennis ball from the bowl on the hall table on the way to the garden. Feeling rather self-conscious, I made a big thing of throwing the ball up into the air just this side of the hedge and catching it noisily. On the third throw, I purposely let it fly over into the road. I followed and had a good look up and down the street while ambling over to the opposite pavement to fetch it. Everything looked alright. There were only the familiar neighbourhood cars dotted here and there and no-one was sitting in a parked car.

Ma was opening the tip-up garage door as I came in off the street. I nodded to her. I watched as she climbed into the car and started the engine. Rose was nowhere to be seen. As the car shot past me in reverse, I caught a glimpse of a form lying wrapped in the green blanket on the floor behind the front seats. Ma waved and said in a voice that was far too loud, "Toodle-oo, Steven. I won't be long. I'll try to remember to get some bananas as well."

Bananas! What on earth made her say such a silly thing, I thought as I closed the driveway gates and pushed the bolt into a small hole bored into the red soil. Behind my back I could hear the car engine surge down the road, my mother slightly mistiming the change of gears as she wasn't used to driving Dad's car. It took some effort not to turn around and watch her drive up to the intersection of Francis and Innes where I knew the car would disappear from sight as it rounded the corner.

Surprisingly, Ma was back in less than an hour and a half. And she had brought a box of fruit and vegetables with her, bananas included! I knew that she couldn't possibly have driven Rose to the safety of the Swaziland or Lesotho border in such a short time. I also knew it was unlikely that Rose had left by plane. How would she have got through passport control if the police were looking for her?

With Jane out at a party and Perry at the university on bush baby duty, we were alone in the house that evening.

"Where did you take Rose?" I asked her at the supper table, breaking a cardinal family rule.

"You know it's not safe for you to know such things, Steven," she answered apologetically.

"No, that's not it," I interrupted. "I'm worried about Rose. Is she safe?"

"I hope so. I only took her on the first leg. There are others who will take her further."

"Like in the Underground during the Second World War, right?"

"Right."

I could read Ma's thoughts from her face and the way she worked the corners of her mouth. How much should she tell me? To what extent should she protect me? Should she warn me? About what?

"It's fine," I assured her. "I don't need to know anything." But it was she who suddenly chose to talk.

"I'd never put you or Jane into any kind of danger. I'm sorry about this afternoon, I really am. I shouldn't have asked you to…"

"Honestly, Ma, it's fine," I repeated. "Did I tell you that Eric's mother had her bag snatched on Rockey Street?"

"It's important that you know *this* in case anything happens, Jane and you will be looked after. I've organised it, so you don't have to worry. You're perfectly safe."

I forked the piece of chicken onto my plate with vehemence, trying to squash the words that burnt inside me.

"We are, Ma, but what about you?" I burst out, losing the battle to remain silent.

She didn't answer for a while and then I knew for sure, she was deeply involved in underground activities beyond merely helping out friends.

"There is a moral imperative to take part in this struggle, whatever the personal cost," she said eventually.

These were words I didn't expect from my mother. They belonged in books, in the editorials I glanced at in my father's newspaper. They were the words of the friends and intellectuals who regularly smoked up a storm in our kitchen but not my mother's, not Lucy's.

"Except for children," she added hastily. "Your job's to go to school and meet friends and have fun and just grow."

She smiled, picked up her empty plate and came past the back of my chair, where she stopped for a while, her hand resting lightly on my shoulder.

"Now tell me about Eric's mother. Is she all right?"

"I'm not a child," I said sulkily.

"You're right," she answered, moving over to the sink. "Parents have a hard time recognising that their children are growing up. I don't know what it is about us … some kind of selective blindness. But you are still too young to get involved in all of this. There's no need for it at all." The dishes were slopped into a sink of hot, soapy water which William had filled before he went off duty and the conversation was at an end.

The Driftwood were rehearsing at our house that night. Neville and Dennis and I jammed in my small bedroom. Neville was using a bucket, suitcase and pot instead of the drum set which he obviously couldn't bring along and the volume on the amp was turned down as far as it could go. Even so, it didn't sound too bad. Our repertoire had been slowly growing over the months and the newer songs were getting progressively more challenging. Still, it was Dennis who was the class musician and who showed Neville and me the ropes. We were very willing to be directed for being part of a band was not only a musical thing for us, it was a matter of social prestige, a passport to making it with our peers.

Being a school night, we packed it in just after ten when the two of them were fetched by Dennis's dad. Jane came back from a party soon afterwards. She was in a rotten mood. She flung herself on the sofa, kicking off Ma's shoes which she had borrowed for the night.

"It's like at first I really want to go. I'm all excited when I'm invited and then after a while I think to myself, it's going to be boring, I just know it is," she moaned to Ma and me. "And then I force myself to go. After all, who am I to pre-judge? Give it a chance, give people a chance. How am I ever going to find people I like if I don't put some effort into it?

"But when I get there, immediately I know it's a mistake and I'd rather be at home with a book. All those stupid people, talking rubbish with drinks in their hands and pretending they're interested in you when they aren't, and pretending they're not interested in you when they are. All I could think about was Dad sitting in jail and it's a bloody cold night and have they given him enough blankets and food?"

"Not sure whether to be sorry for yourself or for Dad?" I said.

Ma put her arms round Jane. "Don't be hard on yourself, Janey. You'll find like-minded people soon enough. We've just got to keep reminding ourselves that we are not unique. There are hundreds, no, thousands of families in the same position in South Africa and elsewhere. And we've got a whole lot of advantages most of them don't."

"Like what? I can't see them," Jane mumbled into Ma's jersey.

"Like being white, for instance," I put in. "That's a big one in this place."

"Come on, sweetie, go to bed," Ma said soothingly. "I'm bushed myself. It's been a hell of a day. I wish I could wave my magic wand and make everything right for you two. No-one tells you just how difficult it is to say the right thing to young people. I wish I could adopt the simple philosophy my mother had. She believed that if you weren't an adult (her definition was 21 and over) you simply had half the brain, half the needs and deserved half the attention. We children just got on with it."

"Those were the days before Spock," my sister said.

Before the three of us got to sleep, a car pulled up in the driveway with a jerk and a jolt and Perry rushed indoors. Ma came out of the bathroom in her flannel nightie; Jane emerged from her room in her pyjamas.

"What's wrong?" Ma asked. Perry's clothes were awry, his hair mussed, the usual unruffled manner completely gone.

"My thesis, my thesis, I'm ruined!" he yelled. "Someone left the cage unlocked and they've escaped. The security guard and I have been searching for bush babies everywhere in the building. There are still six missing, God knows where. They could be anywhere on the campus, just anywhere. I've come to get some help. How about it, Steven?"

"It's a school night," my mother began, but I took no notice.

I grabbed a thick jersey and a couple of torches and rushed out into the night with Perry. I was keen for an adventure. It was exactly what I needed after a day of little tugs this way and that which had disturbed me more than I would admit.

Perry's Cortina backfired before we catapulted away. All the way through Hillbrow and down Empire Road to the university, Perry talked to himself, his thin beard bobbing up and down. Bursts of mist billowed out from his mouth and there were beads of moisture on his top lip. He stopped reluctantly at each red robot that caught us, but only for as long as he needed to insure it was safe to pass. I kept my eyes peeled for traffic cops but there were none. Here and there night watchmen huddled round small fires in perforated drums.

We parked behind the science block and I followed Perry as he crossed the tarmac and went down a narrow alley, the weak beam of the torch wandering over a line of dustbins and piles of rotting cardboard. After a hurried fumbling with the keys, Perry let me in through a metal door. The sign on the front said "NO UNAUTHORISED ENTRY".

The door shut behind me with a whine and a click. Inside it was completely dark. Although I could hear Perry moving up ahead, the dark seemed to have swallowed him and his torch. I stood still; overpowered by a primitive reek which I recognised as the rich, rank smell of animals. Only then did I notice the sound of the scrabbling of claws against wire and the grunts and squeaks of disturbed animals. Still, I was not prepared for the sight that greeted my eyes when Perry snapped on the light.

We were in a long room painted a bilious yellow in which every window was painted out a dirty, opaque white. Wire cages of all sizes filled the space on both sides of a narrow aisle. In the cages huddling at the bottom asleep, or pacing up and down, were a variety of monkeys and apes of different colours and sizes. There were about forty of them. Hanging on to the bars with outstretched arms, swinging by their tails or shaking against the wire mesh, they presented a picture of utter despair.

"How can you?" I asked Perry as I walked down the aisle making eye contact with the almost human inhabitants of this nightmare room. He did not answer. He was counting the bush babies which were housed together in a slightly larger cage at the end of the room.

I had overheard Jane and him discussing experimentation on animals at the house a while back. Perry had argued that it was a necessary evil.

How else could man test new medicines for diseases such as TB or malaria which were rife amongst the poor and disadvantaged, he had asked in a logical, cool manner. Abhorrence on the grounds of cruelty to animals was a sentimental luxury, he had insisted. Jane had wanted to know how he could justify a *psychologist* using caged animals. Research into what it was that made humans tick, he said, was crucial for understanding people's needs and creating a better society.

It made no sense to me that night in that ugly, smelly place. A large baboon, sitting completely still in his cage, looked at me. Small eyes rimmed in red set in his blunt, weighty head followed my every movement. It was too much to bear and I left the building to wait for Perry at his car. My body felt heavy and numb. I could have fallen asleep upright, frozen like a plank of wood.

Like Jane, I found myself thinking about my father sitting in Pretoria Central, fifty kilometres away. For nearly a year I had pushed away the image of him inside his cell, a cage of sorts. But now it surfaced strongly and hung before my tired eyes overlapping the empty parking lot as if two slides were stuck in a projector at the same time.

Dad was looking at me with the expression he had when he wasn't being funny and he wasn't being serious, like the baboon had, really. Maybe it was exhaustion, maybe that awful yellow room or the memory of Rose in a blanket behind the back seat of Dad's Peugeot, but I felt like lying down and howling. I climbed on to the back seat of the Cortina. I stretched out on it, then pulled up my knees. I used my sleeve to wipe my running nose and eyes. It was a relief to hear little crying sounds coming from me, to feel the tears running freely from my eyes.

When Perry got back, he was a lot calmer than he'd been earlier.

"Sorry it's so late, old thing," he said to me while starting up the car (his habit of using quaint old-fashioned phrases had returned). "I made a bit of a miscalculation. Only two of my pets were missing, and guess where they were? Snuggled up under the others where I couldn't see them, under the cage."

"What time is it?" I mumbled.

"Gosh! After one. Will you be all right getting up for school, Steven?"

"Sure," I said, sitting up.

SIXTEEN

They arrested Ma in November. The Security Branch came in the early morning, did their usual thing of throwing books off shelves and searching the cellar and garden shed. They ordered Ma to dress and pack a small bag of clothes and toiletries. Then they marched her off to their car, which was parked across our front lawn and a little into a bed of Michaelmas daisies which William had planted out after the spring annuals were over. She sat on the backseat with a policeman on each side of her while two others continued searching the house.

"Don't worry," Ma mouthed to me from behind the closed car window.

I smiled and gave her the thumbs-up sign. It was very early. Birds were making a racket in the trees as they do at dawn in summer. The heavy dew on the lawn on was making my bare feet cold. William was a little distance away at the gate. He was wringing his hands. I think he was crying.

Jane came out of the house with the last policemen and stood beside me. We watched as they climbed into the car and reversed it with a whoosh of flying dirt and a jolt, turned on the lawn and drove out through the front gates past William. Jane and I ran out into the road. We could see Ma turn around in her seat to get a last look at us. Then she was gone.

Perry arrived at the house an hour later. "Your mother knew this might happen, "he told us. "She discussed it with me and I agreed to live here and keep an eye on you two until she gets back."

"God!" Jane cupped her hand over her mouth. "Aunt Grace. I haven't phoned her."

She ran to the telephone in the passage, leaving Perry and me alone in the kitchen.

"Gets back when?" I asked.

"I don't know. A couple of months, I'd imagine," he answered gravely.

We sat in the kitchen in silence for some time. Perry looked round. An air of helplessness flapped about between us. Dishes from supper were piled on the draining board. My school uniform was hanging from a hook on the back of the door. I could sense that the consequences of the promise he had made to my mother were only now sinking in.

Jane returned. "They've just changed the law. A person can be held for up to 180 days without being charged. And from what I understand, there's no food or washing to be dropped and picked up either. Lucy's on her own."

"What did Aunt Grace say? "I wanted to know. Aunt Grace was my father's sister and although she shared none of his political convictions, she was our only blood relative in Johannesburg.

"She kept saying, 'oh dear,' over and over. And 'how could Lucy have got herself into this kind of trouble with Ivor away for five years?' She'll be here this afternoon, so she says."

"I wonder if they'll put her in solitary confinement." I was thinking out loud.

"Most probably. But Lucy knew what she was getting into." Jane's manner was matter-of-fact, almost brutal.

Perry turned to Jane. "I'll give you a lift to varsity in a while, Jane. And you too, Steven. But I've got to have a serious discussion with you two first. Lucy has organised it so that we receive a monthly stipend from the lawyers for groceries, William's wages, lights, water, rates, etc. I'm sure Aunt Grace will be given some sort of power, a veto, to ensure I don't make off with the Carter millions." He snorted. "Actually, there's going to be a whole lot less money about, I'm sure, and it will take some effort to keep this boat afloat. I've never had experience in looking after a house and family, so you chaps better help me out."

"You can start your duties with William," Jane said sarcastically. "He's cowering in the back convinced that we're all going to starve and he'll lose his job."

When I got back in the afternoon, Aunt Grace was at the house. Although Jane and I never discussed it, we were united when it came to Aunt Grace. A force to be reckoned with at the best of times, she would very likely insist on taking us to live with her in her rigid, impeccably tidy home in the Southern suburbs. There was absolutely no way we would do that.

We'd given way to her on some things in the past, like the importance of exchanging Christmas cards and good table manners. But not in a month of Sundays, were we prepared to let her win this particular battle. It took all my and my sister's combined wiliness to persuade her that everything was FINE.

Were we sure that Perry was mature enough, at home often enough, aware enough of the responsibilities of running a household and looking after teenagers? This was not the time or place to voice my own niggling doubts. Of course, I assured her. It would only be a couple of months. We would be quite all right with him. Obviously, Ma had taken him on for just this eventuality. He was a great guy. We all got on terribly well.

"Don't forget," I said, "there is William as well."

Were we aware that she was now our legal guardian and the final responsibility was hers? How could she exercise this responsibility if she lived and worked on the other side of town and it took her half the afternoon getting across town what with the traffic? It was totally unnecessary for her to come except for a visit now and then, I said. She was welcome to come whenever she wanted, when it was convenient for her, I hastily added.

It would be less of a disruption if we stayed on, I continued. This was our home and we were fairly close to my school and varsity. The effect I was after was a tone that, on the one hand stopped her feeling unwanted or that we were hiding something from her, and, on the other, was mildly sympathetic about the extra burden my parents' disappearance was placing on her. It was a fine line to tread, but, as the survivor I had become in a single day, I knew my future depended on it.

My aunt waited for Jane to return with Perry in the late afternoon and swooped on them with her advice and barely hidden anxieties. I left them to it with much relief, only too glad to hand over the baton to my sister.

I sat on my bed strumming my guitar, randomly changing from one chord to another. I remembered Jane saying after one of the infrequent family gatherings held at Aunt Grace's house, "How anyone can live with those clocks and chimes and cuckoos going off all the time? And as for glass vases standing on doilies filled with water and semi-precious stones, it's frightening!"

"It's just a matter of taste, Janey," Ma had said.

For me the hours spent at my aunt were a kind of slow torture. She had no children of her own and held very strong opinions about how children should behave. To live with her or have her live with us would have been a kind of death.

SEVENTEEN

And so the Perry-in-the-house period began. In the early days, Perry would often fly into the kitchen in between his bush baby duties with a couple of bags of groceries, cook a mushy mixture he called "hunter's stew" and rush off again into the night once we had eaten. When he had the time, though, he made a point of offering to help us with my homework or Jane's varsity essays, generally being available. He was careful to ask if we needed a lift anywhere and took Jane for driving lessons in Lucy's Beetle. Perry glued a roster on the fridge. There were three horizontal columns with the headings, WHERE? WHEN? and NUMBER, and three vertical divisions with our names PERRY, JANE and STEVEN arranged above.

"It's so that we all can keep tabs on where everyone is," he told us. "If you leave the house, fill in where you're going, when you'll be back and the phone number."

For the first week or so, the atmosphere was one of cheerful co-operation, we asked if we could help and even offered to make others a cup of tea when we made our own. The roster was filled in religiously by all. It was like children playing house.

Little by little, cracks emerged. A phone account remained unpaid until the line was cut. Fear that Aunt Grace would try to phone and discover this glitch drove Jane and me to pester Perry till he eventually got round to paying it. Filling in the roster on the fridge door became a bit of a hit-and-miss affair and, when it fell off, it lay on the kitchen table, unused, before finally disappearing. Not one of us mentioned it.

Late one evening Perry smuggled a girlfriend through the back door after Jane and I had gone to bed. I heard the whisperings and door closings in the passageway and smiled to myself. The next morning, the girl was gone. Jane was her usual blunt self.

"Have the courtesy of introducing us to your friends next time you have them over, Perry," she said. "By the way, the headboard rattles with all that bouncing about."

Perry turned crimson and buried his head deeper in the morning newspaper. One had to feel sorry for him.

"I'm not going to be too grateful to him," Jane said crossly after he'd left. "He chose to do it, didn't he? And he's getting a pretty good deal out of it too. Free bed and board, not bad, I'd say."

She banged the bedroom door in my face. Her bad moods were as common as the rains in summer.

Slowly, almost imperceptibly, Perry's absences from the house grew longer so that it was the exception rather than the rule to have him around in the afternoons or evenings. At first he told us where he'd be, then slowly he just drifted off with vague explanations or none at all.

On the odd occasion he and I found ourselves at the house at the same time, he would fire off a string of questions, as if my presence had triggered an attack of guilt. Was there anything I needed? Clothes? Personal toiletries? Companionship, perhaps? Was everything all right at school? Was I remembering to clean my teeth every night? Could he advise me on my reading? What was I presently reading? Did I consider this to be suitable reading material for a fourteen-year-old? Sorry, fifteen-year-old? When were my exams? Oh, had I already written them? How were they? Did I need any information about sex? These bursts of attempted parenting revealed one thing to me: Perry was floundering.

Aunt Grace visited us fairly regularly, giving us at least a day's notice to get our act together. My parents' friends, Izzy, Abie and Rita, also popped in periodically. After a couple of minutes of questioning Jane and me on this and that, they would land up chatting with Perry if he was home. Perry would hold court from Dad's armchair, sucking on his pipe, combing his fingers through his young man's beard and talking in his usual pedantic, intellectual manner. My parents' friends would leave, their minds at ease that the "orphans" were in good hands. It was a conspiracy maintained by all three of us, each of us played our part in presenting the image of a smoothly functioning household with Perry at the helm.

Increasingly though, it was Jane or William who ran things. I moved into the discipline gap with the ease of water running through an empty channel. I did little or no studying for my end of year exams and diverted my report straight from the post box into my drawer without showing it to anyone. Surprisingly, no-one asked and I didn't let on. In it, the numbers with red circles were more numerous than the ones without.

With no holiday plans presenting themselves for December, I hung about friends' houses hoping to be invited for a solid home-cooked meal. I didn't mind too much if I wasn't because at home I had the freedom to eat tomato sauce on bread for three days running if I felt like it. I was out most evenings with Eric, Dennis or Neville starting to circle around girls and to gate-crash parties.

Transport was a major problem. We began to hitch-hike to get around town and there was no-one from whom I had to hide this fact, except Aunt Grace and she was duped fairly easily. Jane was busy with her own socialising and conscientiously studying as always, while Perry was an increasingly distant figure.

After the holidays were over, I returned to school in body only. I had been promoted to standard eight by the skin of my teeth. Extra maths lessons were a thing of the past. I quickly copied homework from friends' books before class. I scrunched up marked tests returned to us so that I would not have to think about them again. Luckily, no-one seemed to have twigged to the fact that my mother had been arrested. Only Eric, Neville and Dennis knew and they picked up on my cues and hardly ever mentioned it.

What I cared for most was going out, hanging out with my friends, and the band. The Driftwood practised in Ma's exercise room, Neville on the full complement of drums, Dennis and I strutting our stuff with wailing Fender and Stratocaster guitars plugged into an amp turned up sky high. For two weekends running we practised night and day. When she overheard me making plans for a third, Jane put her foot down.

"No way," my sister told me.

"What d'you mean 'no way'?"

"You heard," she said. "You don't expect me to study while that din's going on, do you?"

"Well, it's just too bad because we'll be playing here on Saturday and Sunday, like it or not. You can go to the library at varsity if you've got to swot," I insisted.

"No, I'm staying here. It's my home, isn't it?"

"Where else do you want us to go? Where can we practise?" I asked angrily.

"Anywhere but here," Jane snapped.

Perry looked up from his plate of take-aways. "Can't the others in the band have a chance to host the practice?" he asked mildly.

"It's not fair, "I retorted. "If Lucy or Ivor were here they'd let me."

"They're not here, we are," Jane answered. "At least *I* am."

Perry looked away sheepishly. He had been away for four days running.

"Go suck eggs!" I spat at her.

"Go lay chickens," she answered, laughing.

Without the peace-making Lucy around, our arguments were more frequent and vicious. Frustrated beyond rage by my sister's sounding "so right" (it made no difference that I knew that she *was* right) I punched her on the arm as hard as I could and ran out of the room.

"YOU FUCKING LITTLE SHIT!"

Jane's scream echoed through the house. Then a door banged shut so hard it was like a bomb going off.

EIGHTEEN

I always loved girls. I distinctly remember, when I was no older than four, standing and watching a group of little girls in their bobby socks and beautiful swishing dresses skipping and chanting in the nursery school playground, and wishing … wishing for what? To be noticed by them? Perhaps. To join them? No. That was girls' stuff and I was a boy and liked being a boy. I had a gun and a holster, a dinkie car and a play-play knife with a blade that bent. No, it was a feeling that had no name, a tug with no wish attached to it.

The memory of it has got mixed up with the slimy sensation of wet, cold pumpkin in the pocket of my shorts. This is what would happen at Mrs Hall's Play School: we would be served a small bowl heaped with cooked vegetables and maybe a fish cake, and a full glass of milk which we had to finish before being allowed to go play outside. I took the only escape I could think of. Later on in the morning I'd forget and ram my hands into my pocket. Squelch.

All through primary school, the feeling lay underground. I was at an all-boys school where the excitement of marbles, scuffles, peg-leg (you used a real knife for this game), stealing penny sweets from the cafe and swopping comics crowded out other concerns. Jane's friends and the girl children of my parent's friends were like flowers in a neighbour's garden, easy to trample in my haste to get to the fruit trees.

I teased and baited and chased girls as well as any boy of my age, all the while sensing that I'd much rather be relating to them differently. Not knowing how, I staved off the feeling and had fun with my friends. Secretly, I was in love with a number of the girls whose lives I made miserable.

About a year before Dad went to jail (I must have been twelve) he called me into the lounge to have a chat. From his opening sentence, I knew what I was in for.

"Girls are different from boys," he began. "You see – their bodies are different from ours."

I knew that he'd been set up by Ma to talk to me after I'd locked Jane and a friend up in her bedroom all afternoon long, peeping in through the windows and being a general pest. Embarrassed for Dad, I dived behind the lounge curtains. I did not want to witness his struggle.

"You must be gentle with girls, Steven," he continued manfully. "One day, you are going to want to be friends with them, more than friends. Maybe you are already starting to wonder about it all. I know you know how babies are made but there is more to it than the mechanics. Maybe you have started noticing changes in your body, maybe you spend a lot of time thinking about girls. Ma seems to think you like girls very much but don't know how to treat them. I can see your shoes sticking out of the bottom of the curtains and I'll continue, because I know you are listening."

I squirmed. Looking up, I saw tiny scraps of paper pinned to the linings of the curtains. On them, in my father's handwriting, were bank account numbers and details of a safety deposit box.

I forget what else Dad said to me as I stood behind the curtains. Perhaps I even blocked my ears. Eventually he packed it in and let me go off to my room, red-faced and smarting from embarrassment. I can imagine him shrugging as he reported failure to my mother.

"I tried," he would have said, pouring himself a brandy and Coke, relieved that he would not be asked again.

The December holiday after I turned fifteen, Neville organised a visit to two girls he knew in Orange Grove. Numerous telephone calls were made by both parties and there were many changes of plan, but in reality it was a simple operation. The parents of one of the girls were going out that Saturday afternoon, and Neville and I were to pitch up, alone, at the house, at two.

I tried on a whole range of outfits for Neville when he came to fetch me. We finally chose a pair of pale jeans and a striped T-shirt with a straight neckline, the best from a wardrobe that was getting scruffier by the month. It was fashionable to have torn and ragged bits, Neville said enviously; his mother wouldn't let him leave the house in anything like that.

We left my house at one. It was quite a walk to Orange Grove: down a short dip and up a long steep incline, past the home for unmarried mothers, where we couldn't resist whistling at the girls crocheting

104

booties at the window, past Marist Brothers College on the crest of the *kopje* and all the way down Louis Botha Avenue. It was a sweltering hot day. The thumbs we held out to passing motorists were ignored and sweat began running freely down my forehead and pricking my neck. I kept sniffing my armpits wishing that I'd had the courage to ask Perry to buy me the toiletries he kept asking about.

Still, we arrived twenty minutes early. The house was typical of Orange Grove, made with marmalade-coloured bricks and full of nautical touches, rounded walls, porthole windows edged in white, gutters and trim painted a sky-blue. Three hundred miles away from the sea, and that's what people chose to build – little brick steam boats, I've always thought. We checked the number on the gate and made off to a nearby park, wary of being spotted hanging about from behind the net-curtained windows. We passed the time by chewing our way through a box of Spearmint Chiclets which Neville had conveniently brought, and I was given a few tips, too.

"If you run out of things to say, just show them your profile. You've got a damn good profile," Neville said.

Eventually, at ten minutes past two (we didn't want them to think we were too eager) Neville pressed the front door bell. From behind the door came the sound of a rush of feet, then some giggles, and then nothing.

"They don't want it to look like they've been waiting," Neville whispered to me, "but I've got the answer."

Sure enough, as we slowly made our way down the short path to the front gate, we heard the door open behind us. Following Neville's cue, I turned back. One girl had draped herself round the doorknob while the other stood in the shadows behind her.

"Are you Neville and...?" the one in front asked.

"Steven," I said.

The girls stood back to let us in.

"Do you want to sit in the lounge?"

It was the same girl who spoke. Although she was bare-legged and barefoot, her dress was smart, party attire. It was a swirl of patterned chiffon over some shiny lining that fell from high collar to mid thigh in a fashionable cut I think they call a tent dress.

"I'm Sarah," she said, "and this is Janine."

"Sure, anywhere," Neville answered.

At first glance, Janine seemed the mousier of the two. Following the three of them indoors, I stole a look at her back. She had long dark blonde hair that fell in a shower over a blouse of some stretchy material. Her skirt was not short and not long, and she wore heavy, clunky shoes.

As we entered the lounge, the awkward business of where to sit or to be accurate whom to sit next to, overtook us. There was a large sofa and two easy chairs in a dark fabric with tassels at their base. From a tiny nudge of his head, I got the message that Neville had opted for Sarah and Janine was mine. I headed for the relative safety of one of the armchairs. Across from me was a glass display cabinet filled with Spanish dancing dolls and china dogs.

Once we were seated, all four of us were silent. The click, click of a grandfather clock sounded very loudly through the room.

"It must have been a hot walk. Can we get you anything to drink?" Sarah eventually suggested.

"Yes."

I nodded.

With visible relief, both girls went off to the kitchen. Neville waited until they were out of earshot to begin a furtive session of whispering.

"Well, d'you dig her?"

"I haven't really looked at her," I lied.

"What have you been doing, then, you idiot?"

"I don't know what I think of her. She hasn't said anything."

"Neither have you."

I suspected that a similar conversation was going on in the kitchen.

"Shh! They're coming," I warned Neville. I was sweating although it was cool in that dark, gloomy room.

I took another look at Janine as she and Sarah put a jug of orange squash on the glass-covered coffee table and arranged coasters on little tables brought out from a nest of tables ranging from small to tiny. She had a sort of weasley, pinched face, but not ugly. I still did not know what I thought of her.

Neither of us had said a word to each other.

Neville draped his arm around Sarah's shoulders as they sat together on the couch. Later, out of the corner of my eye I could see them kissing.

"Um, what standard are you in?" I asked Janine.

"Six," she answered so softly I had to lip-read. She was pulling hard on her skirt hem. Perhaps she was regretting her choice of clothes.

"I'm in eight," I said, "but school's school. Have you ever been to The Spot? It's a dance club on Jan Smuts Avenue."

She shook her head.

"It's tit, really tit."

Janine got up and whispered something to Sarah, who disentangled herself from Neville. The two once again left the room.

Neville groaned. "Have you made up your mind about her? I'm telling you, Steven, she's not bad as far as girls go. You could do worse. If she's anything like as hot as Sarah, then," he gave me the thumbs-up sign.

"I don't know," I said. "Does she want me?"

"What does it matter? Just start, you know, cuddling her up."

"I don't want to unless she wants me. She must say first."

"Okay, okay, I'll ask Sarah. Meet me at the back in a minute's time."

I wandered down the passageway looking for the kitchen. On the way, I decided I needed the toilet. I opened three doors before I found the right one. One was the main bedroom, a place of terrifying twin-bed formality, the next a young girl's room done up in pink sweetie-pie bows and the third a linen closet with the sharp smell of mothballs. I stumbled into the toilet with relief, stepped onto a deep shag rug cut into a moon shape to hug the base of the toilet, and lifted the matching furry lid. My wee tinkled loudly into the bowl so I aimed for the sides. The toilet made a violent woosh when I pulled the chain and I left it, shamed for no other reason than being heard to be using the toilet.

Trying to hold in the claustrophobic panic that was building inside me, I burst into the empty kitchen and out the back door. I found myself in a shabby cement-covered backyard ringed with little outhouses and servant's rooms. Neville was waiting for me under the washing-lines.

"What took you so long?" he asked. "Sarah says Janine won't say. She wants to know if *you* like *her*. I said I'd find out."

I shook my head. It was a stalemate. I wouldn't say first and neither would she.

Neville was irritated.

"God, Steven I took all week to set this all up and you're such a baby, you don't know how to take advantage of a good wicket. Humour the girl, man, and you can dump her tomorrow."

Again I shook my head

"Let's go," I said to Neville, trying not to plead. "These girls are really boring."

Neville continued to grumble for a few minutes but he relented and we said goodbye and left that awful house. I was disappointed with myself, with my inability to carry out what I imagined others found so easy, but my overwhelming emotion was relief. It was a relief to get back on the streets with Neville and twirl round lampposts. It was a relief to get away.

I achieved my first French kiss at a party a couple of weeks later. The lights were dim, the Seekers were singing "I'll never find another you", and the girl was close and willing. It wasn't all that pleasant. There was spit and mouth and tongue everywhere and the girl, who must have been more experienced than I, pushed her tongue into my mouth so forcefully I felt like gagging. Yet I came up for air triumphant. My career as a lover had been launched.

NINETEEN

One afternoon when tennis practice had been cancelled, I came home early and nearly rode right into George, William's son. I was coasting in through the gates, now kept permanently open, and was executing a particularly spectacular flying halt when a figure materialised out of nowhere. I swerved, lost my hold on the handlebars, and the bicycle and I parted company. The momentum carried the bicycle across the lawn and, wobbling along riderless, it entered a great big mound of yellow jasmine which opened and closed behind it as if it were welcoming a visitor from Toyland. I, on the other hand, had landed with quite a bump on my bum. For a split second I was confused, maybe even scared, but then I saw a pair of shoes on the ground before me and they were the spiffiest pair of mahogany Jarmines I had yet seen. The little pin pricks that decorated their highly polished surface were in whorls as elaborate as a starry sky of Van Gogh's, and between turn-ups ironed into shapely perfection and the shoes themselves, I noted a flash of silky grey sock. A quick scan up the legs belonging to the shoes and socks and my instincts were confirmed. Brushing off his immaculate suit and readjusting his fashionable string tie was George.

"Shame. How're you, Steven?" he asked as he helped me up.

"No, fine, George."

"Sorry about the *baas* and madam. It's a bad thing."

I shrugged. As William had gone off to the shops, I let us into the house with a key and we sat in the kitchen drinking tea.

"So, George my man, what you got to say for yourself? How long are you staying?"

The cool lingo was an attempt to throw a warm blanket of friendship over an encounter with a man only a couple of years older than me but whose life was largely impenetrable to a white schoolboy from the northern suburbs.

George looked at me sideways. "I've been living here a month," he said ingenuously. "There," he jerked his head towards the outside courtyard where William's room was.

I was amazed. The penny was dropping. The recurring crises when we ran out of milk, bread and sugar and accused each other of "gutsing", William's distracted air when he shut the door in my face when I came to his room to ask him something, it all started to make sense.

"You didn't need to hide, George. William should have told us. There's no problem with your staying here. It doesn't matter about your pass. You know we've never cared about that sort of thing in this house."

George looked straight at me. His face was beautiful: regular, clear features, limpid eyes, high cheekbones, perfect teeth. It lit up the shabby kitchen like some kind of exotic lamp. He wore an expression that managed to exude a friendly openness at the same time as it remained inscrutable, hidden.

"Don't tell me. You're in trouble with the police again."

No answer, just that cheerful, blank stare.

"What is it? What do they want you for?"

"Murder," he answered in a clear voice.

Sheer disbelief and a kind of admiration clashed in my mind. After a long moment, a strangled, "What!" emerged.

George was fiddling with the cuffs of his striped shirt.

"Did you do it? Did you actually murder someone?" I asked, incredulous that I was saying these words out loud in my own kitchen.

"Yes," he answered.

"Who?" I asked.

"My girlfriend's friend," he answered. "I caught her with him. I cut him badly with a knife. He died by the hospital the next day. I left when I hear from my friends that the police are asking for me in the township and I came here."

I had no idea what to say next. It needed a leap of imagination to turn this impeccably dressed, young man-about-town into a knife-wielding murderer. I picked Puss up from the floor and made a show of petting her while I plotted.

"If Perry and Jane find out you're living here, or rather *why* you're living here, I don't know… But it's cool with me. I won't say a thing, even to William. Just carry on as you were, George. Keep a low profile and maybe the whole thing will blow over."

Of course, I knew that it was unlikely that murder charges would be dropped but what else could I say? Our standard seven, English set-work had been Albert Camus' *The Outsider* and the hero in that committed a pretty senseless murder. He killed a total stranger on a beach in Algiers for no reason that I could make out and ye he still was a nice guy. It had something to do with the philosophy of existentialism but I couldn't quite get the hang of it. George's crime had to do with the appalling conditions people lived under in the townships, I rationalised, the poverty, the fight over limited resources, the unemployment, the stupid pass laws. He could count on me not to tell anyone.

We spoke of other things, the nightlife in the township, the music he was listening to (the big band sound was hot) and we went into my bedroom where we took chances on the Fender and the drums until the door opened and William came in.

"Ho!"

William's face creased into a harsh grimace. I had never before witnessed such a distortion of those calm, benign features. Ignoring my presence completely, he showered George with bursts of angry words. I didn't need to understand to get the gist of what was being said.

George said nothing in his own defence. He lowered his head and averted his eyes, enduring the tongue-lashing. It was a cunning ploy, one I should have used myself when my own father lost his temper with me. Instead, I found myself throwing out whining explanations, which only extended the argument, providing him with new targets. By submitting so passively, George had turned the thing around, both absorbing and deflecting his father's rage. George put down the guitar which he had been playing on the bed, got up slowly and left the room. William followed him, berating him all the way down the passage. I hurried after them.

"It's all right, William, "I said. "He's told me. I won't tell anyone, 'strue's God, honest, I won't. Not Jane, not Perry. No-one. Your secret's safe."

The scolding continued unabated in the kitchen, rising and falling and then gaining in strength once again. Suddenly, William stopped in mid-sentence, and a look of panic flashed across his face. Instantaneously, all three of us recognised the series of sounds from putter to cut-out, from jerk of a handbrake to the subsequent slam of a door.

George and William shot out of the house through the back door at the same time as Jane came in through the front. I was in the entrance hall to head her off while the retreat was staged behind me. She dropped the car keys in the bowl on the entrance hall table with a proprietorial flourish (she had passed her driving test only a week before). A door slammed.

"Who's that?" she asked me.

"No-one, just the wind." I answered.

It was William himself who blew their cover. He sent George away to the comparative safety of Pietersburg, where Martha lived, and once he was gone, confessed to both Jane and Perry one Saturday morning. Jane was sympathetic but adamant that George should not return to Johannesburg. Perry's response was extreme.

"For two months we've been harbouring a murderer, and you, Steven, knew all about it!" he fumed.

"Only for a week or so," I reminded him.

"But don't you chaps *understand*," he said, his voice breaking into a kind of bleat. "They hang people for murder in this country. It's totally irresponsible of you and that fucking gardener to do this to me. I didn't ask for all this crap. In fact, I hold you two personally responsible for putting *me* in danger."

I resented Perry calling William "a fucking gardener" and it was no use pointing out that for much of the time we had been as much in the dark as he had.

"It's over, Perry. The man's no longer here. It's history," Jane said.

Perry, however, continued to rant.

"I've had it with you lot!" he shouted. "This is not my problem. You two are not my problem. I don't know how the hell I landed up in this predicament, but I sure as hell am not sticking around any more."

TWENTY

It was no idle threat. Later that day, I overheard Perry on the telephone to Aunt Grace.

"You better do something about these bloody Carter children," he was saying, "because I've had enough. I'm out of here."

I waited for him to leave the house and then made a frantic phone call to Jane who was at the university library. Please, it's urgent, you've got to find her, I told the librarian, our mother has had an accident. She might not make it. She's in hospital. All right, describe your sister, she said. She's short, got short blonde hair, unwashed, stringy, wearing, I dunno, jeans and a T-shirt, most probably.

After a long wait, Jane came to the phone.

"What's happened? Is Ma all right?" she barked.

"Fine. I don't know."

We had heard nothing from Lucy for over three months. Since her arrest, no-one had been allowed to see her, not the lawyer, not Abie. She was still under 180 days.

"But that's not the problem. Perry's been on the phone to Aunt Grace. He's quit, Jane. The bugger's leaving us and from what I heard, Aunt Grace will be here any minute. She's coming over to pack us up. You know what that means."

"I'm on my way." Jane said.

On her way home, Jane had a brain wave, she told me later. She stopped off at Lilian and Solly Shapiro's house in Rosebank and asked if we could board with them. Then she hurried back home.

"They've got this big place that's empty since Jonathan moved out, and they owe it to Lucy and Ivor," she told me when she got back. "I think it's the answer, Steven. We can't maintain this house. Have you noticed the rust on the garage roof and the gutters? It's throwing money into a hole for us to stay on. Aunt Grace has met the Shapiros a few times; she can be won over. Their place is quite close to your school. It's an easy cycle ride compared to your ride now and getting to varsity will be no problem for me either. They were quite willing. In fact, Lilian sounded keen. You've always quite liked them, haven't you?"

I nodded. Lilian Shapiro had the reputation of being one of the leading intellectual figures in the movement, a stalwart of the party, a fiery speaker at public meetings, a rabble-rouser. My parents had always admired her commitment and keen brain. I do remember the odd private crack being made about them, the little asides about poor, henpecked Solly or their highbrow cultural pretensions. But these comments were no sharper than the average gossipy exchanges that flew around a group of friends and acquaintances.

What d'you say?"

"What will we do with the house?"

"Rent it out. It would give us a bit of income."

"And William?"

"He could stay on and look after things here. We could rent it on the condition that they keep him on."

"Puss?"

"Really, Steven. Choose. Either it's Aunt Grace's or the Shapiro's. I know what I'd choose if I were you. In fact I've already told the Shapiros that I'm coming. Are you?"

I agreed.

Aunt Grace was flustered and anxious when she arrived, eager to do the right thing and take us under her wing once and for all. We were ready with our story.

"It's better, this way, Grace," my sister explained. "The Shapiros are eager for us to live with them. They're coming over in a little while so that you can discuss it with them. They should be here any time now. Really, there will be far more supervision of Steven and it will be easier for him to concentrate on his school work if he's living with a family."

This didn't sound so good to me but obviously I couldn't say so.

"Lilian doesn't work so she'll be at home when he gets back from school, I can concentrate on my university work and not have all this," she waved her arms about "to worry about, and you can sleep like a baby in your bed, completely assured that we are being taken care of."

When Jane wasn't grumpy or snapping at everyone, she had a honeyed tongue, masterful at persuading others with a reasoned, mature logic.

But it was the Shapiros who finally tipped the scales. As Lilian came out of the car, she hugged Jane and said laughingly, "I've always wanted a daughter." Both Jonathan and their other son were overseas, one in London doing physics and the other a junior professor at some prestigious university in America. They were older than my parents, non-practising Jews, part of the movement, familiar. They were kind, decent folk and despite their politics, they led conventional lives. There was no trace of recklessness or Bohemianism in their manner with which Aunt Grace could find fault and she finally relented.

Considering the reasonableness of this couple and their eagerness to have us, it was not a difficult decision. I think she was relieved at finding other interested adults who'd share responsibility for the "jail orphans" and an arrangement was brokered. Jane and I would pay a minimal boarding fee, Jane would keep Ma's Beetle and we would both receive a monthly sum from my aunt for our other expenses. Jane's university fees were covered by a scholarship.

While a tight-lipped, white-faced Perry moved out that evening, Aunt Grace marshalled William and Jane to sort through the house and decide what furniture to leave behind for the tenants and what to store in the cellar. It was no small task; the house had been our family home for over ten years and we had collected a mountain of possessions. The books alone took four days to pack into boxes.

With William and me pushing it from behind all the way down Francis Street, Jane eventually got Dad's Peugeot to start. She drove it to a Hillbrow garage where it stood in the forecourt for a month or two, a dusty FOR SALE SEE INSIDE sign propped on the dashboard. An estate agent was called in by Aunt Grace who subsequently met a couple of interested parties. For lack of a better choice, a group of German students who were studying at the Technical College moved in.

The day before we made the final break, Jane drove me to the house to pick up the last little bits and to say goodbye to William. We let ourselves in through the front door and walked through from room to room, faintly surprised by how odd the house felt and looked. Unnoticed before, paint was peeling in great flaking patches off the ceiling, and the skirting boards and door-frames were battered and chipped. Stripped of everything but beds, a couple of sticks of furniture and the odd carpet, the whole character of the house had changed.

A memory popped into my mind as I walked down the uncarpeted passageway and past the open bathroom door, my footsteps crunching on the bare floor. I was very small and I was entering the bathroom.

Someone with my mother's voice said to me, "Hullo, Stevie-boy. Have you come to visit me?" I stopped in my tracks as she turned in the bath. Clinging dark, wet hair was stuck to a skull with blotches of white foaming stuff growing from its top. I screamed. Here was someone who was my mother and not my mother at the same time. Spooky, like an empty house.

William was outside scooping leaves from the pool. The water was bright green, the colour of my guilt.

"Hullo, Steven," he said. "How is your new place?"

"It's fine. Have you met the new people who are moving in here?"

William nodded.

"What are they like?"

"They are young and strong," he said. "But I don't know what they are saying. When they talk, I say, yes, yes but I do not understand them." He laughed uncertainly.

"You've got the Shapiro's number but here it is anyway," I scrawled out the phone number on the back of a school notice I'd shoved in my back pocket.

"If you need to speak to Jane and me, you can anytime. And you've got Aunt Grace's number. Listen William, if these guys give you a hard time, or start smashing up the place, well, then we can come and sort it out. We'll chuck them out and find other people to rent the house. It's no problem."

William stopped his scooping and his eyes sought my face.

"I promise, Steven, I will look after the house and the furniture and everything. When the madam and the *baas* come back from jail, they will ask, where is this, William, where did this thing go, the stove, the fridge, the carpets your mother she love so much, the one with the colours in the lounge. They must still be here when the *baas* comes back."

It was mortifying to hear him. His loyalty to our family was comforting but it also made me uncomfortable. It was too Uncle Tom's Cabin, too "yes-mastah, no-mastah".

"But you must be happy, too. Will you go to Pietersburg this Easter?"

"To Moriah," he answered, Moriah in the Eastern Transvaal where thousands of pilgrims from the Church of Zion congregated every Easter.

"And George? Have you heard from him?"

William gave me a quirky, cocky smile.

"She is far away but safe. Martha has a letter from him. She is in Rhodesia, working in the copper mines."

Jane came bounding through the Zulu hedge.

"Oh, there you are. We've got to get back. The Shapiros eat at seven, exactly. I'll see you next week, William, when I come to fetch the post. Come on, Steven."

"I had a dream about a big fish, William. What number is that?"

"Number?"

"For fah-fee, to put money for a bet with the Chinaman."

"Steven." Jane pulled at my shirt.

"Ah. A big fish. I think it is thirteen, Steven. Yes, thirteen. But fah-fee is not for men. It's a game for old women."

Jane turned around and marched off.

I gave William a friendly punch on his forearm.

"Listen I've got to go. Put ten cents on number thirteen, anyway. I think it will give you good luck, I've got a feeling in my bones."

"Bye," I shouted from the top of the stairs at the kitchen door.

"Bye-bye, Steven. Number thirteen on Friday," William's voice boomed through the hedge.

As we made our way back through the house, Puss came sliding through the burglar bars of the bathroom window and set up a yowling at our feet.

I looked down at her.

"Germans don't eat cats, do they? Not like the Chinese."

Jane had the front door key in her hand. "Stop faffing, Steven."

"Who's my pussy, puss?" I crooned, belly-lifting her soft form to dangle up in the air.

"COME ON!"

I dropped Puss onto the bare floor where she landed with a thud, and joined Jane outside. She shut the door and checked that it was locked by shaking the door handle. It was a habit she'd picked up from our parents.

The Perry-in-the-house period had come to an end. It had lasted just under three months.

TWENTY ONE

A week after our move to the Shapiros, a letter arrived for us at the house in Francis Street. Luckily, Jane picked it up in time. It was official notification that the next visit for prisoner number 5446932, one Ivor Sydney Carter, was at 8.30 a.m. on 12 February 1966. A maximum of two visitors would be allowed for the half-hour visit. Visitors should present themselves at the main gate ten minutes before the appointed time. No physical contact permitted and neither could we bring the prisoner any food or gifts.

Children under the age of sixteen were not allowed visits but Jane and I decided to risk my going with her.

"There was a chap who looked about twelve last time Ma and I went, and there were no questions. He was let in at the same time we were," she assured me.

We set out early on Saturday. More asleep than awake, I huddled against the side of the passenger seat of the Beetle and allowed all that my eyes saw to wash over me in a kind of blur. Walls and gates and hedges lining the streets and pavements of the suburbs passed in a broken rhythm of brick, tar, chain-link fence and painted plaster punctuated with a profusion of greenery.

Only a few people were awake, mostly Africans, men and women walking fast or riding bicycles to work. A domestic worker was putting out a bag of rubbish on the roadside before the garbage trucks arrived. I caught her eyes as she turned away from her task but the contact hardly registered. A few more lurches and turns (these must once have been the rocky crags on the summit of the *kopjes* of Johannesburg) and we were in Louis Botha Avenue. I almost missed the traffic cop propped up on his motorbike a little way off the shoulder of the road under the trees, but the gleam of his boots registered through my grogginess and I was instantly alert.

"Jane!"

"Um."

It took an effort not to turn around in my seat to check if the cop was following. Although Jane had her license, she looked too young to be driving and had been stopped often. She was short so her head hardly reached the top of the steering wheel and the seat was adjusted so close to the pedals, it was ridiculous.

"You should wear make-up and do something to your hair," I said.

Jane pulled a face. She had misunderstood me.

"I don't need to tart myself up. I'm doing fine in that department."

We passed "death bend" and I paid close attention to the road surface. The turn was sharp but experts blamed the high accident rate on the incorrect camber of the road which tipped cars in the opposite direction to the curve. As the Volkswagen accelerated through a green light, I saw glittering shards of glass and dark, oily stains on the tar.

"Don't even mention George," my sister said.

"Of course," I replied, irritated. "What do you take me for?"

"He's going to be particularly difficult, with Lucy in jail, so let me handle him."

"Okay." I was more than happy to let Jane take the lead.

We drove on in silence. I tried hard not to think about what I'd say to Dad. I hadn't seen him for a year.

The prison was one of the first buildings you come to when entering Pretoria from the south. It was a solid structure in red brick with a massive steel-studded door set dead centre. It had been a fort during the Boer War and a brass plaque near the entrance identified it as a national monument.

Jane marched up to the imposing entrance and knocked on a small door tucked into the corner of the steel-studded one. I thought she was joking but almost immediately a little oblong aperture set in the metal facade slid open and an eye peered out at us.

Jane stood on tiptoe to reach the opening.

"Two visitors for political prisoner number 5446932," she said referring to the letter she had in her hand.

The peephole slid shut. There was a deep woody thud, a rasping of metal against metal and the delicate sound of a key turning in a lock. With a melodramatic groan, the door swung open. I expanded my shoulders, put on what I imagined was a mature expression and followed my sister.

We entered a small courtyard, quaint in a way, partially covered with a pitched roof. Rows of wooden benches and a small glass booth occupied one side. Two guards dressed in khaki, rifles in their hands, stood at attention at either side of the back of the gate, as if on parade. Jane made her way to the booth. She pushed the letter into the slot at the bottom of the glass partition, spoke a few words to the official inside it and signed what looked like a register. Then she joined me on the bench where I was waiting. We were the only civilians there.

Her face sought mine. So far, so good, it said.

We waited less than a minute before a door opened on the far end of the courtyard and a guard appeared. He nodded in our direction and waited for us to make our way over to him.

"Mind your head," he warned at a midget-sized doorway leading to a steep flight of worn, stone stairs. At the top of the stairs, we were handed over to a second guard. Fleeting glimpses of passages blocked off by grilles opened up right and left. We passed a black prisoner on his hands and knees, polishing the floor. He didn't look up.

Until that moment, the inside of jails were known to me only through films. Prisoners being led to their cells; brawls in the kitchens or laundries. Befriending cockroaches, moulding lumps of bread into chess pieces in solitary cells or rearing birds (The Birdman of Alcatraz was one of my all-time favourites). The glimpse I got of a real jail neither confirmed nor refuted this view. I couldn't take it in, so intent was I on following the guard ahead of us. He was dressed in impeccably ironed khakis. The crisp, knife-edge creases parted and swung together over his shoulders and beefy bottom in a complex rhythm that took us along as if he was a magnet dragged through iron filings.

I had lost all sense of direction when he finally led us into the visitor's room. It was narrow and dark and separated into two strips, one for visitors and one for the prisoners. On either side of the divide were rows of wooden cubicles. Except for the last cubicle, where shuffling and human voices indicated another visit was taking place, the room seemed empty. In each cubicle, an enormous sheet of thick glass divided the visitors' section from the prisoners'.

The guard led us into a cubicle and then stepped back. We stood on tip-toe peering through the greenish glare of the glass. Through the gloom of the room on the other side, we saw a door from where it now became obvious prisoners would emerge.

The guard coughed for our attention. He had brought a low wooden box on which we could stand. It was rather kind of him. As I stepped up on it, I felt like a young child on a special outing, something like my first chance to buy stamps at the post office on my own.

Suddenly my father was across the glass from us.

"Hullo my girlie, Janey. Hullo, Steve," he was saying.

He was also wearing khakis but they were ill fitting, tight around his armpits and short at the sleeve. The hands which stuck out from the frayed cuffs gripped the edge of the counter, the knuckles white. One clutched his glasses, the other a pen and piece of paper. I had a sense that I was seeing the whorls of black hairs on the back of his hands for the first time. They were really rather extraordinary.

"Stevie, Stevie."

I forced myself to look up.

"That's better. God, you two have grown."

Except for a few more grey hairs and a slight hollowness in the cheeks, it was a relief to see Dad's face as it always had been. He was smiling in an unfocused way.

"I wasn't expecting you, Steven. It's a surprise."

His voice seemed a bit strangled. Maybe it was an affect of the clutch of little holes drilled into the glass through which it came to us. Then I saw the guard standing only a foot behind and to the side of him. He was staring into the middle distance, almost embarrassed to be doing what he was, listening in to pathetic scraps of conversation between prisoners and their visitors.

"Are you managing at the house? Who is staying with you?" Dad asked. "Brian came to see me. He said foreigners were answering the phone at the house and didn't know where you two were. What the hell is going on?"

Brian was my father's younger brother and an officer in the police force in Kimberley. I imagined that the prison authorities were surprised to receive a request from a policeman to visit my father. Maybe that's why he was allowed a special, non-scheduled visit while we were limited to once every six months.

Jane filled Dad in on the Shapiros, letting the house, the arrangement for William.

"I'm surprised Aunt Grace didn't let Brian know," she said.

Dad looked a bit lost.

"Are you sure you're okay? I feel so helpless here. It's as if life is running away without me," he said. His false teeth dropped in his mouth momentarily before he sucked them up again. My father had all his teeth out in his early twenties. It was a result of a childhood of abject poverty with no visits to the dentist, my mother said.

"We're absolutely fine," Jane said. "Look at us." She beamed at him, knowing the effect it would have. She had always been such a daddy's girl.

"What's on your list?"

Dad put on his glasses and focused on the piece of paper in his hand. He seemed thankful that Jane had allowed him the semblance of being in charge. It was a dual thing: he needed to think that he could help us and we needed to believe he could. It was the way it had always been in our family.

"I want you to contact Peter Philips," he said. "I can't remember the number but he lives in Brixton. Highbury Road, something like that. Look it up in the directory. He owes us about a thousand rand for hampers that he sold. Threaten him with a debt collector, the whole bang shoot, if he doesn't cough up. Get Aunt Grace on to it. Put the money into a special account for your university books and stuff for you, Steven. I can't sleep thinking that you haven't got enough."

My father had always been a superb organiser. From jumble sales of clothing to fund-raising trips that managed to reach every wealthy Indian shopkeeper in Durban. His skills for getting things done were legendary.

"Now Janey. There is the question of the policies I have with the bank. I want you to follow these instructions to the letter," he said.

As he detailed the procedure Jane should follow, I found my attention wavering. It was understandable, this need of my father to be in charge, to fill up the precious half-hour. For six months he would have been planning what to say, making notes so that he would not forget, creating some reference from which he could draw comfort when the brief visit was over.

"And, now for family business," he continued. "Have you heard anything about Rebecca's daughter? How's she?" he asked.

It took Jane and me a second or two to understand whom he meant. Rebecca was the name of our mother's mother. She had died four years previously.

"No, the same problems with Rebecca's child. Still not talking, although the experts expect her to," answered Jane, impressing me with her quick thinking on her feet.

Hopefully, my father would understand from this that Lucy was planning not to testify at the trial of their friend Florrie although the Security Branch were expecting she would. It was Florrie's arrest after a long period underground that had led the police to Ma, as each member of the circle who had sustained him had been rounded up, interrogated and broken. Only Rose, who was in London, had escaped in time.

My school results came up next. Jane did not let on for a second that there had been a bit of a glitch in this regard.

"No, he's doing really well, aren't you Steven?" she said. "He got a B for geography in the finals last December. Or was it biology?"

I nodded.

"Maths?" My father caught my eye. I tried not to squirm.

"It's okay, Dad. Not my best subject, of course."

"The money for extra lessons. If you need money..." and he was off again with a string of exhortations and directives. His words required only this from us: nods, looks of concentration, the odd "Yes, Dad," and sheer staying power. It was our job to appease him, to assure him, to calm his worries. Without ever having discussed it between ourselves, in the most natural way possible, we fell into it perfectly. It was a reversal of the parent-child relationship but it was crucial we did not let on. Neither Jane nor I could bear to have him lose face. It was extraordinary how united we were in this, the usual tension between us temporarily laid aside.

His personal requests were small.

"We are applying to the prison authorities to allow us the right to study. If we get the go-ahead, I'll need books. I'll let you know which ones when we find out finally."

He ticked off this point with a short little pencil that he fished out of a top pocket and started on the next.

"In the Red Cross parcels over Christmas they sent us… "

"Time's up."

The guard on his side of the partition moved closer. My father ignored him.

"…they sent us a small chocolate and some knitted socks amongst some other pretty dreadful stuff. The chaps would love some of those chockies. Phone them, they've got offices in town. See what you can do."

The guard took my father by the arm.

"Time's up," he repeated and he began turning Dad around in the booth. But my father was hanging on, a look of stubborn determination on his face. He had nothing more to say but he wouldn't leave. There were tears in the corners of his eyes.

"Bye-bye, my darlings. I love you. You're just incredible. I'm so proud," he called out, turning his head to get a last look at us.

Only as he was led out did I notice how much weight he had lost. Seen from behind, his entire body seemed to have shrunk. The gruff voice of the guard who was prodding him in the back with his swagger stick and the sound of doors being unlocked and locked again drowned his last words. He seemed to be saying, "Give your mother a kiss for me," but we couldn't really tell. It was awful seeing him slip into uncharacteristic sentimentality.

The guard on our side of the cubicle cleared his throat and Jane and I stepped off the wooden box we had been standing on. The visit was over.

As we were relayed back through and out of the maze, each footstep we took seemed to stretch the thin connection between my father's life and our own. By the time we found ourselves outside on the blazing pavement, expelled from the building like the ink squirted out by an octopus as it withdraws under a rock, it had snapped. Dad might as well have fallen off a cliff once he left that room. Once again his life had slipped into the fictional realm.

TWENTY TWO

From the minute Jane convinced me to accept living with the Shapiros, I recognised that there would be a radical change to the shape of my life. I resigned myself to the fact that my freedom would be restricted, that I would have to accommodate a new set of domestic arrangements. Outwardly, I bristled at the thought of it, but there was also a small feeling of relief. I could hardly admit it to myself, but part of me was disturbed by my plunging marks at school and the messy state of my affairs. It was a reprieve of sorts to hand over charge, to duck responsibility, to be saved from myself.

I didn't expect how soon or with what strength the changes would be enforced. One of the first things Lilian did when we moved into their house in Rosebank was to go and see the headmaster. She came back filled to the brim with "an agenda".

After a private talk with me she chose to announce her plan of action at the supper table. "Steven and I have had a little chat and we've come up with a plan to improve his school marks," she declared. "I myself am going to tutor him in science and English. At school, I got the prize for chemistry, physics, mathematics and English. Not that one should boast. I can't tell you how pleased Mr Muirson was to see me. They weren't in the least aware of Lucy's arrest, although a staff member had come to him about what she felt was a change in Steven."

"Three afternoons a week, Steven will do a different subject and I will supervise. We'll get on like a house on fire, won't we, Steven?" She smiled across the table at me. "A friend of Jonathan's – Tim Adams – has kindly agreed to come and help you with maths. I'm a bit rusty after all these years. How many is it since I was at school? Twenty-five? Thirty? Gosh!"

Jane looked up from her plate. "You told me you were doing fine, Steven. You've never needed help with English before."

Lilian answered for me.

"Mr Muirson fished out a copy of Steven's last report. It was much weaker than he thinks that someone of Stephen's potential should be attaining."

"But which subjects *did* you pass in December, Steven?" Slowly, the realisation was coming to Jane that she had been tricked.

"I can't remember," I mumbled. I poked at the fried fish with my fork.

Once again, Lilian answered for me. "Geography and biology fully in the green so to speak, English and Afrikaans were a bit iffy, just below 50% and maths and science, well…"

"You mean you only passed two subjects at the end of last year?"

"Let's not concentrate on the past, shall we, Jane dear? What's important is that Steven is committed to working hard and there's no doubt in my mind that he'll do really well this year."

"Umm," said Jane. I knew she'd give it to me later when we were alone.

Meanwhile, from across the table, Solly was throwing me those little lifeline grins people use to buoy up flagging spirits. Every now and then he'd say, "I know you can do it, Steven," and "It's just a slight adjustment of attitude, nothing major," and "Steven's a sensible chap," etc. It was mortifying.

My sister did not believe in fussing. Her style, however, was equally terrifying.

"You never did show me that report, did you? I'm just telling you once," she said to me after supper was over. "You better pull your socks up otherwise I'll apply for a special visit with Dad on the grounds of a family emergency, and you know what a fuss he'll make."

"There's no need for you lot to go off like that," I said. "No-one bothers to do any work in form three. It's not as if I'm in matric or something."

Jane twisted her mouth and lifted her eyebrows, miming disbelief. Ja, tell me more, she was saying.

"All right," I said, "just get off my back, all of you."

Reluctantly, then, I let go of the life of freedom I had made for myself in the absence of my parents and bowed to a new regimen of rules. I was to be home before ten on school nights and twelve on Friday and Saturday. If I went out, I was required to tell either Lilian or Solly where I'd be. I'd have to let Selena, the maid, know whether I'd be missing any meal so she could adjust the quantity of the food she cooked and set the table accordingly.

Every Tuesday, I was to hand over my dirty washing to Selena and make sure that when it was washed and ironed and left folded on my bed,

I put it away in the cupboard, pronto. I was expected to shine my own school shoes in the scullery, making sure that I covered the floor with newspaper. Unless I was involved in sport or other school activities, it was home straight after school where I would immediately change out of my uniform and have a sit-down lunch.

Lilian had an illogical obsession with daily conventions, the meals and clothing and etiquette for each occasion (bourgeois concerns from such a political revolutionary, I felt). After lunch I had to set to work.

"I think routine and structure are good for children," Lilian told me when she first laid out how things would run. "It can only be beneficial to your school work if your life runs smoothly generally."

My first battle was with my messy, incomplete school books. As I flipped through them, Lilian at my side, it was as if scales fell from my eyes. Lilian kept her tone positive but, after raising two academically bright sons, she must have been pretty shocked herself. How had I let it get so out of hand? It wasn't a conscious decision to opt out. Rather an accumulation of little split-second choices such as to go to a party rather than finish a grammar exercise, or loll about playing the guitar rather than face factorisation. Small events in themselves, they had multiplied by a hundred and created huge holes which I now was required to fill. What a task!

Lilian and Tim were thorough teachers. I had always had the attitude that once I understood how to do something I should quickly move on but Tim's methods blocked such escape routes. He gave me more examples to do, which revealed that I hadn't really understood in the first place and the whole topic would need revision. My long history with a variety of maths teachers who had tried to make me think mathematically, was resumed.

Again and again I faced my own stupidity, racking my addled brains around equations, bullets coming out of guns at this speed, solutions poured into test-tubes in that proportion, Greenwich mean time and intersecting lines over the equator, enzymes that broke down proteins as opposed to the ones that did the starches.

What made some people clever, I fumed? Jane, for instance. Her intelligence was a box out of which she brought fine tools. I could see them, little slide-rules and metal triangles etched with neat figures and symbols, a set of Allen-keys on a ring, a nifty manual and a whole range of odds and sods, each one ready for the particular problem it could unlock. Inside *my* tool box, just as heavy to carry, was nothing more than a massive blunt hammer, to smash things, and, well, perhaps a whistle.

It seemed so unfair that what mattered most at school was to be accurate, while my strengths in being creatively inaccurate (telling fibs was my best) were allowed expression only every two weeks when the English teacher set us an essay topic. Even then we were strongly advised against flights of imagination. Write about what you know, we were told in class. If you already know about something, I'd think to myself, why bother to write it down. Writing was only fun when you set up your fishing rod, baited a hook (blew on your whistle to relieve the boredom or lure the quarry, whatever) and waited for the big one to bite, a perfect subject around which to weave a spine-chilling tale.

This was my medium, not the orderly configurations of figures that Lilian and Tim left on numerous scraps of paper calculating angles, proportions and powers. "QED, quite easily done," Lilian enjoyed saying to me at the end of a long demonstration.

"Yes," I sighed inwardly, "for some it is."

The new regime meant changes around friends – Eric, for instance. We had known each other since nursery school and he was invariably the friend I chose to join us on family holidays to the coast. ("Smooth holidays are ensured by a prior visit to the library for Jane and a friend for Steven," my mother liked to say.) I still saw Eric at school but socially we were drifting apart. Maybe it was because he wasn't interested in girls (or girls in him, it was difficult to say). Maybe it was because he lived quite a distance away from the Shapiro's. Also, he was not a member of The Driftwood while our drummer, Neville, who attended Highlands North, lived in an adjoining suburb and was my mentor when it came to girls.

Neville and I saw quite a bit of each other. We rehearsed, played in gigs together, visited girls he knew and hung about at his house. On the odd occasion when he'd turn up at the Shapiros, I'd quickly whisk him upstairs to my room, shamed that he might connect me with the old-fashioned starchiness of the place and notice how tamely I had fallen under Lilian's discipline.

It was an illogical feeling. Neville knew my parents, knew my situation. Still, I could not quell my uneasiness when visitors arrived, except for Aunt Grace. For her, the more conventional, the better.

A big problem for me was that I didn't like my bedroom. I never understood why Lilian didn't put me in Jonathan's room (after all, he was in England). She said he disliked people getting into his possessions and put me into a small inter-leading room connecting the passage and a sort of makeshift pantry, a walk-in cupboard filled with tins of food, bottles and boxes of cleaning materials.

My room was cramped and dark, filled with ugly bits of furniture. I put my guitar on the kist at the end of the bed, and stuck my Jaques Cousteau diving books on the shelves of a display cabinet but it didn't help. When Lilian moved in a desk, I could not find the words to ask her to remove the hideous items and so the room was crammed.

I couldn't close the door to the pantry without moving the chair at my desk, nor could I open the cupboard doors without banging into the side of the bed. Except for the single chair, there was no place for friends to sit. Mostly, Neville and I lolled on the bed but we were never truly relaxed. I had the sense that such sloppiness would be met with disapproval if we were interrupted so I'd get Neville to jump off at the least noise outside my door.

Sometimes Selena would come in to fetch spare linen from the kist or groceries from the pantry. Other times, it was Lilian telling me she was about to leave or didn't we want to come for tea. It wasn't that the arrangement was unbearable, just awkward enough for me to never feel easy.

I would lie in the dark on the unfamiliar mattress and blame my insomnia on the slight scent of soap powder that pervaded the room. It was the difference of the smell of this place compared to home which most affected me. (Jane, typically, had the pick of the accommodation, a perfectly private room of a reasonable size, tucked away in a quiet corner. This, I took note bitterly, was despite the fact that she was not there nearly as often as I was.)

When she wasn't tutoring me or overseeing my studies, Lilian spent her afternoons listening to opera records. She was a devoted fan of the opera and would sometimes join in with the arias. Neville and I thought this quite funny but not funny enough to dispel the stuffy atmosphere of the household. We also both developed quite an aversion to poor Selena.

Whenever she was greeted, she would bow her head and whisper a reply as if she were a slave on a southern plantation. She spent her day gliding silently through the house, dusting, folding linen and cooking in the kitchen at the back. She resisted being engaged in conversation, whether out of shyness, fear or repressed anger I never could tell.

Soon after I moved in, I spent an afternoon in the kitchen trying to recreate the warmth and camaraderie I had often felt in the company of servants, but with no success. You could never avoid the distortion of relationships between black and white in South Africa, a distortion between server and served, oppressed and oppressor, the poor and the rich, one culture and another. Apartheid had entrenched the inequality and it lay deep within every one of us, causing us to speak to each other loudly through what seemed like very thin straws. And in a language that was ours, never theirs.

It was one of my parents' greatest regrets that they did not teach us to speak an African language. Of all the white political figures I knew, it was only my father and mother who could engage Africans in fluent Xhosa and Zulu respectively.

On the day I hung out in the kitchen, Selena stepped behind her role as servant and pushed me back into the role of "young master". She answered my questions politely but distantly; in the same tone I heard her use with Lilian, a kind of ingratiating simper. I tried a little longer hoping to break through the barrier, to touch in her the forgiving nature I had observed in so many Africans. I was amazed at how they gave of their humanity to people who had collectively withdrawn their own. It was out of the goodness of their hearts, I thought.

I watched Selena squeezing large beetroots into a big aluminium pot filled with water, bending the curling roots which dangled from the fat, round bodies like the tails of drowned rats. Then I gave up and went to my room. I recognised the failure to connect with Selena as mostly my own fault, or should I say the fault of my pink skin. On the other hand, it did not make me feel more at home.

TWENTY THREE

The Driftwood was playing at a social on the night I met Sally. I'd known who she was, Donny's sister, the one with pigtails. (Donny had three sisters, a stroke of fortune which boosted his popularity at school no end.) But she was no longer wearing pigtails when I saw her at the social.

In contrast to the other girls at the party, most of whom had teased their hair into beehives, her brown hair was mussy and it looked as if she hadn't bothered to comb it at all. Neither had she made an effort to dress up for the occasion. She wore a plain navy top, dark, baggy pants and no make-up. Yet, I noticed from the stage as we played the first set, she was no wallflower.

She chatted with friends and danced often, even without a partner. Once she seemed to be demonstrating a form of the Twist to her friends. She got down so low, her bottom nearly swept the floor, while her arms swayed up in the air in counterpoint. I increased the tempo of the beat and Dennis and Neville followed suit.

Normally, I played willing second string to Dennis's lead, but I had a sudden urge to impose myself, to make myself more noticeable, especially to her. I increased the tempo of the beat and Dennis and Neville followed suit. Two or three times she went down low to the whistles and claps of an admiring group crowding around her. It was quite a feat to keep it going and not lose her balance. When the number ended, as it eventually had to, she seemed to laugh off the attention. She unselfconsciously hitched up her pants, wiped the sweat off her forehead with a grungy sleeve and went back to her friends. I found her utterly mesmerising, so different from the other girls, dressed up to the nines, nervous and stiff as lacquer dolls.

Unfortunately, despite all my efforts, which included pressing forward on to the stage, lifting the neck of my guitar bronco-fashion at appropriate times and holding my head sideways to show off my profile, she seemed oblivious of me. Not once did I catch her casting her eyes in my direction.

Neville saw straight through me. When I turned my back to the dancers on the fading notes of the last number of the set, a routine we'd rehearsed, Neville looked down at me from behind an extravagantly executed drum roll. He made a slight jerk of the head in Sally's direction and gave a knowing wink.

"Go for it," he said to me as we packed up after the party. As we carried our equipment to the parking lot, I scanned the place for a glimpse of Sally. Then I saw the sedate white Peugot of the Shaws sliding into sight and I ducked round the back. I didn't want to be spotted by the ever polite and concerned Mr Shaw. When it was in my interests, I was not above accepting the help of my friends' parents (I even, one day, accepted quite a sum of money when it was offered to me by Neville's mother). But this was another case. If he saw me, Mr Shaw would definitely trap me into accepting a lift with him to the Shapiros.

There was a small huddle of giggling boys and girls sharing a joint deep in the alley. I sidled up to them hopefully. A boy offered me the reefer smoked down to the fingers.

"There's one more hit," he said, generously.

"Naah, not tonight."

I had never tried pot, but tonight was not the night. If Sally had been there it might have been different. I wandered back to the edge of the building and peeped round the corner. I checked my wristwatch, actually dad's. It was already close to twelve-thirty but I didn't care a damn about Lilian and her rules. There was no sign of the Shaw's Peugot or Sally so I ambled casually to the front. If I could just get to say hullo to her, if she hadn't already left, I thought, then the rest would come. Please let her still be in the hall.

At that minute, I saw her striding out through the doors, talking to a couple of girls who seemed to be leaving. For a couple of seconds, she was on her own and I knew that I had to make a move. I boldly walked over to where she stood, looking past her as if I was scouring the place for someone else.

"Aren't you Steven Carter? From Don's school?" Her voice was direct, loud.

I nodded. The crude ploy had worked; I couldn't believe it.

"Have you seen Neville, the guy in the band?" I asked, still pretending to be looking for someone.

"Hasn't he left with the stuff?" she said. "I thought you were helping to pack it up. The rest of the band were. I saw them."

"Ja. I suppose he must have got a lift with Dennis's old man."

Resolving this little made-up issue finally gave me the opportunity to do what I had wanted to do from the beginning, to bring my eyes to rest on Sally and finally engage her, one on one.

"Your band's not bad. You guys are quite good," she said.

I felt prickles of excitement run through my body. Up close, Sally's scrubbed, unadorned face was even more desirable. Her features were in fact rather plain. Brown eyes, brown hair, a slightly odd, short nose which crinkled into a squidgy blob when she laughed, lips a bit too thin. Yet…

"Thanks," I said.

"How are you getting home?" I asked.

She looked around, a strand of her hair flying against her mouth and staying stuck there. I hadn't noticed the others leave and except for a couple of complete strangers sitting on the steps at the entrance, we were alone.

"I dunno. I think Jenny's gone. We came together but maybe she's found someone. I'll walk home. It's not far."

"It's dangerous on your own."

"Um," she made a little sound as if this hadn't occurred to her.

She looked a bit distracted, and then faced me head on, an intensity in her eyes.

"Aren't you the guy whose parents are in jail?"

I nodded. I didn't mind in the least her mentioning it. If that was what made me stick out of the crowd, I would take it.

"Why?" she asked, bluntly.

Normally I found this question tedious but I liked this girl's directness. There was none of the carefulness in her tone that I found so irritating. She genuinely wanted to know, same as wanting to know anything else. I found myself answering her more fully than I usually did. Sure, a good deal of it was a tactic, an attempt to reel in the fish once you've jerked the hook in and you know you have at least some chance of landing it.

"My father was found guilty of being a member of a banned organisation and disseminating propaganda against the State. They tried to get him on charges of treason, trying to overthrow the government, that kind of thing, but luckily that didn't stick, otherwise I reckon he'd have gone to the gallows. I know my father wouldn't have got involved in blowing up pylons and violent stuff like that. My God, he lectured me no end on the need to find peaceful solutions and not to resort to physical stuff with my friends or sister. I can't imagine him being violent. My mother is under 180-day detention. They don't need to charge her with anything in court. They have the power to do that sort of thing…"

All this was true, if a little overdone. I'd heard Jane uncharacteristically do this exaggerated bit with a friend once and found myself using the same words, the same phrases.

"But listen, it's getting really late, I mean early." I shot a look at the phosphorescent hands of Dad's watch. "Shouldn't I walk you home? Did you bring a jersey or bag?"

She shook her head.

"Which way?" I asked.

"There," she pointed. "Down that street till you get to Tudhope Avenue and then a bit further, Jamieson Avenue."

We began strolling down the road. Sally was talking about my parents again, but in a frank, bold way. So many people started dredging up stories to show off their own liberal beliefs when they found out about my parents. How they too were involved in politics in their youth, or their contributions to the African Feeding Scheme or bursaries for Sowetan schoolchildren. One woman bragged of her generosity to her maid, who was "allowed to make tea or coffee for herself anytime of the day". That was with adults, though. With people my age, it was different.

"So where are you living? Don't tell me you're alone at home without parents. That's too good to be true."

"No such luck. I'm living with some friends of my parents, the Shapiros. Anyway, I've got an older sister, Jane. She's at varsity."

"Does she live with these people too?"

I nodded.

We walked through the deserted streets of the affluent suburbs of Johannesburg, the lush grass and smooth tar of the verges providing contrasting textures underfoot. An odd sensation began to hit me in waves, causing time to stick and then rush past. Perhaps I'd inhaled some of that pot, I decided.

Sally was asking about the Shapiro household. It was all right at the Shapiros, I wasn't mistreated, I told her. (I couldn't, of course tell her about the worst embarrassment of living with "strangers", the pyjamas I washed out by myself in the scullery in the early morning or the sheets I rolled up into a tight ball before stuffing them into the washing basket.)

It wasn't completely dark and the air was balmy. For the whole week there had been an unseasonable heat wave in Johannesburg and the papers were full of photos of priests, rabbis and imams leading prayers for the long-awaited summer rains. There was a national drought, agricultural catastrophe, the Vaal dam less than one-quarter full.

A waning half-moon sailed behind a couple of scudding clouds, emerging again to splash the hedges and gates, shrubs and trees with a silvery sparkle. The streetlights provided a string of evenly spaced, brightly lit mini-worlds through which we passed, markers that I hated reaching, because each one meant we were getting closer to Sally's house and I would have to leave her.

"All we've done is spoken about me. Tell me something about yourself," I said.

At first I congratulated myself on sounding so mature but instantly I was riddled with doubt. Sally gave a little laugh and didn't answer, leaving my words hanging in the dark between us. I groaned inwardly. I could have kicked myself for being so forced and stuffy, as if I was quoting from a book on how to converse with girls.

Oh, to find the right words, I lamented. Why was it always so difficult for me to know what to say? All my life I seemed to be borrowing other people's words. Only when I was angry or when I yapped or imitated Mickey Mouse or made what my family called rundy-bundy noises, did things pour out of my mouth as easily as they seemed to for other people. But I was not a child any more. I should be able to communicate sensibly. Girls expected it – I expected it, for goodness sakes.

There was this other worry too. Sally was at least my age, perhaps older. I wasn't sure. Would she want to associate with a boy younger than herself? Somewhere far off in the city a motorbike broke into a roar that reached a crescendo and then fell away.

"Ag, there's nothing interesting about me," Sally eventually responded. Had she been chewing over my question all this time? I squirmed with embarrassment. "Fights with my parents, school, brothers and sisters. There's nothing else."

"Well, if it wasn't for my parents, there'd be nothing much I could say about myself either," I assured her.

135

"You're in a band," she said.

"Only to back Dennis. He's the musical guru. What standard did you say you were in?"

"Eight."

"Same here," I said, relieved that it wasn't nine. I was mulling over the possible age gap between us when we turned into Jamieson Road.

"It's that house, one from the corner," Sally motioned to a low house behind a high curving wall punctuated with slits through which shrubs stretched out leggy shoots. The wall was finished in bagged brick, painted white. It was an architectural style that was becoming popular in the northern suburbs at the time, a modern design that was comfortable, tasteful and modestly African.

"Bet your dad designed the house. Or your mom?" I said, desperate to keep her with me.

Sally looked round from the heavy barred gate which she was unlatching. A blaze cast by the entrance light above the gate lit up her broad smile.

"Don told you, didn't he?"

"No," I lied. "It was a guess."

"Ma said she was inspired by the Zimbabwe Ruins," Sally said.

The gate swung open and she walked into a bricked courtyard edged with lush foliage. I stayed behind on the street side of the open gate. This was it. This was the moment I would turn my back on her, walk away and make my way home. Hitch a ride if I could. Walk, more likely. An hour and a half, I reckoned it would take me to reach the Shapiros on foot.

"Bye-bye."

I closed the gate Sally had absentmindedly left ajar and pushed the steel bolt home. Still I waited, the wrench of leaving too painful to make. Ostensibly, I was waiting until Sally had found the front door key she was searching for under some flowerpots and was safely indoors.

Then the improbable happened. Instead of going directly inside after finding the key, she called to me in a clear voice, "Come, Steven." Simply that. Come, Steven.

If I had conjured up the scene that followed, I couldn't have made it better. In a second, I was at Sally's side and she closed the front door behind us with the softest click. I felt a wildly growing excitement as I crept through the entrance hall and down the darkened passageway behind her, horribly aware of my shoes squeaking on the polished quarry-tile floors. We stopped at the sound of a cough from behind a closed door.

"Is that you, Sal?" a hoarse voice called out. "What time is it?"

Sally pulled a face at me and held up her hand to show crossed fingers.

"Not that late," she called out. There was a "humph" from behind the door, then nothing.

Sally put her hand in mine. Her skin was surprisingly cool in the hot air. It was the first time we had touched that evening and we both knew it.

"Wait," she whispered and left me, disappearing into a deep puddle of shadow on my right. I did as I was told, waiting, my heart beating with the deliciousness of the moment. She seemed to be gone for hours. I stood all alone in the dark in an utterly strange house, lost, powerless and unbelievably happy.

Then she was back leading me through the kitchen and out the back door into a small back garden. Because of the drought and water restrictions, a couple of the shrubs looked as if they'd been shocked and turned grey overnight. Moonlight showed up tangles of straw like witches' hair. Sculptures on heavy plinths were set here and there in between the plants. Sally trailed a finger over one that we passed.

"I always do that," she said. "It's Shona, from Rhodesia."

I stopped. In the weak light, I could just make out a torso made up of interlinking stone forms piled on top of each other, some shiny-smooth, some roughened. Then the stones lost their separateness to form a hugely pregnant woman with bare breasts, her body arching forward, the neck outstretched. The blank slits of her eyes in the huge stony head faced upwards as if she was surveying the stars.

"Your parents aren't prudes, that's for sure," I said, laughing.

"Not in theory, anyway."

Sally laid out a blanket to shield us from the scrubby, itchy lawn. I sat down beside her, carefully putting my arm around her shoulder. We kissed. I'd worry about Lilian later. Much later.

TWENTY FOUR

A couple of days later, Jane pulled into the school grounds to fetch me after hockey practice.

"What's up?" I asked as soon as I'd thrown my tog bag onto the back seat.

"Can't a big *sussie* fetch her baby *boet* without arousing his suspicion?" my sister teased, as she steered down the driveway in first, revving the engine well beyond the point she should.

Boys in navy blazers flashed by the window. On the edges of my vision I recognised Reggie Nutfield, who waved to me with a shout. Unlike the day they arrested my father, I felt not a tinge of embarrassment at piling into what was frankly a rusting wreck. Who cares? I thought. I was no longer a piddling standard six boy.

"Out with it. It's Ma, isn't it?"

"Yes. Abie phoned Lilian today. They're bringing Ma to Florrie's trial on Monday. She's going to testify as a state witness, or that's what *they* think. She's being held at John Vorster Square and you and I have a special visit in…" She consulted her wrist watch, "…an hour and a half. A full three-quarters of an hour, contact allowed, no guards inside. They're treating her with kid gloves. She's their major trump card, the star of the production. God, Steven you'd better wash the minute we get home. You pong something awful."

I sniffed my armpits.

"I can't smell a thing."

"You know Ma," she said.

It was true. Ma was a stickler for cleanliness. It was her only major obsession.

When Jane and I pulled up outside John Vorster Square, I was washed, brushed and neatly dressed. We were pleased to see Abie waiting for us at the front desk. He smiled and I was surprised to see his lips stretch over a keyboard of new, bright-white teeth.

"Long time no see. I've been meaning to pop in at Lilian's and Solly's to look in on you chaps, but the political cases are mounting up," he

138

didn't finish the sentence, and drew us away from an approaching policeman. He whispered something in Jane's ear, a single word, and then passed us on to the policeman who accompanied us to the lifts. Abie rushed back to us as we stood waiting. "Give Lucy my best," he said and then he was gone.

We stepped into the first lift that arrived and were surprised that the policeman didn't follow. Instead he put his hand round from outside, located the buttons by feel, running up the bank until he hit the second-last for the fourteenth floor and barked at us in Afrikaans, "Go to the office on the right. Ask for Sergeant Meyer." He retracted his hand as the doors began to close. It was like a hairy crab scuttling behind some rocks.

"At least it's not the seventh floor. That's where they threw Suliman Saloojee out," I said to Jane as the lift shot up.

Jane put a finger over her lips and pointed to the grille on the ceiling. Of course, silly me. A full contact visit, without guards, with the star witness on the eve of an important political trial. It was obvious that they would be listening to us.

After we found Sergeant Meyer, it was a matter of seconds before we were led into the room where our mother was being held. She jumped up when she saw us.

"Oh my, oh my, oh my," she repeated over and over, throwing her arms around us and burrowing into us with her head. She alternated between pulling back to have a good look at us and diving back in with hugs and kisses and tears. Snatches of garbled words bubbled out from her mouth. "So big", and "both of you", and "so long", and "my two sausages".

She took my lower arms in her hands and squeezed. I willed my body to stay soft in her arms, to appear welcoming, aware that this was how people who love each other might behave after a separation of over six months. I even put my own arms around her shoulders. I sensed that Jane was fighting a similar battle. Inside me was an immense pressure, a welling-up, but I could not translate it into anything but the most awkward motions on the outside. I could not bear the thought of bursting into tears. I wished Lucy'd get a hold of herself.

Eventually she did and we sat down on some chairs spaced some distance apart.

"I'm being really soppy," Ma said, "I'm sorry. You've grown so, Steven. Almost four inches."

"Are you alright?" My voice broke into a squeak.

"And other changes too," my mother continued, "more mature around the jaw. And Jane," she shifted her attention between us like a spectator at a tennis game. "You're looking lovely. Those spots have cleared up. A genuinely handsome young woman."

Jane squirmed in the upholstered chair. She was wearing quite a short dress and you could hear the "zip" as she peeled the bare flesh of her thigh away from the vinyl seat.

"Are you alright?" I repeated, my voice level this time.

"Yes," she said. "Fine. Just missing you two and Ivor. How is he? Did you take the other visit with him, Jane? Tell me how he is."

Jane took over the conversation with Ma while I walked over to the plate-glass window and its view of the city. She gave Ma a sanitised version of events: the house and Perry, William, the visit we'd had with Dad, the set-up at the Shapiros. Everything fine, school, varsity, money? No fine, yes, fine, fine, no, yes, of course. Was there any one special? Yes, boyfriends. Was that plural? Laughter. I was only half-listening.

"Steven," my mother came over and put her arm around me. "It's extraordinary the way Joburg is changing. All this development and building, a boom town. The whole economy's going through an…"

"Upswing?" I said.

From the corner of one eye, I watched Ma survey the panorama ahead and below. It struck me that this was probably the first time in months that she'd seen anything of the outside world. Yet there was no inkling in her manner that she was feeling sorry for herself. There never was with my mother. She seemed to make a point of maintaining an interest in the world about her, of facing everything that life threw up before her with a kind of survivor's naiveté. As soon as I had formulated this thought, her open, anxiety-free air shifted.

Some people unconsciously stick their tongues out a little when they are concentrating on a task. My mother chews her lips. Looking deliberately first at Jane and then me, she moved to the desk and positioned herself with her back to the door. She put a finger to her mouth, wet it and began tracing something on the table surface.

"Yes. An upswing," she said.

Jane and I stood around the desk, watching closely to see the letters she was spelling out, one after the other. I, then F, then a wipe of the hand, miming the cleaning off of a blackboard. Y, O, U. Another wipe.

"Well, it's true," Jane said. "The rand has never been stronger."

D, O, N, T, wipe, W, A, N, T, wipe, M, E.

"Tell me more about Aunt Grace's plans to move. Are they causing difficulties?" Ma said as she continued.

T, O, wipe, D, O, wipe I, T.

Aunt Grace, of course was not planning any move we were aware of. I could see that Ma, increasingly frustrated with this laborious means of communication, was looking for a new way to get her meaning across.

"No," Jane put in at the same time as Ma burst out with, "I *won't* have her mucking things up." My first thought was how odd, muck was the last thing you associated with my aunt, but desperation had led my mother to say the first thing that came into her head. Then it dawned on me that Ma was asking our permission for her to refuse to testify at Florrie's trial and risk the very likely possibility of being returned to jail.

Jane answered, "She's always done what she thinks is right. It doesn't affect us."

My mother turned to me. "And you, Steven, how will you be if Grace moves?"

"There's no difficulty," I answered slowly, for this double-speaking needed careful thought.

"If she's not here, we'll be fine. She has her reasons. You know what she's like, her principles and stuff."

If the Branch were eavesdropping, as we were pretty certain they were, it was unlikely that they would decipher these vague allusions. The brains of the police force were not held in great esteem by the left. In fact, their stupidity was the butt of many jokes.

Ma looked relieved.

"That's what I thought myself, but I needed to hear both of you say it," she said softly, and immediately changed the topic.

For the rest of the visit, Jane and I could find nothing to say. Lucy suddenly thought of the dentist and asked when we'd last been. Jane and I had to admit that we hadn't got round to it. "We will, definitely," Jane assured her. I didn't think it was likely.

My mother asked if we minded terribly if she just sat and held us a bit, and I endured. I was starting to realise just what a strain these visits were and were likely to be for the next few years. Then, mercifully, it was over.

There was a knock on the door (I noticed that there were no footsteps preceding this) and Sergeant Meyer came in. My mother put on a brave face as we were led out.

"Bye," she said in a breezy tone as if she was going off to a film society meeting and would be back later. She was led down the passage and disappeared round a little bend.

"God, her hair looked awful," I said to Jane in the lift.

"Well, what do you expect? She's not been on holiday, Steven. They don't provide perms and tints for detainees."

We reached the ground and walked out the building.

"And thin," I said. "She's quite a lot thinner."

Jane reported to me on Monday evening about what had happened at Florrie's trial.

"You could see that they couldn't wait to get Ma up on the witness stand – the wife of a prominent lefty, a prisoner himself, turning state witness. It was a real scoop for them. But they got the shock of their lives.

"Once she was sworn in, the prosecutor asked his first question, something silly like how she spelt her name. Ma ignored him totally and faced the judge. 'I refuse to answer any questions, M'lord. I will not testify.' She said it in a strong, clear voice.

"There was quite a twitter about the place. Florrie just beamed at her from the dock. The judge tried to dissuade her, telling her that he would have to sentence her for contempt of court if she persisted. She sat bolt upright, her face as calm as anything and said not another word. She was bloody magnificent!"

"I can imagine," I said. "It's that face you get when you've gone too far with her, a wall."

"Ja," Jane agreed. "I don't think I've ever been so proud of her. I mean until then I don't think I knew what she was about. I sort of took her for granted."

I smiled to myself. Jane and Dad had the closest parent-child relationship in our family. They were both intense, intellectual types; talkative, interested in everything around them but also given to sudden piques and displays of uncontrolled temper. Ma was more like me, ordinary, unambitious, a background person. Jane's admiration felt like a tiny personal triumph. Our type also has merit, I thought to myself. It gave me great hope for my own unformed and confusing personality.

"What's she got?" I asked.

"A year, like we thought. But I think they're going to bring her back and charge her on her own. Being a member of a banned organisation, disseminating unlawful propaganda, all that again."

"Christ, I hope she doesn't get five years like Dad."

"No, they can't possibly do that. She's really only been on the periphery of the movement."

Jane was right. Ma was tried for being part of an illegal organisation and was sentenced to three years minus the six months she'd already been in detention. To save themselves from being charged, two members of the movement whom she had thought of as friends had agreed to testify against her. It was not what they said, because the State really didn't have much on her.

"Still," Jane said, "it was the only time Ma looked upset during the trial, when they called the state witnesses. I think Ma felt sorry for them or disappointed, it's hard to say. Not me, though. I know exactly what I think. Bloody cowards and traitors."

Ma was transferred to Barberton Women's Prison, a drive of about four hours from Johannesburg. As a category D prisoner, she would be allowed one visit and to receive and write one letter of 500 words in the first six months.

TWENTY FIVE

Around this time I struck up a friendship with Cedric van Zyl, the former bully of form five and my tormentor. I had heard that he'd got a job at a branch of Recordia in Hillbrow after leaving school, but thought nothing of it at the time. Then one Saturday morning, as I was leafing through through stacks of records on the trestle tables outside on the pavement, I heard his unmistakable voice from behind me, above the pumping thump of the Rolling Stones.

"Steven Carter. Wheels. Stevie, my china."

Twisting around, I looked up, resigned to facing the expected hostility.

"Cedric."

He stayed back a couple of yards.

"Good to see ya."

"Ja, same," I said cautiously. Could it be that he now wore his hair long, in a ponytail?

"What are you looking for?"

"Sonny and Cher."

"They're up here," he said. "Which album? *I got you babe?*" He crooned the twangy American vowels. "Have you heard *The Carnival is Over*? It's a new one by The Seekers. Oh, here it is." He passed it over.

"Have you got the later one with 'We can work it out'?" I asked, instantly regretting extending the contact.

"No, man. I don't think so. Maybe it's out on a seven single. The Seekers are a bit soft for my tastes. Have you heard 'Get off my cloud'? Now, that's up my street. The Rolling Stones at their baddest best. We've been playing it all day. D'you want to hear it?"

He motioned to the LP I was holding in my hand.

"Okay," I said, and followed him to the back of the shop where a row of turntables stood with earphones dangling from hooks above them.

He took the record from me, slipped it out of the cover, flipped it expertly onto the rubber bed of the record player and deftly dropped the needle in place.

"Enjoy," he mouthed.

For an hour or more, I listened to tracks from a stack of different LPs, The Hollies, The Rolling Stones, Cliff Richard, the Beatles (of course I already had all *their* records), The Byrds, Sonny and Cher, even some folk songs, Buffy St Marie and Donovan. Cedric changed the albums for me, walked around the shop, doing this and that, a king in his domain.

After a while I took off the headphones, chose three albums from the pile beside me and laid them out in a row, still undecided which one to buy. Cedric left the till to the assistant and sauntered up to me. I tensed up, waiting for him to pounce. But it didn't happen.

"So, Steven, how's life treating you?" No hint of sarcasm that I could detect.

"No, okay," I answered.

"And school?"

"Fine. You're not very busy for a Saturday morning." It had struck me almost immediately how empty the shop was. I had once been to the town branch of Recordia on a Saturday and it had been jam-packed.

"Depends on the time of the month. The quietest time is the third week of a month," Cedric explained. "Round pay time, it gets crazy."

He offered me a Lucky Strike, shaking the pack so that a single cigarette jumped half out. We lit up, blowing satisfying little twirls of blue smoke. I found myself slowly relaxing. After a few puffs, I asked him how he'd got out of going to the army.

Conscription was the dreaded thing waiting for every white male in South Africa after school, or, if you managed to defer it, university. Quite a few guys left because they couldn't bear the thought of serving. But this meant they could never return to the country. That was unthinkable for me; it was not a choice.

Cedric said, "I signed up for Commandos. You go on basic training for a couple of months and then a few camps a year. It's the best option. The camps aren't too bad but the basic, God, that was awful!" Cedric let smoke come out of his nostrils, a trick I could not match as a beginner smoker.

"I think I'll go for that myself," I said.

"I saw things in the army," Cedric mentioned. "I've got a good idea what our parents were up to. Is your father still…?" He let the question hang.

"Ja. D'you still hang out with Baby?"

"Dave Dodson? No, man. He's joined the police force, can you believe it? He's fully into barracks life, partying with the *ous*, shining up his pistol and taking pot shots out the windows. He's gone *magoeloe* if you ask me. He brought a couple of his new friends to my flat once, I have a flat just round the corner in Jorissen Street, and they were out of it, hanging from the balcony by their bootstraps, smashing the place up a little. I thought of calling the police, except I remembered they *are* the police. He hasn't been round since."

I looked down at the records on the counter.

"Why don't you take the three of them? I can put them aside for you. You can come in next Saturday for the other two."

"Thanks."

"Hey, you're not looking for a Saturday morning job, are you? Gary over there's leaving and we're looking for someone. The pay's not much, but you get to hear the latest records before anyone else."

I nodded. "Ja, man. I'm definitely interested."

"You get R5,00 a morning, and a 10% discount on any records you buy. Still interested?"

"Ja, sure." What luck!

"Leave these – I'll put them under the counter – and you can work off the cost with a couple of mornings' work. Just make sure you come in next Saturday at eight sharp and I'll introduce you to Mr Stagermann – he's the boss. He comes around first thing in the morning and just before we close in the afternoons to count up the shekels. But really, Wheels, he's no problem. He thinks I'm the best thing since Cassius Clay beat Sonny Liston."

The next week, I began my first job (not counting the addressing of envelopes, packing Christmas hampers and manning jumble sales for my parents, sometimes for a couple of bob, sometimes not). It was a sought-after position, as I found out from the number of youngsters coming to ask for casual work. Record shops were a social hub, attracting all sorts: members of the Lebs, a gang of Lebanese youth well-known in Johannesburg for their mod dress and bad attitude; their foes, the equally vilified Hell's Angels; smartly dressed African men on the prowl for the latest American jazz; serious music fans of all persuasions; giggly school girls whose gyms were turned into the briefest minis by a quick pinning as soon as they left the school gates.

146

There was also the glamour of being one of the first to handle the recently unpacked imports, the first to hear many of newest songs. Even at "home" (if one could call it that), many of the phone calls I received during the week were from Neville or his friends to ask if the latest Stones album had "landed" or to book a particularly popular seven single. Records were a real connection with Neville and Dennis after Dennis's father had put his foot down over his slipping marks and suspended The Driftwood.

During quiet spells at the shop, Cedric and I would take a smoke break, and he would get incredibly talkative. He often spoke of the six months he'd spent in basic training.

"It's a bad scene, I tell you Steve, BAD. The officers really get off on driving you into the dust, making you feel *this* small. They drill you non-stop, up and down the parade ground with your full kit on until your legs feel as if they've oozed out of a rubbish dump. But it's what they do to your mind that's the worst. Wake you up in the middle of the night and call you all into a room where they talk *kak* for hours about the red peril and terrorists and how every black man you see walking down the street wants to give it to your sister. Then they pull out maps of black Africa with labels all over, dictatorship, cannibalism, rape of nuns, 10,000 fed to crocodiles. All crap."

By the time Cedric invited me to his place after work one Saturday afternoon, I was convinced that he was genuinely reformed, politically, that is. When I arrived, he was expertly rolling a joint between his fingers. He had been promising to introduce me to pot for ages. His flat was a tiny one-room hovel and we both sat on his bed, a mattress on the floor.

"I started smoking *zol* after the army, bottle-neck after bottle-neck," Cedric said. "It changes you that place, I tell you. I wasn't the same person. This racism they've been pouring into our heads since we were *laaities*, it's wrong man. Wrong."

He shook his head and brought down some matches from a tomato box beside the bed.

"Let me get it going for you." He inhaled sharply, holding the smoke in his lungs for as long as it took the lit end of the reefer to draw back along its fiery length with audible crackles. When he finally let go, the sweetly scented smoke raced into the air where it hung in seductive spirals.

147

"Go easy, it's your first time. The chap I bought it from at the garage swears that it's DP." DP, Durban poison, the best grade. I took my first puff and immediately began to cough and splutter.

"Careful there. You alright?"

When the reefer was too small to handle, Cedric placed it carefully between the prongs of a hairpin and re-lit the end. We took two more puffs each and, when it was good and dead, he took the tiny charred remnant, popped it on his tongue and swallowed. Then he rolled back onto the mattress and stared at the ceiling while I leaned back against the wall, cushioned by a block of mouldy foam.

"There was this guy in the army with me who was, you know, a weakling, a mommy's boy. The *ous* in our tent gave it to him, man. They wouldn't leave the guy alone. I couldn't take it in the end, Wheels. Yes, big bad Cedric himself. It got to me so that I asked to be moved to another tent. There was nothing I could do to help him, nothing. Only watch. At school, you know, I was the man, the main man. You remember? In the army things are different man; it's for real. I saw people die, actually die."

Instead of coming out his mouth, Cedric's words seemed to be reaching me from the walls in his flat with their garish posters, from the grimy carpet, the ceiling. They hung like tangible objects suspended in the thick atmosphere. If I so wished, I could reach out and pluck them out of the air in front of me, examine them and throw them back to bounce about in the room as independent beings.

So this is what it's like to be stoned, I thought with a sense of triumph.

Cedric's eyes were closed but he continued to fill up the room with a slow stream of words. "D'you know that painting with the old American couple standing outside their wooden house? The old guy with a pitchfork and the woman looking as if she'd swallowed vinegar? Could be my old man and lady except that he'd have a rifle in his hand and she would have a brandy and Coke. They taught me all the shit I had to unlearn."

I had lost the thread of how we'd got onto Cedric's parents, but it didn't matter. There were as many connections in the room as I wanted to make. We were bathed in meaningfulness, colours and textures just a little bit different, growing and glowing. Spaces and angles seemed a shade out of alignment, as if the world had been joggled just a little bit, and for once you could see what was behind things, you could peep round the corner.

Cedric stirred and opened his eyes. He turned his head towards me and fixed me with a knowing look.

"What?" I asked eventually.

"What do you think of the green weed, Steven?" he asked with a little smile.

"Profound," I answered.

He laughed.

"Wait till tomorrow. All the great thoughts you've had today will seem like drivel. Don't let me put you off, though. I'm pretty partial to the stuff myself even though I've been talking *kak*, morbid *kak*. Next time I'm going to ask that petrol attendant for the laughing variety."

He made a great effort and swung off the mattress.

"Two things," he said. "One, I've got the munchies and I'm not sure there's a thing to eat in this dive, and two, I'm *lus* for a spot of Hendrix, Jimi Hendrix, the undisputed best. Which one should I go for first? Now there's a big, existential question."

TWENTY SIX

The Shapiro's kitchen was large and was in need of renovations. An enormous Aga stove which needed regular feeding and stoking, dominated one end. A separate scullery and laundry room led off from the left, and from there a back door opened onto a courtyard where Selena and the gardener had rooms. Everything in the kitchen was painted a shiny, cream enamel but it was chipped and covered with a sooty deposit, especially on the funnel of the stove and where it entered the ceiling. There was a fetid, gassy smell to the place, which Jane identified as the odour of burning anthracite absorbed over the years by every surface. Although it was by far the warmest part of the house, I hardly ever entered the kitchen. It was Selena's domain and she had made it clear that she did not think it was the place for me.

Selena was off on Tuesday afternoons, and one cold Tuesday afternoon, after a numbing ride home on my bicycle, I was drawn to the heat of the fire that Selena had banked up before she left. I did some illicit scrounging for food in cupboard and fridge (the cold lunch left for me wasn't great). I was sitting with my feet up on the metal bar that skirted the base of the stove, leisurely consuming a bowl of Post Toasties with boiled milk and lots of sugar, when I heard Lilian's voice.

I had known Lilian was in the house from the opera wafting through the air, but I hadn't been too concerned. She didn't go into the kitchen very often. Now I jumped up, grabbed my shoes with one hand and balancing my bowl and spoon in the other, crept stealthily across the kitchen to the scullery, where I wolfed down the rest of the cereal. I heard another voice. A visitor? The next thing they'll be coming in to make tea, I thought.

I heard the kitchen door open, and Lilian and her visitor stepped in. I immediately recognised the other voice. It was Sheila, an acquaintance of my parents who was on the edges of the movement. What I should have done, of course, is come out immediately, greet the two of them and leave. That would have been the natural thing to do and would not have aroused the least suspicion.

But I missed the moment and anyway something in their conversation hooked me. Could they be talking about Lucy? Once I'd hesitated, it was impossible. If I emerged, it would be obvious I'd overheard them. If I left via the back door, they'd hear me. I was trapped.

"The thing is," Sheila was saying, "there's no conceivable benefit to the movement from her languishing in jail. With Ivor, it was a considered risk. But this! I think it just blew up in her face."

I heard the kettle being switched on, the opening of the cutlery drawer. Then Lilian's voice again. "It's not a sacrifice I would make. I could never have left Brett and Jonathan when they were quite that young. Will you have Earl Grey, Sheila, or ordinary?"

"Ordinary, thanks."

"Jane seems all right. She's old enough to cope." "Yes," Lilian said, "she seems a stable type, clever and forthright. How odd, Selena's left this dirty saucepan on the stove. I'm seeing Jane grow in confidence every week. She's an independent girl, focused."

Another little lull, then the words I knew were coming.

"Steven is another matter, though."

"Oh."

Sheila was fishing, waiting for Lilian to elaborate.

"Well, he's vulnerable. In actual fact, I think Steven has always been a worry to Ivor and Lucy. For one thing, his schoolwork is shaky. And he's an odd boy. He never looks you in the eye when he talks to you, and he shuns any attempt to get close to him. It's as if he's on his guard, doesn't trust a soul. I think his wiring's a bit muddled. He picks at his food at meals and then I find the inside of a loaf of bread hollowed out as if a mad rat had gnawed it. He refused to go to Lucy's trial even when Jane and I offered to try get him special permission, and when he heard Lucy's sentence, I'm positive I heard him laugh."

"Laugh?"

"Yes, it was odd. And then he sulks when you ask him to do the smallest thing around the house. I can smell cigarette smoke on his clothes. I shouldn't be saying all this to you, Sheila, the poor boy's parents are both in prison."

"He is a teenager at the worst possible age, Lilian. Perhaps it's nothing to do with Ivor and Lucy, but just growing up. A late maturer, something like that."

"Mmmm. I can't help thinking it's not the average teenage thing. I am worried about him, Sheila. So, might I add, is the school. The headmaster told me that the English teacher had been to see him about the gruesome essays Steven hands in. Murders in the night, that sort of stuff. The headmaster said the teacher thought Steven's quite talented as a writer. But he was worried by the content!"

"Have you spoken to Solly?"

"Which biccies should we have, Lemon Creams or Digestives? Of course, but you know men, they don't like that kind of personal analysis. He tells me to back off and let him be. That's difficult to do, especially with the boy in the house. Anyway, I can see Solly also struggles with Steven.

"Any attempt at daily chitchat and Steven acts as if you're interrogating him under torture, so you back off and then you feel as if you're ignoring him. It's so damn difficult. He just zips his mouth or says whatever he thinks you want to hear. I have a feeling we don't know half of what he's getting up to. He often gets in late on the weekend and I don't know where he's been or with whom. He doesn't bring many of his friends to the house, so I can't tell. Yes, it was very brave of Lucy, sticking to her principles like that. But the cost! Should we take our tea through to the lounge?"

As I heard their voices disappearing down the passage, I slid on to my bum on the floor. It was a melodramatic gesture, I know but I was in desperate need of relief. Then I got up, crept out of the kitchen like a thief and went to my room.

Lying in bed under a mountain of blankets that night, the soapy scent of the room itching my nostrils and sparking a hot, white anger deep inside me, the conversation I'd heard in the kitchen came flooding back. In many ways I agreed that for Lilian and Solly I had not been the easiest of foster-children, house guests, lodgers, whatever the word was.

They were doing what they thought was the right thing and finding it more difficult than they had expected. I understood that. And it wasn't the first time I had been called a late maturer. What was painful was not their criticism of me. It was what they had said about my mother.

It made me furious that they judged my mother and found her wanting. Despite the praise that the surviving local political figures were lavishing on Lucy in public, despite the accolades she was earning from those overseas (we had received letters from Rose and been flooded with cards from complete strangers from as far afoot as Denmark and Sweden and the States), in their heart of hearts many held another opinion. No good mother would choose to do what my mother had done.

It wasn't fair to sit in judgment of Lucy when she wasn't around to defend herself. I fumed. She had been in Barberton for four months now, and how long in solitary confinement – six months before that? What about her? And anyway, we were not the only ones in this position, I reasoned. Thousands, no millions, of African families were separated by harsh laws and harsh economic realities. Children were regularly sent back to rural areas to be brought up by grandmothers while mothers and fathers toiled in the city. Why had Lilian and Sheila not tempered their position with that fact?

It was not as if we were babies in nappies, requiring a mother's twenty-four hour care. Jane was nearly nineteen and I would be sixteen in September. Old enough to care for ourselves. I remembered watching a documentary about Sub-Saharan herdsmen, children, some younger than nine, taking off alone into the scrubby edges of the desert with their families' prized flocks, for weeks at a time.

I thought of Bertha telling us of how her father left his family in Lithuania at the age of twelve, setting out to seek his fortune. He eventually landed up in South Africa, working as a *smous* in some godforsaken Karoo town.

It was unfair to accuse Lucy of being a poor mother. It was not as if she had abandoned a nest of naked, vulnerable chicks. On the contrary, my parents had shown great confidence in us. (I latched onto this thought with relish, raising my voice to convince the hostile audience I was addressing in my mind, answering Lilian with words I knew I'd never have the courage to express out loud.) My parents believed that they had brought us up well and given us a moral and emotional basis to face the world. However much we might flounder on the surface, we would turn out fine – of this they were sure.

From the second that both of them were gone, in the pit of my being, I was certain of this unshakeable faith they had in us. It was a challenge to live up to and yet I could not fail. Whatever I did, I could not disappoint them in any fundamental way.

Sure, they worried about my less-than average marks or the company I chose to keep. I was sure my mother and father worried endlessly about us in prison. It was only human. Yet, deep down, both Jane and I knew that they were confident we would be alright, and that freed them to fight for a just society, to go to jail for what they believed in, to stick to their principles.

None of the four of us had needed to say these things out loud. In fact, until the painful attack on my mother, these thoughts and feelings had never been expressed in words. I could not allow myself to believe that to my mother, politics were more important than us and that she was a lesser mother because of her choice. It was too loaded, too dangerous a thought. You could not be anything other than a superb mother if you were a superb person, I told myself. It was as simple as that.

Twenty Seven

9 September 1966

Dear Ma

Hullo to you on the day after you know what. Thanks for the dosh which Solly gave me on your and Dad's behalf. I haven't thought what I'm going to spend it on, maybe a small portable gramophone for my room.

I haven't worn the jersey you gave me the last visit *very* often. I'm not sure if it's not a bit jazzy, if you know what I mean, but it's the thought that counts. Maybe the Germans who donated the wool could give you wool of one colour to knit a *plain* pullover next time. No stripes.

What I can't wait to tell you is this: yesterday morning, Lilian called me downstairs to the front door and there were Eric and Barney (do you remember Eric's younger brother?). I was totally surprised because I haven't really spent much time with Eric for ages. They sang Happy Birthday and then Eric said come and see what we've got round the corner.

I went out in my *broeks* and t-shirt because I'd been lazing in bed thinking how nice it is when your birthday falls on a Sunday and I hadn't bothered to get dressed. So I went round the corner and parked in the driveway was a brand new 50cc Honda, bright red, shiny, the latest model.

"It's yours, Steven," Eric said and I said, "No, man, it can't be." And then he said, "Get on it," and I did. I couldn't believe it. D'you know what Eric said to me then? That he'd saved up and bought it for me because he'd never forget all you and Dad had done for him and all those holidays in the Transkei and Plettenberg Bay we'd taken him on.

It's so beautiful, Ma. I can't wait to zoom all over town on it.

That's 300 words.

Now Jane's chance.

15 September
REPLY TO SPECIAL LETTER DATED 12 SEPTEMBER
Dear Ma,

Of course I won't drive the motorbike without a licence and only after I really know how to handle it. At the moment I'm just practising in the driveway and just a tiny bit into the street when there are no cars about so I can get the hang of it. I know that I have to be very careful and not show off, etc. And, yes, Eric brought me a crash helmet which I will wear EVERY TIME I ride.

Lilian was a bit worried but you know what a fusspot she is. I think she is coming round to the idea since it will mean less bother for her and Solly. Aunt Grace doesn't know yet because she came the night before my birthday to wish me happy birthday.

Even Dad wasn't totally against the idea. We saw him on Friday. Now that he is Category C and I am 16, it's much easier to organise visits for me. Dad said was that he could see that it would make me far more independent and less reliant on Jane and Lilian and Solly for lifts but I should act responsibly. Which I will do. Promise. So don't worry.

Lots of love, (200 words)
Steven

15 November
Dear Dad,

We had a terrific visit with you on Friday. I noticed the tan. Must be the sport they're letting you play, or the gardening?

I've already told you how Ma looked but I'll tell you again: very well and as always young. She's very proud that they didn't believe her when she filled in her age on some form in the prison.

About the Honda. Ma wasn't at all against it. She can see that I'm not a small boy any more. I'm 16, remember. So please don't write to her about it. The issue goes round and round and everybody gets into a tizz and there is no need. Eric says the place in town where he bought it gives new owners a set of free lessons and I am organising to go in the holidays. I phoned the licensing department and there is a test I need to pass. So I'm swotting up all the road signs and traffic regulations like a responsible citizen.

Until then, it sits in a corner of the garage. Even Solly wants a spin, can you believe it!

The teachers have given out our marks in class although it is not official. The ones I can remember are: English 63%, Geography 51% and Maths 47% (grotty, but it's a pass).

I have not thought about what I'm going to study when I leave school, but now that you've made me aware of it, I'll turn my mind to looking at careers. I'll discuss it with you again. (250 words, half for Jane)

Lots of love
Steven

20 December

Dear Jane,

How's the conference? I'm sure absolutely grand seeing that you students swung it so that it takes place in Cape Town in the height of the season. This is typical. Why not solve the world's problems (the poverty, political oppression, etc., etc.) from a comfortable position, with good mountain and sea views? And with a whole troop of guys to entertain you. Dave's with you, isn't he? And Mark and Leo and Peter B. Admirers vying for my popular sister. All this while your little brother is stuffed up at the Shapiro's house for the whole hols, all his plans to go away coming to naught.

Dennis's ma had an operation for a burst appendix so my plans to get to Plett with him have crashed. Once again The Driftwood have nowhere to practise and, anyway, Neville is away, so that's that. I think we're drifting apart (excuse the pun).

Ma's sisters in Zululand phoned and said they were terribly sorry but they couldn't have me stay as there's been a death in the Bramwell family and all of them are needed to look after an ailing aunt, or something like that. They promised they'd send up a train ticket in Easter. So, this is me, stuck in Joburg and hating every minute, because everybody is away, except the Shapiros who never seem ever to go on holiday.

I am still under a strict injunction not to ride the Honda until I pass the test. It's not my fault that I failed the learner's the first time. Full of stupid questions like when you come to a stop street and wish to turn, indicate in what order you would do the following: a. reduce speed b. remove foot from foot rest c. indicate d. rev the engine, etc., etc.

I absolutely hate it here, Jane. I can't bear to stay much longer. Last week Lilian accused me of bringing ants into the house, can you believe it? I told her they were sheltering from the summer rains, but she said that it had taken her ten years to get rid of them (why bother?) and my taking food up to my room had attracted them again. What possible reason did I have to eat in my bedroom, she wanted to know? As if leaving food lying about was the worst sin in the world.

As for Selena! No proper Christmas holidays for her, just a week over Christmas and New Year. We couldn't cope without her, Lilian said, not the three of us, the emphasis on *three* as if it's me who's the burden. And Selena simply grates me, her simpering yes-sir, no-sir, three-bags-full-sir. I think I'm going crazy here with all the petty rules about meals on time and leaving phone numbers and bringing my laundry at the right time and not helping myself from the fridge without asking. Opera and nagging, I hate both.

I think I've finally worked out what they're singing (in Spanish, Italian?). It goes like this: Didn't you say you'd practise some trig? Some trigonometry over the holy, holy holidays? Gooooooooing out again? Then the chorus comes in with, he has forgotten to put down the seat of the lav. I lie dying, I die, I die, sings the hero, I die from nagging.

How can I live with a woman who calls her ample bosom "the girls" in public? Tell me that!

When you get back, let's…

TWENTY EIGHT

"More chicken, Steven? You haven't told us much about your stay in Cape Town, Jane. How was the conference? Sorry, Solly, I've told Selena millions of times not to keep the roast potatoes so long in the oven. Don't bother to get it. Steven, could you reach down and fetch Solly's potato? No, not on his plate – put it on this side dish here. So it was a success, was it? They passed resolutions on which issues?

"I can't understand why people don't recognise that population growth is the most pressing problem in the country. It takes simple arithmetic to work it out. Are you finished, Steven? Oh, I thought you were because your knife and fork... It doesn't matter, just a silly thing..."

Supper at the Shapiros and the usual monologue that went for conversation. Mercifully it was drawing to a close and I was planning to bolt to my room the second the pudding bowls were collected from the table by Selena. But then Solly caught his wife's eye in what seemed a pre-arranged signal (the look between them positively fizzed) and he turned to Jane and me.

"Lilian and I would like to have a chat with you two. Let's go through to the lounge for tea."

We trooped out of the dining room and into the lounge, Lilian balancing the tray of tea things. It was a room that was rarely used, a formal place with a full lounge suite in a pale green chintzy cloth and a horde of china knick-knacks on little tables. Solly took the nearest chair and cleared his throat.

"I don't believe that good food should be spoiled by difficult words. Sit down."

It was now our turn, Jane's and mine, to exchange glances. We sat down together on the sofa. Lilian busied herself with the tea, fussing over the right amount of sugar and how-much-milk? Her manner at the table had lulled us into believing that things were the same as usual tonight and yet there had been this little chat, waiting for us all along.

"What have we done, now?" Jane asked with a forced laugh.

"It's not what you've *done*," Lilian put in.

Solly ran his hand along his flanks and rocked back in his seat, looking for a way to start. "Lilian and I think that things have gone a little awry with this arrangement of ours. You've been living here for nearly a year and things are bound to need sorting out periodically," he began. "I know Lilian has her own issues with you and she will have her chance in a while, but from my side, I must say I am a little disappointed.

"Perhaps the fault has been partially ours. In the beginning we were really delighted to help out your family. Ivor and Lucy are our good friends and we've known you two from when you were this high. But we, um, underestimated the tensions that can emerge when you've got four people living together, thrown together artificially, four strong characters with their own agendas.

"You are not our children and your parents had a different, how can I put it, parenting style than we do. You probably think we're a couple of sticks in the mud, but we have certain standards of behaviour that we are accustomed to. We feel we have been pretty reasonable with our requests. We expect you to observe a few basic rules and show a modicum of respect towards us. Manners are not outdated virtues, they are the grease that oils all social intercourse."

Jane interrupted. "What are you saying? That we've got no manners?" She laughed.

"Um. Not quite, well, different, yes, different standards of conduct."

Jane looked a bit incredulous.

"Give us specifics and I'll be able to make sense of this but I honestly don't know what you're complaining about. You're obviously unhappy with something we're doing."

"Well, firstly, there's Steven out on his motorbike at all times of the night and day. It's simply not safe."

"I thought we'd been through that before. Anyway, what's that got to do with manners?"

"Letting us know when he's coming home, whether he's eating with us or not and playing that infernal music! If the gramophone hadn't been a present from Ivor and Lucy, we'd have asked him to take it out of the room permanently. It's not pleasant having to ask Steven constantly to turn it down. You'd think he'd have got the message by now."

"And?"

"The manner in which you two treat Selena."

"What about it?"

"Lilian has noticed that you take her for granted, all the washing and cleaning and cooking that she does."

Jane shrugged. "What else?" she asked.

"Don't dismiss Selena so lightly. She's an important person."

"I'm not dismissing her," Jane answered, "but I want to hear it all before responding."

Solly's hands moved in the air, searching for words.

"Your general attitude towards Lilian and myself, that's the only way I can put it. As if you resent us. *Are* you resentful? How do you feel about living here?"

"It's fine by me," Jane answered. "I can't see what the problem is, myself. And you, Steven, how are things for you?"

"It's okay," I answered cautiously.

I could see no purpose in complaining about things that I knew would never change.

"I could be given a bit more freedom," I added quickly (rather hopefully as it turned out), "like a later curfew on the weekends."

At this point, Lilian, who had been restraining herself, burst out.

"Christ! You never keep to the one we agreed on. You're late four times out of five, so why bother asking for it to change! Ignoring it hasn't bothered you until now."

Her head twitched from side to side, as she gathered force to throw out the next words.

"And you aren't *okay* about living here, Steven. I can feel you hate the place, hate us!"

She brushed a china ballerina with her elbow, and it wobbled on the glass-covered table at her side.

"Oh," I said.

"Oh," said Jane.

The room was silent except for the descending notes as the ballerina completed her pirouette and froze.

"If it's come to this, there isn't anything to discuss then, is there? I'll find somewhere else for Steven and me," Jane eventually said in what I thought was a very adult tone.

Solly objected. No need to take such an extreme line, really not necessary, sure to work out once the air is cleared, merely assurances needed all round, that kind of thing.

Once the ugly words were out, however, there was no going back. The sour mood was palpable. No-one could look at Lilian.

Jane turned to me.

"I know you haven't exactly loved living here, Steven, but since Lilian seems to have it in for you in particular, it would be interesting to hear what you have to say. For the record."

I squirmed in my seat.

"Of course I don't hate you Lilian," was all I managed.

"I know differently," she sniffed.

"Know or feel?" Jane had taken up the cudgels in my defence!

"Know. People have told me that you speak behind our backs. After what we've done for you, I think the word ungrateful isn't inappropriate."

"Which people?" Jane asked. "You're accusing us of being ungrateful and talking badly of you to other people, so I think it's only fair to tell us who."

"Of course I can't tell you it's this one or that, "Lilian said angrily. "I've seen it for myself, in black and white, written down."

Jane and I gaped at her.

"Steven wrote a letter to you when you were in Cape Town."

"What letter?" Jane asked. "I didn't receive a single letter in Cape Town."

At first, I didn't have the foggiest idea of what she was on about. Then I realised and my jaw dropped.

"Carry on," Jane was saying, but Lilian had clamped her mouth shut and was staring off into the middle distance. A white hot fury exploded inside me.

"She's been going through my stuff, Jane, that's what. HOW DARE YOU READ MY LETTERS! That letter's in the drawer in my desk! Your wife's been rifling through my private stuff!" I roared at Solly.

He winced.

"Let's not let this get out of hand," he said. His expression told us that he deeply regretted the tactical error his wife had made.

Jane was still confused.

"What letter?" she asked again. "I didn't receive any letter."

"I never sent it," I shouted. "I don't think I got round to finishing it. As for your standards of behaviour," I was addressing Solly again (I couldn't even look at Lilian I was so angry with her) "how about the fundamental one of respecting people's privacy and NOT SNOOPING!"

I jumped out of my seat.

Solly had turned a pasty sort of colour; he was really unused to angry scenes. Meanwhile, Lilian was mumbling a long explanation. I heard perhaps every third sentence, I was smarting so bad, I was hopping about the room, getting ready to leave, but staying so that I could have a further chance to vent my spleen.

"I found a polony sandwich green with mould in that very drawer a few weeks back so I thought I would check… It's unhygienic, this eating in the bedrooms, it attracts cockroaches … and it was just lying there, wide open on top of everything else… I obviously didn't mean to read it but it felt as if he left it there for me to find … you wanted me to find it, didn't you, Steven?"

NO!" I thundered. "It was none of your bloody business!"

"It was very hurtful the things you wrote about us. Solly and I have done all we can for the two of you. Everybody thinks we have been marvellous, opening our house to you and providing you with a stable home. I feel I've treated you like my own children."

"Well, poor them, that's all I can say. I suppose you snooped on them too. No wonder they live overseas. I'm glad you read what I wrote, it serves you right. You're a nasty old bag!"

"No, no, no. This I cannot have."

Solly had stood up, as if he intended to thrash me. He pointed to the door.

"You may not speak to my wife in that manner. Out." He enunciated each word with precision, his rage held in check only by supreme self-control.

"Don't worry, I have no intention of staying," I retorted.

Jane had also got up from the sofa. As I flew out the room, I heard her addressing the Shapiros.

"Look," she was saying with a mature, conciliatory air, "you guys have really helped us out, but it's time we moved on. The best thing is to find another place for Steven and me. It's no-one's fault, but it would be better all round, and I have a few ideas. Give me a week or two and I'll have us both out."

TWENTY NINE

The suburb of Parktown in Johannesburg has an illustrious past. It was here that the mining magnates and other entrepreneurs of the colonial era, made rich on the gold and opportunities of the Reef, built mansions befitting their fortunes. No expense was spared by the architects. Facades of brick, plaster or dressed stone were modelled in a variety of imaginative forms, trimmed with *broekie* lace and windows of glowing stained glass and filled out by deep, cool verandas. Roofs were liberally adorned with dormer windows, turrets and towers, creating romantic, fantastical silhouettes against the skyline. Substantial gardens surrounded these monuments to success, gardens the size of smallholdings with driveways that went in and out on separate roads.

As the years went by, the suburb lost favour and wealthy families relocated to houses in more northerly suburbs where they built homes with all the modern conveniences lacked by Victorian construction. The houses they left behind fell into disrepair. Some were converted into offices, one into a nursing home, but most were rented out as they were, in marvellous, shabby grandeur. They were favoured sites for communes set up by an assortment of youth, many of whom were university students whose campus was a short walking distance away.

It was into one of these set-ups that Jane and I moved from the Shapiros. This time Aunt Grace was no problem at all. Jane phoned her and told her of the move a week or so after the day we had piled our few possessions in the Beetle and carried them up to our rooms on the top storey. Aunt Grace seemed to accept the arrangement as the decision of another adult, for Jane had certainly become that, and promised she'd bring us a couple of things we needed, some bedside light fittings, that sort of thing. As for the rest, beds and desks and bookshelves, some form of cupboard for our clothes, we raided the cellar of the house in Francis Street (one of the German students kindly agreed to bring the stuff over in a *bakkie*) and were offered a range of cast-offs by David, whose parents were moving to a smaller house.

Once I'd swept away the last vestiges of the previous tenant, torn and empty LP covers and piles of dusty notes and odd clothes, and arranged my own sticks into various corners of the enormous room, I surveyed it with a sense of happy expectation. The spaciousness, the gentrified style of its high pressed-iron ceilings and bay windows pleased me enormously. I had a sense I could make myself over in this space, become a new me.

There was another joy, what's more, a real surprise. I forced open a pair of French doors that had been painted shut with thick orange paint and discovered a quaint little balcony with a curly, rusty iron balustrade, an astonishing bit of luck, I thought. It was tucked into a V formed by the complex slopes of the roof and was completely hidden from ground level. The view was absolutely terrific. Spread out below the slate tiles and sagging, tussocky gutters at my feet, lay a vast neglected garden. With its waist-high grass it was more a field than a garden. In the middle of it I could just make out the faint outline of what was once a rose garden, like the relic of an archeological site waiting to be dug up.

Beyond were other gardens and roofs poking out from behind large, arching trees especially those colonial favourites, palm trees, grown wickedly tall and wide. Viewed from ground level, they were planted as symmetrical focal points to individual formal schemes, but from my vantage point on the roof the repeated pattern of their distinctive fronds led the eye to the horizon where the towers and high-rise flats of Hillbrow met the sky. Perched up there, with pigeons cooing at my toes, the sun and air wheeling about me in my private crow's nest, I felt as if I had been given a fresh chance. I was filled with a sense of new beginnings.

I had made a mess of the last period of my life, of this there was no doubt. Despite more effort, I had done only slightly better in the end-of-year exams. Worse, I had left behind a muddle of resentments and gossip flying around the tattered remains of the movement. I could hardly bear to think of this.

I had heard that my father's good friend, Rita, on hearing of our fall-out with the Shapiros, would have nothing more to do with my sister and me whom she labelled as selfish. I had failed to protect my parents from the worry and upset that they would experience when they got to hear of our difficulties in letters they received from others. Both my father and mother, who had also recently graduated to category C, could now write and receive letters more frequently, so they were bound to hear about our woes. Solly and Lilian were sure to feel obliged to explain their side of the matter to my parents as soon as they had the opportunity.

Here I'd start afresh, un-hassled by parent stand-ins, simpering maids or the opera, I would get things right. I'd get through matric. I'd steal the heart of Sally Mitchell. I'd work out the firm shape of a future career. I'd be a different person, grown up and responsible, yet free too, free to entertain Cedric in my room, free to roam the streets of Hillbrow by day or by night. Yes, I'd handle both of these seemingly contradictory aspects with aplomb.

"Steven? Where are you?"

Jane walked out on to my little balcony.

"Wow! This is amazing."

"Don't think of it," I said quickly. "You've made your choice."

Jane laughed.

"Move up."

She punched a cardboard box into a flat square, laid it on the shit-stained floor and joined me where I sat, legs dangling through the railings. There was just enough space for the two of us.

Jane threw back her head and closed her eyes against the bright light.

"Ummm, feel the sun," she murmured.

After a while, she dug into her pocket and pulled out a packet of ciggies. She lit up and inhaled.

"You'll have to keep sweeping this stuff off your balcony. I read that quite a lot of diseases are carried in bird droppings."

"I will. Give me one."

Jane looked at me but handed over a cigarette and the matches without a word.

"It's tit here," I said, watching the little cloud of smoke we were making drift over the roof and beyond. "I've got a good feeling about this place."

"It's not the places we've been, it's the people who have been the problem. What do you think of Agatha? She's a bit way-out, isn't she?"

Before we moved in, we had met the six or so students who lived in the house at a party to which we had been invited. In order to be vetted by them, I'm sure. No-one asked us questions, though. It was more subtle than that, just a friendly student banter, joking, irreverent and sophisticated to my schoolboy ears. They were a little like my parents' friends but far more youthful, with-it, experimental.

"She's a bit odd," I said, "but harmless, I think."

"Umm, very odd. And she's got the hots for Kevin."

What I had immediately appreciated about the students in the house was their neutrality. They were neither terribly helpful nor out-and-out rude. There was a friendly indifference in their dealings with us, which I found refreshing. Kevin was the only person who was visibly home when we moved in. "Need a hand?" he asked, when he saw the German and me struggling through Jane's doorway with her bed. After helping us get the angle of our approach right, he drifted off with a "call me if you need me". Other people's concern often translated into invasion into our lives. I liked it better to be around these students who were totally absorbed by their own social and academic concerns.

"You're not a bit sweet on Kevin yourself?" I asked Jane.

She flicked her ash to the floor and stood up to stretch.

"God, no."

David had been at the party and I had seen her with him most of the night, huddled in conversation on the fringes, even dancing for a short while. But her body language said something else. While David greeted me in his usual jocular way, Jane, who was at his side, took the opportunity to scour the room, and it was on Kevin and Agatha, in a clench in a dark corner, that her eyes had come to rest.

"And David?" I asked.

"Not him either."

Dave fitted the profile of a "convenience date" very well. He was obviously besotted with Jane but too much of a gentleman to impose on her. He was clever, considerate, kind and funny, but with his short, podgy body and extra-thick glasses, he simply wasn't the type girls, especially popular girls, fall for. Everything about him said that he did not expect success in this area.

"He's lots of fun," I said.

"Yes, he is." Jane slithered back down beside me.

We ground out our cigarettes in unison. She pointed to a clutch of spires emerging from the trees in the middle distance. "Is that red brick building the clinic we passed on the way, d'you think?"

It was rare, this easy, relaxed talk flowing between us. So much of our interaction was thorny, hurried, with Jane doing the bossing and me the complaining. She was quick to lose her temper, quick to point out my faults and quick to threaten that she'd tell Ivor and Lucy about my offences, unless they stopped immediately. That she never actually did was no consolation, for the slightest possibility that my parents would hear of me in a bad light, was for me the worst punishment.

I could not bear to think of their disapproval of or their disappointment in me, nor could I carry the guilt of knowing that I was causing them to worry when they were so helpless. There was already the mess with the Shapiros. I knew that Lucy would side with her children, if side is the right word, but how much better it would be if they got only a sanitised version of events from Jane or myself, and we could stop Lilian from bothering her with a letter.

"It was much easier when Ivor and Lucy were category D," I had told Jane the week we moved.

She misunderstood me but agreed.

"Far better. We'll be schlepping to Barberton every second month now and I can't ask Dave to drive us every bloody time."

I looked idly at the red brick building Jane had wondered about but didn't care if it was the clinic or not.

"Probably. You know, I wouldn't mind being a doctor one day."

Jane's mouth dropped.

"What made you think of that?" she asked incredulously.

"Dave. Yes, I know what kind of results you need, academic brilliance and all that. I most probably am not doctor material but maybe I could do be a medical technologist or something. After the army. There's *that* first, although I've been thinking, Jane, they might exempt me on the grounds of, well, you know, being a potential spy or commie, or something. That would be a relief! But about this medical thing, I've been reading a book about the Curies. I'd like to play a part in ground-breaking research, even if it's small. Finding the cure for awful diseases, malaria or TB."

Jane lit another cigarette and made to chuck the dead match at a pigeon attempting a landing at her feet.

"D'you know Lucy told me that when you were small you wanted to find a cure for death. You were about four or so and had only just discovered that you were going to die one day. You cried inconsolably and asked her if clever people could ever find a cure for it. Ma said she didn't think so and you said, I will, when I'm big, I will!" She chortled. "I don't suppose you remember."

"Vaguely," I answered, "but I mean it, you know. Okay, it's true that after I read the Cousteau books I wanted to be a marine biologist…"

"Deep sea explorer, wasn't it?"

"And I went through that game-ranger stage but medicine seems, I don't know, important. I think you can make a difference to people's lives. Don't look at me like that! It's not as if you're heading for great things yourself. With a BA people usually land up teaching. BA stands for bugger all."

"The last thing I want to do is teach. Just imagine me shut up with a class of stupid children. But a lot of the courses I'm doing are fascinating. Social anthropology is my favourite this year and the English has improved too. I view this degree as a finishing touch to my general education. As for the future," she shrugged. "But I'm glad you're thinking ahead, Steven. Maybe you can come up with a plan for both of us."

"This place seems good for starting to work on that. I think I'm going to begin by painting my walls, green or blue."

"Better green. Blue can be cold, especially if your room is south-facing. Remember the spare room at the house. It's fine now but I don't know how we'll warm up these grand rooms in winter." She stood up lazily and dusted off her pants. "I better be getting on with my own plans. Won't you come a bit later to help me move the bookshelf? I think I've found a better place for it."

"Sure. Give me another one." I motioned to the pack of Rothmans that she was tucking into her shirt pocket.

"Don't push it," she said curtly, and left.

THIRTY

We always lived in a swirl of political talk. It was the medium in which we were raised. A hubbub of words was the lullaby that filled the air as I lay in my darkened bedroom waiting for sleep as a young child. It was the background commentary when we played cricket with children of my parents' friends, the source being a knot of adults on garden chairs ostensibly watching us but in reality deep in serious political discussion. It accompanied us on holidays and social visits, on fishing and shopping trips, at the swimming pool or in the car.

Odd-sounding words such as "bourgeoisie", "the lumpenproletariat" and "Trotskyites" dotted these conversations and took on the nature of exotic charms, like Rumpelstiltskin or the Baba Yaga. What could a word such as "lumpenproletariat" possibly mean? It had the sound of a brand name for a lumpy foodstuff, like Wall's Eskimo Pie or Baker's Tennis Biscuits. Even when the words were understandable, they meant something else. When taken literally, "state machinery", "the iron curtain", or "class warfare" conjured up humorous or magical images which made me giggle to myself.

Slowly, through simple explanations in response to my questions, through a process of osmosis really, I learnt to ascribe realistic meanings to the words. I still could not follow everything that was being said, and neither did I want to, as I often found the discussions rather boring. Yet, there was the always the possibility of drama where disagreements over interpretation, viewpoints, ethics or strategy might lead to a slinging match, and there was much teasing and joking to dispel tensions. By the time my parents were taken to jail, I had learnt to listen and take in, but I did not dare to participate, as Jane with her superior knowledge and confidence could do.

The talk continued at the house in Parktown at parties, over dinner, in little groups in the lounge, over coffee till the early hours. The voices were younger voices but the concerns were the same. Floating up in nearly every conversation would come the big question: what lay in the future? How would it all end or, more worryingly, would it ever end? How would the situation in South Africa play itself out? How long would we have to endure rule by this sickening government? How would we ever get to live in a sane, reasonable and democratic country? Were we doomed forever?

"When Verwoerd was assassinated, for a moment I thought, at last, it's here, the people have had enough! And what does it turn out to be? No heralding of a new age, but a madman who thinks he's swallowed a tapeworm. A bloody worm that ordered him to kill. And now we've got BJ Vorster who is just as bad. All I know is this: when change comes it's going to be because the majority stand up to the system, not an act here and there by a couple of individuals."

It was Jane who was holding forth late one weekday night after devouring a meal that Paddy had prepared. Everyone was still sitting round the kitchen table, except me; it was my turn to do the dishes, and I was busy scraping off the pile of supper plates over the dustbin before plunging them into the soapy water in the sink.

"And it's going to be violent, more violent than anything we've seen before," Kevin was saying. "You can't carry on with these inhuman policies and lock up everybody who opposes you forever. Eventually people say, it's enough, no further. It's melodramatic, I know, but I predict a bloody revolution. It's only a matter of time."

I looked over my shoulder in time to catch Agatha shuddering.

"I can't imagine how we will live through it. Violence frightens me," she said, her small actress's voice wavering.

"Then I don't know why you don't leave the country," Jane's aggression was held in check by a measured delivery, "since we are already living with it every single day."

My sister had no time for tender-hearted, sensitive types, especially when it came to politics. "Amnesty International rated us as the country with the worst human rights record in the world. You don't get that label by boxing the ears of your opposition when you disagree with them or threatening a couple of journalists."

"It could get a lot worse," Agatha continued.

"What you mean is that it could start to affect us, the whites."

This was from Mary, the new girl.

"Quite."

Jane looked chuffed, as if she'd scored a point. She had a way of gruffly ending conversations before they had a chance to get going. I sighed and fished around for the steel wool in the murky depths of the dishwater. It was the same story, over and over, the conversation falling into the usual patterns, ruts gouged into the road from frequent travel. Even the dead ends were familiar to me.

I hauled out the frying pan from the bottom of the pile of dirties, sprinkled some Vim into the bottom and set to. Round and round, until the burnt crust gave way and shiny, circular scratches of aluminium beamed back at me.

"Anyone for tea? Pass me the bowls," Paddy was up on his feet.

"But where is it, where is this carnage and mayhem? I just don't see it."

Bruce, our resident conservative, was an accountancy student who lived in a small back room in the garden in what was once the servant's quarters. He smacked his spoon against the edge of the pudding bowl for emphasis before passing it down. He was intent on resurrecting the conversation.

"If you read the papers you'd soon see…"

"The little that is in them," Jane couldn't help but interject.

"Yes, I'm sick to death of photographs of that one-eyed pirate, what's-his-name, Dayan, crowing over his victory. All we've had is the Six-day War for weeks."

Agatha's voice was vague, distracted. Kevin, who had gone uncharacteristically quiet, was looking at her sharply.

"The local stuff is down to a couple of lines on the fourth page," Mary added.

"If you read the papers," Bruce repeated, "you'd soon realise that criticism is tolerated to a greater extent than in the rest of Africa or under your beloved communists, for example. You people go on as if we were living under the Third Reich. The Nats are a bunch of regressive idiots who are intent on ruining this place but they're not exterminating the black population, they're not sending blacks to the gas chambers or anything."

"You're a naive idiot to expect the papers to report the whole truth. It's in the liberals' interests to be mildly critical, all the while…" Jane shrugged.

"No, they prefer to watch them die of starvation where they dump them in the middle of nowhere after forced removals, or in those homelands they've set up," Kevin said, responding to Bruce's point.

"Or send innocent people to jail," I surprised myself by saying.

Most of the dishes were on the drying rack by now. I only had the bowls and spoons to go.

"I'm a foreigner and my opinion most probably counts for naught," Paddy said, pouring out the tea at the counter at my side, "but I think it's spurious to compare one kind of evil with another. I don't come from a society people would deem normal myself but, looking in from the outside, I'd say it's a pretty sick place, South Africa."

He placed a clutch of mugs on the table.

Agatha nodded.

"I agree, we are living in a society that has distorted us so much we can't see it for ourselves. Why, how many black friends have we got, Kevin?"

"Lots."

At the same time Bruce was saying, "What's that got to do with the price of eggs? A person is free to be friends with whomever he wants. If I choose primarily white people who share my interests and background, whose business is that? I am not a racist."

"No-one is accusing you," Jane said. "Why are you so defensive?"

"We've got side-tracked," Mary said. "The million-dollar question is how it's going to pan out. Something's got to give, but what?"

That's all I wanted to know, too. I was tired of the uncertainty of it all, the endless discussions, the wordy smokescreens. Surely one of these really clever people could lay it out for me: "This is what I see will happen: first this, then that and lastly…"

Kevin shifted up on the bench and made space for me.

"Look into the crystal ball and what do you see, Mary?" I asked.

"A blank."

"History tells you that it can't possibly carry on and yet I can't see it changing, or rather *how* it can change. There's no middle ground."

Paddy shrugged, Bruce shrugged, Agatha sighed.

"God only knows," she whispered. "Let's hope that they come to their senses before it's too late."

THIRTY ONE

"You lucky fish, you."

"A charmed life."

"Some people!"

It was difficult not to gloat over the envy of my school friends. And it was true, my life did seem just dandy: I had a shiny new motorbike on which I sailed into the school grounds; I lived in a commune with bohemian university students with lots of possibilities for party-going; and (the cherry on top) I didn't have to put up with any parental control.

Most of the sixteen-year-olds I knew were in a kind of war with their parents. Some avoided direct confrontation and did their rebellion underground. In most cases, though, I got the feeling from bits and pieces I heard, that sparks flew at home. There were fights about hair, clothes, politics, parties, cars, drugs and sex. The generations were at war in each and every middle class home.

It was even given newspaper coverage. "Youth in Revolt against the Establishment" was one of the posters I saw on a telephone pole. "In the USA and England, and now spreading to South Africa, parents the target of their children's scorn," the blurb read. For people my age, parents were obstacles in the path of what they wanted to do. They were there to be outwitted, deceived, very often despised. Except for me, of course, whose parents had been conveniently removed from the picture.

The greatest fear of the older generation was that their children would "drop out", and it hit me one day: that was exactly what my parents had done. "My parents are drop-outs, teenager reveals."

The Parktown commune was perfect. When Perry was living with us at the house in Observatory, I had a similar freedom but it had not felt the same. It had been a muddled, furtive type of freedom and I had suffered awful bouts of guilt about letting down my sister, my parents, myself. Perry had seemed distant, unreachable, and it was as if the four of us, Jane, Perry, William and I, had been cast adrift from the normal flow of life.

In Parktown, there was the whole world to gain. A host of interesting people came in and out of our lives. This time round I was at the hub, in the midst of the flow of things, not on the edges. Instead of a dangerous spinning-off into space, the freedom I had in Parktown seemed inside me. It was as centred as the Zorba dance we liked doing at parties, standing in a row, bending at the knees – taking it slowly at first.

It was a freedom summed up by Bob Dylan's *The times they are a-changing*. His debut LP played day in, day out, filling the house with rhyming couplets of a visionary, almost biblical nature. They were ambiguous enough that every person could read into the songs what they wanted: left-wing protest, social satire, faith, love, the journey of self-discovery, the drug culture. It was exciting, heady stuff; yet it was strangely comforting to me.

When they visited, my friends couldn't help but be impressed by the young, sophisticated crowd with whom I lived. A dazzling array of students traipsed through the house wearing torn or strange clothes, talking up a storm on politics, psychology, philosophy. We were mere school boys, often still dressed in school uniform, but they accepted us as equals, were interested in our opinions. With no neighbours within miles on all sides, our celebrated parties would last well into the early hours of the morning and then start up again, as guests who had taken catnaps in any corner they could find, woke up and congregated in the kitchen. The record player would soon be back in operation.

It was on a Sunday morning after one of these parties that Sally arrived, out of the blue. There had been a warning "klonk" at my bedroom door before it flew open and she was right inside, talking loudly.

"God, Steven, you'd think that they'd at least close the front door. It was wide open, just breezed in, and came upstairs. Not a soul about except a strange girl with long hair who looks a bit battered. God, there must have been one hell of a party here last night! Pity you didn't invite me."

I opened one eye from under the bedclothes. I felt appalling. I tried to sit up and look as pleased as the rest of me felt. I failed and flopped back on to the mattress. Sally was unperturbed.

"This is an amazing room, Steven. I love it! You're a lucky fish to live here."

"Sally," I said, closing my eyes against the painful light. I'd given up on her but here she was, in my room. "Mmmmm."

175

"What, Steven? Are you awake? I've always loved bay windows. Ma thinks they're only good in old buildings, she's strictly contemporary, form follows function, that stuff, but I disagree. If I had a house it would have rows and rows of bay windows, like … the udders of a cow!"

She spluttered with laughter.

"Oh, come on. Aren't you going to get up?"

I rolled over and flung out an arm.

"You come here."

She sat down heavily, her bottom making the mattress bounce up and down.

"Not like that," I said.

I smiled from the pillow. After our night kissing in the garden I had taken Sally out once (we'd gone to see a movie) and then her interest seemed to wane. The few times I went to her house afterwards, she was out, and when I did get to speak to her on the phone, she was friendly but evasive. Through little hints dropped by Don at school, I realised that she was dating someone and then someone else. It was agonising to hear. I imagined her dates as young sophisticated men rather than boys, driving her around in their own cars. I had got off with a few other girls at parties but no-one appealed to me in the same way as Sally. And now, here she was.

I took her by the arm and pulled her down.

"Come into my little den, said the spider to the fly."

She snorted and I saw the way her nose crinkled up and her hair flew about her face in an untidy flutter. Then she lay down beside me and kissed me hard on the mouth. As she pulled her head away, a fine gossamer string of saliva joined my lips to hers, like a life rope. She smiled, I smiled and the string broke.

"Steven, get up, man."

"Mmmm."

"No, really. I've brought you some stuff and it's going to melt if we don't get it into the fridge."

It was only then that I noticed two bags of groceries and a sack of oranges leaning against the wall near the door.

"Once more," I bargained and Sally obliged, with greater passion.

This was better than I could dream up. For Sally to walk back into my life, unannounced, and start up exactly where we had left off six, eight months ago, was bliss. I had worn nothing but a T-shirt and underpants to bed and the buttons of Sally's blouse were digging into my chest. Somehow we managed to get off the offending garment, and Sally's bra was hitched up above her breasts.

I say "we" because the wonderful thing about Sally was that I didn't have to do the moves on her. Unlike the other girls I'd kissed at parties, who passively tolerated my fumblings to a point, Sally made it more like a partnership. She didn't hide her bare breasts; so beautiful to touch, I thought I would burst. She was neither bashful nor brazen, just perfect.

Suddenly, she sat bolt upright in the bed, and said in a matter-of-fact voice, "That's it, Steven. There's no way I'm getting pregnant."

She jumped out of bed, pulled down her bra, fished her blouse from under the sheets and put it on.

"While you get dressed, I'll take these to the kitchen."

She scooped the bags up and left the room.

For a second or two, I continued to lie in bed, groaning. Then I got up with a major effort and pulled on a pair of jeans. I poured some water over my hair which was sticking up awfully, and brushed my teeth more thoroughly than usual (I had been worried about bad morning breath during the entire kissing session). Then I hoofed it downstairs, the *babelas* from last night's party completely dispelled.

Sally was in the kitchen talking to Paddy, the medical student who had a room on the second floor. He was telling her how back home, in Ireland, he would prepare rabbits for the pot after a day out hunting. Sally was still lazily unpacking the groceries into the fridge.

"It sounds like the life you read about in books. We don't eat rabbits in South Africa, I can't think why, just habit I suppose. Here's a plain old chicken though."

A stab of possessiveness assailed me. I remembered the rumour that Sally had been seeing a racing driver in the last months. Paddy was a second year student, sophisticated, foreign and in his twenties. If guys like him went for sixteen-year-old girls, what chances did I have?

"Don't mind me, Steven," he said in his Irish lilt, "talking crap on a beautiful morning. Can't get over how blue the sky is. Have you been outside?"

I made a mental note to show Sally my secret balcony and then began plotting about how I could get rid of Paddy and have Sally all to myself.

"You didn't bring this huge tin of coffee, Sal?" I lifted it in the air. "Must have cost a fortune. It's imported from Brazil."

"My parents gave me the money happily. It's the only time they've said yes to anything I've asked them all week. They couldn't resist the poor orphan story. Anyway, it's only instant."

"I'd keep it in your room if I were you, chum. The hordes will fall on it." Paddy lingered at the kitchen table, carefully crossing his feet at the ankles.

The thought was going through my head that if my major draw card with Sally was the glamour of my missing, heroic parents, so be it. If she wanted me to be the poor-boy-whose-parents-were-in-jail, who needed looking after, I'd be that. I smiled to myself. Paddy might have an enchanting accent and be four years older than me but he didn't have my political orphan mystique.

"Where should I put the coffee Steven? Does each of you have a shelf of your own?"

"Peter Pan's Wendy, a real little mother," Paddy teased.

"No, just anywhere in the pantry. It's genuine socialism. Feed me and you feed them all. But can't we try it out now? Would you like some, too, Paddy? "

Unfortunately, he nodded. As the three of us sipped the rich, milky brew, I explained our housekeeping arrangements to Sally.

Bread and milk were delivered daily and, once a week, usually on a Friday, a huge shop was done by two residents whose names came up on a roster. Whoever came home first, or felt like it, would cook the supper, which meant that some days there wasn't a meal at all, but we were welcome to help ourselves to whatever we found. Breakfasts and lunches were usually solo affairs, and everybody was responsible for cleaning up after themselves. Tensions surfaced now and then, but it worked pretty well.

"What about your washing?" Sally asked.

Iris, a huge Xhosa lady, came to the house on Tuesdays and did everybody's washing but no ironing. This was only a problem when it came to my school uniform. I was conspicuous in my creased flannels, frayed shirts with missing buttons and grubby blazer. But I had always been careless of my appearance at school. "Slick Wheels" was another version of my nickname.

Sally and I were chatting on about such matters (Paddy had gone into a kind of blank reverie, a state that he alternated with spates of chirpiness) when Agatha and Kevin came into the kitchen. It was now an open secret that they had moved in together and that Kevin's bedroom was not slept in.

"Where's Jane?" Kevin asked, after Sally had intoduced herself.

I shrugged. "Maybe still sleeping." I rinsed out the mugs and gestured to Sally. "Come and see the garden, it's a jungle."

Once outside I took Sally's hand. Paddy was right: it was a gorgeous day, the sun bathing the dry grass with a light dusting of gold.

"Who brought you today? I didn't think to ask."

"My father's work is just a little way off. He needed to go into the office, so he offered to drop me off, after I'd returned from the cafe round the corner."

"You must have been the very first shopper. Did you leave in the dark?"

She laughed. "It took me five minutes flat to throw the stuff together."

I pretended to chase her down the rutted tarmac that was the driveway and Sally veered off into the thick grass. When we reached the low, stone wall that surrounded the property, she stopped to pull blackjacks off her jeans, and mine as well. I softened a couple of oranges from the sack that Sally had brought by working them between my hands. We bit into them to suck out the juice. Only then did I screw up enough courage to ask Sally about the racing driver.

"Oh, him," she answered disparagingly, "he was an arsehole."

Jane was slow to realise what was happening. With a hectic social life of her own, including a string of boyfriends, camping trips to the Magaliesberg and marathon study sessions at the university library, she was often away from the house for long stretches. One day, she passed me in the passageway, stopped in her tracks and pointed at my lip.

"What's that?" she guffawed.

"What?" I brushed my lip.

"Come into the light."

She yanked me to the window in the well of the staircase and inspected my face at close quarters.

"You're growing a moustache. And there's hair on your chinnie-chin-chin."

179

I squirmed.

"You'll need to shave in a while. God, who will show you how? That's a father's job. I make a hash of my legs and that's just up and down. Any hair growing on your palms?" she said, opening my hands.

I blushed and jabbed her in the ribs with my elbow.

"Sally Mitchell's been to visit you, I hear."

I shrugged.

"Someone I know at varsity told me you're pretty sweet on Sally."

"So?" I said nonchalantly.

"Oh, just wanted to know," my sister said and walked off.

Later in the week, I found a book tossed casually on my unmade bed. I had to laugh; it was *Sex Manners for Men*.

THIRTY TWO

I don't know if it was because our living situation was easier or because my bike made me more independent (driving me around was a major resentment) but Jane and I were getting on a whole lot better. Occasionally, however, an argument burst out between us. The one that shouldn't have happened was during a visit to Lucy.

I had got permission to miss a school day and we drove up in the Beetle. Jane had to do all the driving, which put her in a bad mood. It didn't help when I kept on telling her that I was more than willing to do some myself.

"You're not driving when you haven't got a licence and don't ask again!" she eventually snapped.

The mood in the car was sour and heavy. Neither of us spoke for hours and the landscape crawled past frustratingly slowly. Familiarity had turned the journey into a Herculean chore, and no roadside sight or scenic view lessened the tediousness of it. On the first rise of the mountain pass to Barberton, we were stuck behind a noisy coal truck belching a thick mixture of black diesel and red dust. Sitting on the flat bed of the back of the truck were a group of grimy labourers wearing coal sacks. They looked straight down into our car with blank, exhausted stares.

"Fuck this," Jane cursed, arching her head to try and see if it was safe to overtake. The strain of the early start and the long drive showed on her face.

"Drop back," I suggested mildly.

"No bloody way am I going to sit behind this lot the whole way up," she fumed, swinging the car over into the opposite lane and, as she lost courage, back again.

"Doubt if you've got the power to overtake," I was saying when a speeding car appeared from nowhere, flashing past in an explosion of red dust. In her fright, Jane overcompensated and pulled the steering wheel sharply to the left. A new terror followed. For a horrible moment we wobbled at the edge of the road, teetering over an abyss of scrub. Each flowering aloe and bush lying hundreds of feet below appeared in technicolour detail. I could hear someone screaming, and I couldn't tell if it was my own voice or Jane's.

Slowly, too slowly, the car righted itself, and the road was where it should be, under our bonnet. The tailgates of the coal truck came back into view. I couldn't help noticing that our near-death experience had not even registered with the labourers.

"God, God, God," Jane was mumbling quietly to herself. She was stricken and had to stop at the side of the road to wait for her hands to stop shaking.

"I didn't see it. It came out of nowhere. I'm sorry, sorry."

"It wasn't your fault," I told her. "It wasn't going to crash into us, anyway. You were back in the left lane. You just got a fright."

We soon set off again, and for the rest of the way to the jail, the atmosphere in the car was surprisingly better. As I looked out of the passenger window I found myself remembering the first time we drove to Barberton with Jane's admirer David at the wheel of his father's Jaguar.

I had found it magnificent: a dizzying zig-zag on a dust road that left the land below crumpled like piles of discarded tissues. As the road wended its way round and round, we alternated between the more barren slopes and the warmer, northern ones where aloes flowered in spectacular profusion. Unlike the frustrating Beetle, the Jaguar ate into the hills with great power. We threw a satisfying plume of rest dust behind us on that day. It hung in the air over the road for ages so that as we wound back to the same spot each time, only a little higher up the slope, a soft red blurry line marked out our path.

"You know we take it for granted, this," David had said, taking one hand off the bone steering wheel and waving it in the general direction of the landscape we were driving through.

It was Lowveld bush, exotic short, black trees with green leaves and long white thorns dotting the ground. Mud huts huddled in clearings in the scrub and Africans wandered along the roadside, herding goats or carrying water in big paint tins balanced on their heads. We passed a group of barefoot schoolgirls, their dark, thin legs and arms poking out of their school gyms.

"When I was overseas," David continued, "this was what was missing, a whole different life, the villages, the herd boys with amulets round their necks, the women, the beads."

"The exotic primitive," Jane retorted. "It's seductive to the outsider, this form of poverty. We think of it as dignified, as meaningful. For the people themselves, life's sheer grinding survival. To the tourist, it's a snapshot."

"No, God," David turned to face Jane momentarily, "I don't mean it from a tourist's point of view, although maybe as whites we'll always be looking in from the outside. No, I mean the genuine love of it, the understanding of it that your father has. I admire that more than anything. Even more than the political sacrifices and handling jail, I admire your parents for loving this goddam country so much, for caring so much about everything about it. Your father knows its history backwards. He collects books on it. I saw the piles of books in the house in Observatory. He's lived with tribesmen, worked with them at the Native Commissioner's Court in Umtata. South African languages, the diaries of the explorers, the wildlife, the plants, the birds, he knows all of it."

"Don't forget the fish," I said, "he loves those best."

"Braaied on the rocks with lashings of lemon and butter, "Jane added. "You're right, of course, but it's hard to think of my parents in that way. Most of the time I just see them as my parents."

Even arriving at the jail had been memorable. David had waited in the car while Jane and I had set out along the path that bisected the gardens and led to the entrance. The red brick facade of the building was punctuated by tiny windows and grilles, the front spanned by a stone archway with the words BARBERTON WOMEN'S PRISON (and the Afrikaans, GEVANGENIS VIR VROUENS) etched into the stone. There was still no-one about. It made me think of a deserted Mexican town into which the posse rides before havoc breaks loose. Many eyes behind the closed shutters, only the sound of your own horse's hooves (footsteps in our case) on the path.

It was the largest, most imposing building in the *dorpie*, and in front of it was the most incredible vegetable garden I'd ever seen. Rows and rows of cabbages alternating with spinach and pumpkins the size of little houses under enormous hairy leaves. There wasn't a stray weed in sight.

"What amazing tomatoes. I didn't know you could grow them in winter."

"It's the Lowveld, silly. They grow all sorts of things here, avocados, pecans."

183

"Ma must love it."

"I doubt if the prisoners get to eat any of it. They probably do the maintenance, though. It's immaculate, as if a chain gang keeps the place."

"Looks like anybody from town can help themselves, "I said remarking on the lack of guards.

"Just try," Jane answered.

She was right. I'd rather have sung *N'kosi Sikelel'i Afrika* at a Nationalist Party Convention than snap off one of the succulent bean pods that dangled from the cascading runners on wire mesh supports that we passed. As we climbed a short flight of shallow steps and entered the shadow of the doorway, I turned around for a brief moment. The lush gardens shone like jewels in the sunshine.

This time round, I hardly noticed them. Despite the early start, we were a bit late when we arrived at the jail. Ma was already waiting in the visitor's room. She was animated when she saw us, because this was a full contact visit, the first since that special arrangement in John Vorster Square before Florrie's trial. As she kissed us, I did my best to ignore the female warden sitting to one side of the room. Mevrou Bester was a huge lump of a woman with a suitably brutal crew cut hairstyle. My mother had hinted in the previous visit, however, that behind her ferocious appearance was a sympathetic and humorous nature.

I took a good look at Ma while she and Jane were talking. I'd got used to the darker, straight hair and she was still thin, but she actually looked a lot better than the last time we visited. Two other things had improved my parents' lives in jail: political prisoners had finally won the right to study and both my parents had signed up with the University of South Africa; they were also now permitted to write to each other.

"Have you brought me the ten rand I asked for?"

Jane got up and handed over an unsealed envelope to Mevrou Bester, who peeped into it and returned it with a nod. Lucy took it from Jane and tucked it into the hip pocket of her blue prison dress. It was something that highlighted the reversal of roles in our situation, these requests we received from our parents for pocket money. There wasn't much they were allowed to buy in jail. For my father it was mainly tobacco which he rolled into cigarettes, for my mother little things like facecloths and toothpaste. Jane made sure their UNISA fees were paid.

"Aunt Grace wants to know when she can write you a letter," Jane said.

"I've received my quota, one from Ivor, one from Lilian and one each from you two, so tell her maybe next month. Yes, I think it would be a good idea for her to have a chance," Lucy replied.

So the dreaded letter had arrived. Hopefully, it wouldn't be brought up in the conversation again. My parents had taken our move from the Shapiro's to the house in Parktown with relative equanimity, but then they had only our version of it. Jane and I were hoping that was the end of it.

But both of our parents tended to pick up on a single issue and inflate it beyond reason. Often it was something that had already played itself out. Their isolation made them prone to dwell on and exaggerate every little comment inadvertently made during our visits or letters (this is what made writing to them such a chore) and their time-delayed responses were sometimes completely out of touch. My father was more prone to it than my mother but, still, I was tense, waiting for a lecture.

Ma did not oblige.

"How was the drive?" she asked Jane.

"Fine," Jane said.

"Hairy," I said.

Jane shot me a murderous look.

"What happened?" Ma was alarmed. Mrs Bester shifted her huge bulk on the chair and clucked. Her stockings made an odd scritching noise as one thigh rubbed against another.

"Nothing," Jane mumbled, and added, "it was nothing, just a truck on the pass that was a pain to get past."

Ma left it at that, but Jane let her beast of a mood get the better of her.

"What was in Lilian's letter?" she asked, glaring at me. "Did she congratulate you on your only son's manners, tell you how thoroughly she enjoyed his presence in her house? Steven called her an old bag to her face, you know. He even mentioned her big tits!"

"I didn't, you cow!"

How my sister could have broken the unwritten rule between us out of pure peevishness was incomprehensible to me.

"Don't lie!"

Jane brought down her booted heel hard on top of my foot.

"Ow!" I yelled.

Mrs Bester jumped out of her chair, but Ma waved her off.

"Now you're talking." Jane continued, beside herself with rage. "You don't say a bloody word all through these visits – he didn't open his mouth last time we visited Ivor – but oh, he's got plenty to say behind people's backs…"

"Goodness, Jane, take hold of yourself," Ma said. "Lilian wrote a perfectly reasonable letter apologising for the fact that things hadn't worked out. Jane, Steven, sit down, for heaven's sake. She said that she found Steven a little bit difficult, but that's understandable."

"Understandable that she finds him difficult or that he *is* difficult?" Jane said, still furious.

"I don't know. Both. It doesn't matter."

Ma was used to these angry outbursts, but they sorely tested her.

"If Steven wasn't happy, for whatever reason, the change was a good and necessary thing." We were silent, the three of us, and the looming Mrs Bester, in her corner.

"I think these drives are too much of a strain for the two of you. Maybe I should ask Aunt Grace if she can drive you up."

"Don't," we answered in unison but each of us was facing in opposite directions.

Still another pause.

Ma took control of an ugly situation.

"Now, we're going to salvage this visit by talking civilly to each other," her voice had ice in it. "What I'd like you to do for me, Jane, is see if you can bring some knitting patterns for a man's sleeveless pullover. Try Stuttafords, or Emdin's perhaps. Neck size 32. I've been given permission to send Ivor a gift. Promise you'll remember."

"Promise," Jane muttered.

"And you Steven. You can do me a favour too. When you write your letters too, slow down, my boy. I so want to know what you have to say. I squint at the words for ages and sometimes I have to give up. I get the gist of it, of course, but it would be a good discipline for you generally. They say that it makes a twenty per cent difference to your marks in exams if your writing is legible."

Mrs Bester had got up from her chair and was motioning with her head to the clock on the wall. Ma came towards us for a farewell hug.

First me, then Jane. I endured the contact, wishing I could find it in me to apologise, but not able to get the words out. Jane however, looked stricken. Shamefaced, in a small voice, she said, "Sorry, I don't know what got into me."

At the end of our last visit as we left Ma had laughingly sung out, "The dentist, the dentist, don't forget the dentist!" This time the leave-taking was more painful. Ma stroked Jane's hair as she drew her aside. "All that responsibility, it's difficult," I heard her say. She spoke quietly to Jane in the corner of the room for a minute and then it was time to go. From outside the door I overheard Mrs Bester comforting Ma in turn.

"Ag, shame, Mevrou Carter, that your children have come out bad like that, swearing, hitting. Big children, too. A mother can cry but what can she do?"

THIRTY THREE

3 Aug, I can't remember

Dear Dad,

I'm sorry about my mid-year results. I could do better, I agree. I don't think it would be a good idea to write to Mr Muirson, though. In fact, I ask you please not to. It is my responsibility and simply up to me. No other person can do this for me. I'm going to get through matric, you'll see.

As for the burglary at the house, Jane and Grace are busy making a list of stolen items. It's nearly all Ma's clothes and shoes, some of your suits, a camera, stuff like that. They are still negotiating with the insurance company about what kind of cover we have seeing the house is rented.

The new tenants, a family fresh out from England, are okay, but unused to local conditions. Grace and Jane had to insist on reinforcing the burglar bars in the exercise room where they got in. I think the tenants are getting the idea!

We have not told Ma how much they took. Jane and I feel that it would upset her more than it warrants. Please stress it's time for a new wardrobe, anyway. Mini skirts are so short now that overseas dry cleaners are charging by the inch!

The artist Rene Magritte has died. My favourite paintings of his (d'you remember Maish had a print of it in his flat?) is the one of a solid looking pipe painted on a white background with "this is not a pipe" written underneath in French.

Love,

this is not Steven (256 words)

P.S. More bad news. Puss was run over. William gave her a dignified send-off and a grave at the bottom of the garden next to Blackie's.

10 September 67

Dear Ma,

Thank you for the pile of paperbacks. I don't know if you or Dad wrote to Grace about what to buy or whether she chose them herself (I doubt it) but it's a smashing collection. There's Arthur Koestler, *Stone Cold Jug* by Bosman (how apt!) and a Graham Greene and all sorts of odds and sods that a SEVENTEEN-year-old can't wait to dip his eyes into. Grace brought her own gift, a checked shirt, thankfully fairly fashionable, and not made of that hairy, itchy cloth that seems to be in the shops at present.

About the story I sent you, Ma, don't lose any sleep over it, really. I wasn't trying to make a statement about mankind, or the hunting instinct or oppression, or anything. If I was, I forget myself what the point was. It's nearly a year since I wrote it and I honestly don't know what it means myself. It's a childish, stupid story about GIANTS, for goodness sake, and I wish you hadn't insisted on my sending it.

Brian Epstein, the Beatles' manager is dead, an overdose of sleeping tablets. We are all shocked.

Love you,

Steven (200 words. Jane can have the extra)

P.S. I told you about December, didn't I?

3 December 67

Dear Dad

Hullo! I thought you'd like to hear this story that Dave, Jane's friend, told us. He swears every word's the truth. He picked up his suitcase (or what he thought was his suitcase) from the airport round-about when he flew back from London and only opened it a few hours after he got home. Inside was a wooden leg! No-one had reported that they had the wrong suitcase so all he could do was wait. Turns out it belonged to a multi-millionaire who had three spare legs and couldn't be bothered to sort it out right away.

Aunt Myrtle has invited me to Umhlanga Rocks for the December holidays. She's planning to book the train ticket soon because of the Christmas rush. She says all Ma's sisters want a chance to have me. I'm particularly keen to see the farm in Eshowe. I can't remember the last time we were there.

I read that they call speed bumps "sleeping policemen" in India. They are putting them in quite a few suburban roads to slow people down. The traffic in Joburg is just getting worse and worse!

Love, Steven (190 words)

15 December '67

Dear Sally

A picture of a rickshaw boy in full regalia at the beachfront so you know I'm doing the Durban tourist thing and thinking about you every minute. I can't believe you *had* to stay in Johannesburg. I'm putting this postcard into an envelope so no-one else can read it and I can say things like I wish I could kiss you all day and night and other rude, delicious things.

Don't you think the "boy" has the craziest expression on his face? It's disgusting really, demeaning to jump up in the air like that, like a dog for its master, but funny too.

I keep on thinking of Washansky lying in hospital with Denise Darvall's heart inside him. I hope he makes it. Such excitement over the first heart transplant and Chris Barnard and meanwhile your heart has been inside mine for ages now.

Love, S.

December 17, 1967

Dear Dad

You should be here in Natal for two reasons. One, to fish, and two, to work on this family of Ma's which is as right-wing as anything! They vote United Party but their attitude to blacks is appalling. The cane-cutters on the farm still wear nothing but hairy sacks in the fields and bend at the knee when you talk to them. At dawn, they're at the kitchen door, lined up for a bowl of porridge, like they've always done. Uncle George talks constantly about "them".

In the country generally, the laws get harsher by the day. Bantustans, Bantustans, Bantustans. That's all you ever hear. It's such an ugly word. The Vietnam War's worse. The photographs in the newspapers make me sick. The rest of the world's messed up as well. Joan Baez was arrested in an anti-war protest in America. What an awful place we live in. Merry Christmas and a Happy New Year.

Love Steven (158 words)

THIRTY FOUR

There were some big changes when I got back to Parktown. (I hitched home early, made Jane swear not to tell Ivor or Lucy.) Agatha had moved out after breaking up with Kevin and Jane seemed to have something going with him. A black guy called Josiah Nthini had moved into Agatha's old room.

Josiah's only possessions were a couple of bundles, a steel trunk and a folding chair. He had recently decided to give up all other work and concentrate on his art, he told us. Space and time were what he needed. The Parktown house was perfect, the room was enormous, it was a present from God, it was fantastic. And not to worry about bread for the rent, he'd manage, no problem. He'd scrape it together from sales of his work at pavement stalls and "Artists in the Sun" exhibitions in Joubert Park.

I took an instant fancy to Josiah. It was his mixture of enthusiasm and sophistication, his interest in art and music which attracted me. Being in his company was refreshing, a change from the serious talk of white intellectuals who seemed to bring up the same issues all the time, criss-crossing the same bit of veld over and over.

I sensed that, to them, Josiah was a bit of an eccentric. His romantic outpourings on art and humanity did not sit easily with their analytical style. His primitive paintings and the friends that congregated in his room were just a bit too much. It was not that they were worried about breaking the law by having him live with us (that was a matter of principle) and there was a leniency about his rent, too. Rather it was his crazy energy; it was who he was. Even on the student left there is an accepted orthodoxy, I was discovering.

Josiah would come up to my room to bum a cigarette and stay talking for some time or listen to music on my portable gramophone. He would hop onto the back of my bike and we'd go visit his friends in the townships. With him at my side, I was introduced to people I'd never otherwise have met. I, in turn, introduced him to Cedric, and he'd pitch up at the record shop in Hillbrow to flip through the latest jazz recordings, or shoot the breeze with whoever was working at the time.

Often Sally and I would find ourselves lolling about on the mattress in his room as he jumped around from one side to the other, explaining the meaning of the paintings he had done on the walls.

"It saves on paper or board," he'd tell us with a laugh. "And, I can work really big. Those figures are life-size; they can jump out of the wall anytime to visit me. Those legs can really work, man. See how wide they are, and thick! They can take the weight of the body when it moves. You must always check that in a drawing, whether the artist has given the forms *weight*. It's the most important thing."

I would squint at the figure that he was pointing to, and try and see if I could get it. The difficulty was how contradictory Josiah could be. Very early on in our friendship I had gone through the handmade cardboard folio filled with his work and had been amazed by the variety of styles and media he'd tried. It was hard to believe they had been done by one person. There were street scenes and domestic interiors in colourful gouache and pastel; there were semi-religious images, ultra-stylised and geometric; even water-colours of landscapes with a European feel. "Picasso went through every movement before his time before he discovered Cubism," Josiah explained before I'd said anything. "He zoomed through the history of art before he was twenty and then he was ready. I'm twenty-four so I've got a bit of catching up to do. Ha!"

One morning, well after ten, I shuffled down the two flights of stairs from my bedroom to mosey about. A bad cold (I suspected bronchitis) had kept me from going to school. As I turned to the kitchen, I heard faint scritch-scratch noises from down the passage. The door at the end was ajar. Delighted that I was not alone, I pushed it open and found Josiah sitting cross-legged on the floor, working on a large, dark drawing. He looked up fleetingly.

"Hi, you." "D'you mind?" I asked, fearing that I was interrupting him at a crucial time in the creative process.

"Not at all," he said, making large sweeping gestures with the hand that held the square of pressed charcoal.

I edged closer in order to watch him. He was using the floorboards to create a texture for the background to a group of musicians rendered in large rounded shapes. The mouth of a saxophone, emphasised by insistent spirals and a punchy circle of dark, erupted into the viewer's space.

"A fusion of jazz and art, my two greatest loves," he explained.

A spasm of phlegmy coughs erupted from my throat. I drew back, unwound a wad of toilet paper from the roll I was carrying and spat into it.

"What's wrong, are you sick?"

He scrabbled in a tin by his side and fished out an earthy reddish-brown crayon. He began picking out highlights in the white and pale-grey areas, his arm dancing from one spot to the other almost randomly. The red added a whole new dimension to the drawing.

"Uh-huh."

Feeling half-drugged by a haziness brought on by my dreadful cold, I eased myself into a deck chair, careful not to split the old fabric, and watched Josiah finish off the piece. Why choose that spot, and not this, why a sharp mark and not a curve? What makes an artist *know* how to go about it? It was unanswerable in my state, perhaps in any condition. It was like asking why grass grows. All I knew was that, whenever I tried to draw, I would lose my way and the drawing would end scrunched up in the dustbin.

Josiah's flying arm seemed to wind down, the staccato rhythms of his darting and drawing away slowing to an occasional dab or smudge. His attention withdrew from the drawing and he dropped the conte into the tin, brushing off a cloud of black and red dust from his hands by clapping them together vigorously.

"I forgot it was a school day," he said. "You going to the doctor? You sound awful."

"Na," I answered.

"You should, you know," he said.

"Ag, what for? The old geezer would only give me an antibiotic. I believe in the body healing itself."

Another bout of coughing and spitting followed. Under the influence of Sally, who had been speaking to me about such things and provided me with homeopathic powders earlier in the week, I was newly converted to natural cures.

"I use witchdoctors myself," Josiah said, "*sangomas*, I should say, it's the more respectful term."

193

He inclined his head to one side and squinted at the finished drawing.

"Umm… I'm not sure that I shouldn't have left out the second colour. Perhaps it was better all in black."

I was surprised. Josiah had had been sent to an Anglican church school in Lesotho and had been drilled in a syllabus designed for the British middle and upper classes: Shakespeare, cricket and cod-liver oil; Latin, hockey and prayers in the chapel. There had been little attempt to reflect the cultural backgrounds of the children in the school. They were to be turned into little black gentlemen in the English mould. Although, his present lifestyle was a reaction to that kind of rigidity, I did not think that a return to his "roots" would include a wholehearted embrace of tribal ways.

"I've always wondered what witchdoctors do," I mused. "I mean in films, it's throwing the bones and that sort of stuff, but that's just Hollywood, isn't it?"

Josiah was still not ready to disengage from the drawing.

"Too late to change it now," he was muttering under his breath. "What about some tea, hey Steven?"

"What is it that the witchdoctor does when you go see him?" I persisted as we moved to the kitchen.

Josiah looked sharply at me, as if seeing me for the first time.

"You've lived in South Africa all your life?"

I nodded.

"Never been overseas? England? America?"

"No."

"Parents born here as well?"

"Yes."

What was Josiah insinuating? It took a second or two to work out what he was on about. Oh, I got it. I was a foreigner in my own country, I hadn't bothered to learn about the lives of the bulk of the population; I was a typical white, a guilt trip, that's what it was. Instantly I regretted revealing my ignorance to Josiah, laying myself open to this charge.

I had noticed before, in little comments here and there, an angry vein running through Josiah's engaging, charming nature. Underneath the congeniality was a bitterness – and who could blame him? What black person wouldn't be in a state of fury, in a country where whites had taken everything from him?

194

Blacks were disenfranchised, they were forced to work at the most menial level for little pay, forced to live in specified areas, forced to carry a *dompas* (literally "stupid passbooks"), harried and bullied and arrested for the least infringement of the pettiest and nastiest laws. I'd always thought that if I had been black, I'd have turned to violence. I'd never have forgiven a single white person. My bitterness would have been immense.

Josiah's smouldering resentment was understandable, but, on the other hand, it was also true that it was not my fault. Apartheid was not the personal fault of one Steven Carter, seventeen years old, living in Parktown, Johannesburg, going to school, listening to his records on his gramophone, riding his bike, loving Sally, a white boy leading the white life that was mine.

"You know the little bit you know about us from servants, don't you? From Iris the washerwoman and the hundreds like her? You think that at heart we're just a bunch of superstitious children going off to have our fortunes told by some outlandish soothsayer."

I didn't answer. Josiah's transformation from friend to accuser had been so sudden, it left me speechless.

"You're not used to speaking to blacks who are your equals. In your heart of hearts you're not even sure we are your equals, are you?" Josiah spoke quietly.

I had to dig deep for my response. It felt like I was drawing it out of my bones.

"I'm not going to defend myself to you. If you think I'm a racist, then well," I shrugged. "As a matter of fact, Dad brought home quite a number of people from his work, Indians and coloureds and blacks."

I tried to keep my voice light, reasonable. To be the target of his anger towards whites was not a comfortable thing but I knew I could not duck it. In a way I knew that it needed a level of trust for him to voice feelings that were rarely openly expressed to whites. But I was also thinking, stop, Josiah, stop, man. I don't deserve this.

But Josiah had the bit between the teeth.

"Nannies? Servants? How many, did you say? Only one but there was a swimming pool and a tennis court at your house!"

His smooth lips parted to reveal his teeth, and he laughed.

"Jup, all the privileges of the master race," he took a sip of scalding tea.

"Yes, Josiah," I answered, anger chasing away the fuzziness of my thoughts, "it's true that I've led a privileged life. It's true that I don't know a hell of a lot about black people's lives. It's true that we had servants and two cars and that I've never been hungry. Yes, my parents would entertain their friends on Saturdays with braais and tennis and swimming and yes, I got nearly everything I asked for, guitars and records and clothes and diving equipment. I've never known a day of deprivation, it's all true." I was stopped by another fit of coughing.

As I recovered, I saw Josiah shaking his head slowly from side to side and we landed up sitting in silence, drinking tea. Maybe he was chastising himself for hurting me, for bringing us to this point but, clearly, we had reached an impasse. There was nowhere this conversation could go; there was nothing more that could be said.

This was the way things were in South Africa. There was no avoiding it. Both of us waited to see where we would find ourselves, if and when the awkwardness would end. Were we fated to be always on opposite sides just because of our skin colour and our backgrounds? Was our friendship salvageable? Had it ever been a real friendship? Was friendship even possible between a privileged white schoolboy and an angry black man?

Normally people hide a social awkwardness by speaking over it, but neither of us did. Embarrassment, anger and guilt sat between us like a rock. It seemed insoluble, like powdered chalk in water. Yet, somehow, the sourness faded.

It had to happen because there were only two routes possible: to call it quits or to carry on, and we liked each other too much to do the first. There was the tinkle of teaspoons inside mugs and the fleshy slurps of our lips sucking down the spicy tea, and the anger seemed to go. It fled, like a fever that breaks, or a swarm of attacking bees making off in a cloud. I felt as if I had found a sheltered hollow in the middle of a sand storm and, looking up, saw Josiah there also, sharing it.

My thoughts swung in a different direction, towards my parents, in fact. I wanted to tell Josiah something that I had recently worked out in my mind and this seemed the right time to do it. It didn't feel like a dirty trick to bring them up at this point, using their sacrifice to duck from my own moral responsibility, a huffy, "well my parents are in jail if you must know" route.

"I've been trying to fit two images together for a long time," I started. "One is a picture of Ivor and Lucy coming off the tennis court after a game of doubles with friends. My mother wearing a chic little tennis dress with flounces and my Dad is in his natty gear as well. They're laughing and joking about the game, ready to take drinks on the veranda. They could be any rich white couple in South Africa. They could be the parents of any guy in my school. Yet," I stopped to unwind some toilet paper and blow my nose, "there they are sitting in chookie. That's the other picture, two people in two different cells, in two different jails, at two different ends of the country. If I try and put the two pictures together, the tennis couple and the separated prisoners, I get to see the extraordinariness of what they've done. It's because, you see, it wasn't forced on them. They didn't have to do it. *They didn't have to do it.*

"They could still be playing tennis and eating out and doing the things that all the other whites do. They could have chosen to go along bitching and moaning about the Nationalists while playing more tennis and eating out some more, living the good life. But they didn't and it's that what makes them extraordinary, simply that."

I looked up from the patterned plastic tablecloth to gauge Josiah's response. I didn't think that I'd explained myself very well. Yet, glancing at Josiah's face, I felt he had understood.

There was a pause and then he said softly, "Yes, I can see that."

An enormous sneeze rose up from the pit of my stomach and propelled me out of my seat. I jammed all the damp toilet paper I had crumpled in my palm to my nose. Nevertheless, I showered my surrounds with droplets of moisture.

"Bless you!"

"Yikes," I said, my eyes streaming. "I'm spreading my germs all over the place. I hope you don't catch … uh, uh," I exploded again.

"Gee, Steven. That's one helluva cold you've got there. You really should go see a doctor. No, not a witchdoctor. We're not getting into that again. Let's put away this silly argument. It's nobody's fault except that lot in power. I have an idea. Do you think your mother would appreciate a drawing of her son, the one with the distinguished profile? Would she be allowed that?"

I nodded. "I think so, as long as it's small and I can fold it into an envelope. She'd absolutely love it, I'm sure. She keeps on asking for photographs of us which we forget to send or bring with us. A drawing would be a lot more special."

I had a sense of escaping the ugliness that had flared up between us, of running from it, but what could a person do?

"Let's have some more lemon tea and then I'll find some paper, unless you want to go to bed. I suppose you should."

"No, it's utterly boring, and I'm not that sick. I've got some paper the right size that I can tear out of my school sketchbook. Can you get a good likeness? I didn't see portraits in your portfolio."

"I can't promise anything. I can only try."

"I'm sure my nose and eyes are all swollen and red."

"We'll do it in pencil, then. No colour."

"I think you should do one of Jane as well, when you get a chance."

"Maybe. Come, bring your tea and let's make a start. You've never had someone drawing you before, have you?"

"Only Jane and that doesn't count."

I tried not to show it, but I was ever so chuffed.

Josiah said one more thing before becoming the artist again.

"You know, it's hard to fight it. That's when the enemy wins, when you hate people for their colour, and it's damn hard to fight it."

THIRTY FIVE

1 September 1968
Dear Dad,

I'm starting to realise that you and Mom have given us something much more important than other parents give their children. The other guys at school are good fun, amiable, even splendid. A lot are really clever and many are going to go really far in life. But I see now that there's something missing, a moral dimension maybe.

To be really human you have to care about other people beyond your family and your girlfriend and your mates and what you're going to do on Saturday night. Ma and you showed us that. It's not enough to drop sixpence into some beggar's hand because it makes you feel better, or to give parcels of food and clothes to charity.

When you and Ma first went to jail I was pretty angry about it. I don't think I knew how angry I was until now. I was embarrassed because it seemed that everybody was talking about our family and I hated that. But I understand now, I do. A person's conscience is more important than anything.

I don't want you to think that I feel you abandoned us, because I know we've been in your mind all the time you've been in jail, and we've been fine anyway. But I know why you had to do it. It seemed like a big inconvenience, your getting into jail, but you COULDN'T do any different, and you'd do the same if you had it all over.

Some of the other "jail children" resent their parents, but I want you to know I don't. The boys at school with their parents around have not become fully human, because their parents have set them this example: pay lip-service to the right causes but don't do anything that will get you into trouble, don't look beyond your own personal comfort, love mankind in the abstract but money and possessions come first, leave the heavy stuff to others, etc., etc. AND I'M GLAD YOU DIDN'T TEACH US THAT!

Love
Steven

THIRTY SIX

Two months after that letter to Dad, Jane and I moved back into our old home in Francis Street. Lucy was being released on the 23rd of November and we wanted to get it shipshape for her. There had been much talking and writing between Pretoria, Johannesburg and Barberton about other possibilities: Lucy joining us in Parktown or even finding a flat in Yeoville or Hillbrow as a temporary home.

It was becoming more and more likely that Jane would follow Kevin to London where he was taking up a scholarship at the London School of Economics in 1969. This meant that for the next few years, until Ivor was released, Lucy and I would be on our own. If we went back to the house, it could mean that Lucy might find herself rattling around in it completely alone for months on end when and if I went to the army. Also, the rent from the house, the only remaining source of income for our family, would cease – Lucy would have to find some kind of work right away. With the strong likelihood that she would be placed under house arrest and a banning order, starting up the exercise classes she ran before jail would be impossible, even if her clients were willing to risk association with a "tainted" person.

As a banned person, my mother would not be allowed to attend any gathering and this would limit her social and work contacts to a single person at a time. No-one would be allowed to visit her at her place of residence, which discounted the use of the house as a work venue. In fact, despite our mounting excitement at her release, the future seemed rather difficult and uncertain. Finally, though, Lucy came to a decision. She wanted to come home.

The move back to the house coincided with my final matric exams. The very morning Jane had organised a *bakkie* to get our things moved, I was in the school hall, awaiting the Afrikaans literature and comprehension paper. It was with a mixture of trepidation and relief that I viewed the giant hurdle I was busy negotiating: matric, the big exams, the end of school. I found myself swinging between panic attacks and moods of stoic fatalism: I'm doomed, but what the hell. There's nothing more I can do. If these exams are the basis of my future, if they will determine what happens to me in life, so be it. But let me stuff a bit more geography into my head, if it will fit, it's so full.

After the exam I avoided the Afrikaans teacher and the knots of boys who were going over the answers with each other, and headed straight for the bicycle shed. Jane had offered to take and fetch me but, considering what her day was going to be like, I had declined. I puttered down the drive to the stop sign outside the school gates and hesitated there a while. A little marshalling of inner forces was required, a mental effort.

When I eventually turned right, instead of left for Parktown, I couldn't help but register the act with a mental bookmark. I laughed as I thought "The Way Home" or something corny like that, the text on a cross-stitch sampler you were likely to find in Aunt Grace's house. From then on, the sequence of buildings and streets, shops and people was startlingly familiar, as if I'd never gone "home" any other way.

In my previous life on these streets, I had been a pedestrian, a passenger in a car, or a cyclist – a child in fact. I had taken this route on my motorbike once or twice before but never paid much attention to the changes. The butcher had given way to a hairdresser, a corner cafe had been upgraded, at one or two intersections previously guarded by stop signs, robots had been set up.

At the house all was in disarray. The bakkie was standing in the driveway still loaded with all our stuff. Beds and mattresses, boxes and bookshelves, plastic bags and suitcases lay higgledy-piggledy on the front lawn. The front door was wide open but William, Jane and Kevin were nowhere to be seen. As I entered, the mess inside hit me like a physical blow.

There were heaps of rubbish in the lounge between bits of vaguely familiar but very battered furniture. The windows were cracked and smeared, the curtains faded and torn. The terracotta-coloured wallpaper I remember my mother choosing with such care was defaced with white splotches, as if someone had cleaned a whitewash brush on it.

"Jane?" I shouted, my voice echoing through the vacant house.

Where was she? And William? How could he have possibly allowed the last tenants to do this? Why had he not told Jane and I that this had been going on? (We had been forced to accept another group of students after the immigrant family left without paying two months of overdue rent. Jane and Grace had given up trying to trace them.)

I eventually found Jane in the back garden outside the door to the cellar.

"God, just about everything of worth has been taken from here as well. They broke the lock and helped themselves – can you believe it? The yellowwood kist I didn't take to Parktown in case I'd damage it... Oh, hullo, Steven. How was the exam?"

"The place is wide open," I motioned to the front of the house. "D'you want them to make off with that as well?"

"What difference would it make?" Jane fumed. "It's a shambles. I don't know where to begin, and there's absolutely no sign of William."

"Did you contact him beforehand?"

"Of course. It's all too much. And your exams, too. Honestly, Steven, we've misjudged the whole thing."

Kevin emerged from the cellar, brushing dribbles of dust-laden cobwebs off his face and hair.

"I think I might have found the kist. Oh, Steven, you're here. How was the paper?"

"Okay," I said.

Jane grabbed the torch from him and ducked back into the cellar.

Drawing me aside, Kevin lowered his voice and said: "I don't think Jane can pull this off on her own. We're going to need a work party of ten to help her get this place ready for your mother."

"We've got to make a start, collect up all the rubbish, sweep out the place," I began.

"That's the last thing you should be worrying about. Maybe you should move back to the house in Parktown until the exams are finished, while Jane and I make the attempt." He looked past me and addressed the black square of the cellar door as if it were an oracle and help might issue from it.

"I don't think so. What about Jane's exams?"

He did not answer. In truth, getting down on my knees and scrubbing out the house seemed an almost pleasurable prospect. It would release me from my own current form of a prison sentence, studying for exams. (Experience had taught me to be realistically pessimistic about my chances and a valid excuse for doing badly was already taking shape in my mind.)

"Look," I said, "I'll start by carrying the furniture out of the garden."

"No!" Jane was back at our side, banging on her clothes to beat out the dust.

"No, Steven shouldn't, or no, it isn't the kist?" Kevin asked.

"No, it isn't the kist, and no, Steven's not getting involved in any of this. We'll fix up your room first, and you can get on with passing matric." She looked straight at me. "As for the rest, we'll just have to do the best we can."

"What about your own exams?" I asked.

"Don't worry your pretty little head about them," Jane responded, "I've only got one more and thirty per cent in the exam will get me a pass."

"A mere pass has never been good enough for you before," I muttered.

Still, with my bedroom earmarked as a priority, we had identified a starting point and we got to work. While Kevin and I carried in my desk and bed from the front garden, Jane gave the room a cursory sweep and clean.

"You get in there, close the door, and I'll pile up whatever belongings of yours I come across outside the door. I'll send Kevin to fetch some help for us, and some lunch. You must be starving."

I did as I was told, taking to my hastily furnished room with my geography books. Making a supreme effort, I shut out the loud scrapes and shouts coming from the rest of the house (its emptiness amplified sound like a hollow drum) and concentrated on studying.

For a long while, I succeeded in taking no notice of the curious, bleak little *stoep* that had been my bedroom most of my life. But it got to me eventually. Remember us, said the flashing glass doors, the scuffed cement floor and battered cupboard doors, the ceiling so much lower than I recalled, the un-curtained window panes. You are back, *we* are back, give us your attention. We watched you skip and hop from babyhood to childhood; we absorbed your hours of boredom in the day and screened your playbacks of the days' events as you waited for sleep in the dark. While aeroplane models sat drying on the windowsill and you trampolined with Jane on your mattress, we kept safe lost stamps and secret comics.

I thought back over all the places I'd slept in over the last four years, the passageway to the pantry at the Shapiros that smelt of soap, my tatty but palatial quarters in Parktown, the gas-lit guest room on the farm in Eshowe, a tent filled with friends on the beach in Plettenberg Bay, the blanket in Sally's parents' garden. It was a wrench to think of leaving that private balcony to another resident in Parktown but, despite its limitations and its present bare, grubby state, none felt as right as my old room. I was home, truly home.

Yet, I'd no sooner had this thought than an opposing view came into play. Home for now but not permanently, a place in which to briefly touch sides and then set off once again, like a bouncing ball. Maybe I could talk a group of friends into starting a commune of our own, some day. Neville, Eric, Cedric. That would be fun. For now, though, it was geography and Ma, geography and Ma.

I went back to my books but, once again, not for long. Shouts, knocking and bumping, brief blooms of colour and movement behind the frosted glass began to intrude. I pushed back my chair and stood up to leave, noticing for the first time the thick layer of dust Jane had failed to sweep off the top of my cupboard. When last I lived in this room I wouldn't have seen the top of the cupboard, I thought.

No wonder there was so much noise: six individuals were remaking our home! Kevin had rounded up three pals from the Parktown house, Josiah, Paddy, surprisingly free for the day, and Mary. And, to everyone's great relief, William had finally pitched up. He had arrived, both puzzled and apologetic, Jane told me, with a long story about how the previous residents had sent him off on holiday a week or so ago and that he had not got the message that we were moving back on the first. In fact he was told it was the fifth, and he'd come back early from Pietersburg only because there was a funeral he had to attend in Soweto.

He had walked through the house and shaken his head with shame. The students had had a big party, he explained, they liked to drink too much. Jane shrugged when she told me this. Her attitude was now one of resignation. She didn't have the energy to chase up the students who had pulled a fast one on us and sent William away so that they could help themselves to whatever they fancied of our possessions. Right now her major focus was getting the house habitable.

For a while I dusted and passed up books to Josiah who was arranging them on the shelves of the floor-to-ceiling bookcases that covered two walls in the lounge. Although the boxes in which my parents' extensive collection had been stored had also spent the years in the poorly secured cellar, we did not expect any losses in this area. Mostly people don't think books are worth stealing but, for our family, books were everything. Volume after volume passed through my hands, each a memory.

One or other of my parents had read to my sister and me every night, well after we could read fluently ourselves. African and Bushman folk tales, the Norse sagas, *Huckleberry Finn*, *The Wind in the Willows*, the series of Narnia books which stretched over a whole magical year. I remembered the books that had been confiscated by the security police in the early years. To our great amusement they had misidentified *The Red Book of Adventure Stories* and *Biggles on the Great Wall of China* as banned books.

"Why aren't you in your room?" barked my sister, as she came into the lounge bearing yet another cardboard box. "Don't get me wrong," she added, "whether you sit there twiddling your thumbs or studying is none of my business. Pass or fail it's your *indaba* but I'm not having Lucy blame me, so do what you will, but do it there." She pointed to my room imperiously.

As I left the lounge, I got a sympathetic lifting of the eyebrows in the direction of my sister's back from Josiah on top of the ladder. I think he'd always found her manner too forceful, but I also knew, despite the automatic spurt of defiance that her bossiness always caused in me, that fundamentally she was right.

THIRTY SEVEN

Prisoners are released in the city or district in which they were arrested so, much to our relief, Jane and I were spared another long trip to Barberton. The instructions were spelled out clearly in Ma's last letter: "DON'T FORGET, be there half an hour early, make it known who you are waiting for, and bring a book each in case you have to wait."

I got up early on the big day, bumped into Jane in the race for the bathroom, and even greeted her. I noticed that there was no sign of Kevin, who had been semi-living with my sister since we had moved back into the house. We dressed and, morning grumpiness overcome, ate a leisurely and civil breakfast together. I heaped Post Toasties in my bowl and flooded them with milk, while Jane spread out the newspaper to catch the crumbs from her toast as she chewed and read.

With my final exams and school career finally over (I was hoping against hope that I would not have to do a sup in maths the next year) life had taken on a texture of limitless, shapeless ease. I still did not have any definite plans for the future. I had not seen Sally since an argument a month earlier. For the first day or two afterwards I had felt awful, close to tears, but now, it surprised me how little it mattered. Maybe we'd see each other again, and maybe not. Perhaps I'd find someone else (there were other girls hovering).

My school friends had been assigned their army papers or granted deferments for university but the army was still processing my papers. If I was rejected for military service, I might do a BA at varsity and see where that got me (but that required a university entrance pass and who knew if I'd attained that). The most likely plan was to take a year off and get a job to help Lucy out with the finances. Yes, whatever happened, I would need to find a job.

Right now, however, my future seemed in suspension, the choices insubstantial and arbitrary, bobbing about like the curls and twists of cereal floating in my bowl. Everybody had suggestions: Dad, Ma,

Kevin, Jane, even Rose who had written me a letter from Ohio where she was now living. But nothing that anybody suggested grabbed me; nothing lifted me out of this rather pleasant torpor that had overcome me since my last exam.

William came in with a large bunch of hydrangeas picked from the garden. Planted on the shady, south side of the house, these were the only flowers that had survived the years of neglect. William had been watering them for a month in honour of Ma's return. He'd even found a packet of iron chelates in the shed, which he had sprinkled round them, remembering how much Lucy loved blue flowers. With the white roses we had bought and arranged in a jug in the lounge the day before, they gave the house a festive air.

"Okay," Jane said, glancing up at kitchen clock, which surprisingly enough had not been stolen and still kept good time, "let's do it."

She grabbed the small bag she had packed with a selection of clothes for my mother and we left the house.

We didn't speak in the car, perhaps from tension, perhaps from the exact opposite, I couldn't tell. We were in Hillbrow in ten minutes. What we hadn't anticipated was a struggle to find parking.

"What can you expect in Hillbrow at nine o' clock on a Saturday morning? Everybody's hell-bent on getting their Christmas shopping done early."

"You'd think they'd have a proper parking lot outside a jail, not just space for two police vans rammed into the front," Jane said, trying to keep calm.

This unforeseen glitch in the smooth execution of our assignment was leading to one of the small panics which often beset us at inopportune times.

"I can drop you off and look for parking myself," I suggested, as we went round the block yet again. It was stretching the conditions of my learner's licence which I had finally passed in August, but I didn't think it would matter if I drove alone for a couple of minutes.

Jane checked her watch.

"There's still time."

"Why don't we park outside Recordia?" I suggested.

"It's a no-parking zone but I can ask Cedric to keep an eye on the car for us."

207

Jane resisted but, after trying yet another street without luck, she swung the car around and edged through the traffic to the vacant spot I pointed out.

"I don't suppose Ma would mind a little stroll back to the car."

Jane successfully reversed the car into the bay on her initial attempt.

"If she's decided to bring out every stitch of all that ghastly craft she's made," Jane snorted with laughter as she pulled up the handbrake, "I suppose one of us could go fetch the car."

While she waited for me on the pavement, I walked over to the entrance of the shop and poked my head inside. It was crowded. I caught Cedric's attention with difficulty.

"Listen, man, won't you do me a big favour? The blue Beetle outside in the loading zone – it's mine. Keep an eye on it for me. If the traffic cops come, bribe them or something."

"A pleasure, Wheels. But, hey, what's the urgency?"

"Going to fetch the old lady," I sang out and hurried to join Jane on the street. I caught a fleeting glimpse of his face. I think he twigged.

It was some distance uphill to the Fort. When I stopped and looked back to check on Jane, I saw that she was sweating and puffing with exertion. She waved me on irritably with the hand that held the bag of Ma's clothes. The Fort squatted on the crest of the ridge above us like a pockmarked toad.

There were no guards or policemen standing outside but the method of gaining entrance was the same as at Pretoria Central. We banged on the door and a metal slot slid open accompanied by a bark of inquiry.

"Collecting prisoner Lucy Erica Carter, being released today!" Jane shouted into the hole.

"Nommer?"

Jane recited Lucy's number from memory and the door swung open.

Luckily we'd followed Lucy's suggestion to bring books because we waited for Lucy for over an hour in a stuffy little room next to the head warden's office. Jane had read what seemed like half a paperback and I a good six chapters of a science fiction novel before Lucy appeared. But she only darted in to fetch her clothes.

"Not much longer," she told us and was off again.

Jane was worried about getting a parking ticket but I re-immersed myself easily in the futuristic plot I was avidly following. You see – I was doing a little secret research for a story I had been writing in fits and starts for a year or so.

In an exercise-book hidden under a pile of gramophone records in my room were the first and last chapters of a saga that had been brewing in my mind for a long time, an epic where good and evil are pitted against each other on a distant planet. I had the initial plot and the final outcome of the story but the middle section, the filling to the sandwich, was proving difficult.

Divorced from politics, apartheid, family problems, exams, the army, girls, my uncertain future career, the state of the house, getting my broken bike fixed, was another zone. Snatches of dialogue, characters, incidents and images stirred and rose in it. Fantastical cities set in denuded landscapes, skies of peculiar colour, creatures visible only in wavelengths at either end of the electromagnetic spectrum. I had kept this place secret to protect myself from belittlement and disappointment, my own and other people's.

The scribbles with which I had amused myself were a source of great potential embarrassment. To reveal an ambition which I might never fulfill was frightening. To be seen to fail was worse than to fail! And I felt sensitive about my chosen genre.

Science fiction and fantasy, "escapist rubbish", as I'd heard Jane call it, did not fit into the dominant family philosophy. Although my parents were not as rigid as some of their political friends, they were focused very much on the tangible, on the here and now. To them, the realms of fantasy and imagination were a childhood indulgence, something adults left behind. Yet it was the only thing I was half good at and it was the only thing that I really wanted to do. But could I? Would I ever be able to fill a whole book with my words, my thoughts? It was a question I toyed with often.

"I'm ready."

My mother had come into the room. All the forms had been completed, all the official business disposed of. Jane and I got up together and moved over to the door where she stood. I dropped my book into the bag I took from her. As we had predicted, it held the jail letters carefully sorted into bundles and bound with string, and a few bits of knitting and sewing. I even spotted the drawing Josiah had done of me.

Jane and Ma walked out ahead of me, which gave me the chance to have a good look at Ma without her noticing. Dressed in an old skirt and the ethnic embroidered top Jane had bought as a gift, she looked terrific. It was a wonderful change after the years of seeing her in drab prison dresses. How she'd managed to get her hair done I don't know but the curls I associated with her life before prison were styled back into her blonde hair.

As we reached the lobby just inside the gate and waited for the guard to unlock it, my mother turned around and held out her hand.

"Steven?"

I transferred the bag to my other hand and put my arm into hers so that, as the wide door swung open and we walked through, she was supported on both sides. Supported? No, *she* was supporting both of *us*.

A little ways beyond the prison gates, a man stood with some papers in his hands. The clothing, the moustache and side burns, the intention in his languid stance, was unmistakable.

"Mrs Lucy Erica Carter?"

My mother halted and let go of us.

"Under the direction of the Minister of Security, Section 12 of the Suppression of Communism Act, I hereby serve you with banning orders."

Without a pause, he continued to read from the document in his hand, launching into a long list of the conditions of the banning order. I caught only the odd phrase: "Required to report daily to a police station … may not leave the magisterial district of Johannesburg … gatherings defined as a meeting of more than two people indoors…"

My mother stood still and waited till he was done.

"I would like to visit my husband in Pretoria, officer. To whom do I address my application?" she asked in her most proper voice.

The security man shrugged and brought out a pen from his top pocket.

"Sign here." He indicated a spot at the bottom of the pink sheet and passed it and the pen to my mother.

Without something to press on, the nib slipped off the paper and Lucy looked about her for a flat surface. I pulled out my book from the bag and she used that. I noticed how boldly and neatly she wrote out her full name. She handed the pen and form back to the policeman who tore off a copy for her, handed it over, turned round and tramped off.

"We'll find out how you can apply, Ma. It's bound to say in the finer print," Jane said.

Lucy folded the pink form into quarters.

I lifted up the bag from the pavement where I had dumped it and threaded my arm through the loops of the handles.

"Ready?"

We began the short walk downhill in the blazing sun.

"Welcome to 1968," we said to Ma.